ONE AGAINST THREE

Slade drew his Peacemaker as one of the three gunmen fired a hasty shot. It missed Slade by a yard or more, smashing a window to his left and plowing on to strike a tailor's dummy standing in the dry goods store.

A second shot rang out, this one striking the roof above his head and somewhere to his right. Slade pivoted to face his would-be killers in profile, thumbed back his pistol's hammer, taking time to aim.

His first shot struck the gunman farthest to his right, their left. It was a solid hit and staggered him, but Slade guessed it was nothing mortal, since the shooter didn't fall at once. Instead, he fired a quick shot in return, cursing aloud to emphasize his point.

All three of them were blasting at him now, the night aswarm with bullets, breaking glass, and drilling boards on either side of Slade . . .

THE LAWMAN

Lyle Brandt

BERKLEY BOOKS, NEW YORK

THE BERKLEY PUBLISHING GROUP
Published by the Penguin Group
Penguin Group (USA) Inc.
375 Hudson Street, New York, New York 10014, USA
Penguin Group (Canada), 90 Eglinton Avenue East, Suite 700, Toronto, Ontario M4P 2Y3, Canada
(a division of Pearson Penguin Canada Inc.)
Penguin Books Ltd., 80 Strand, London WC2R 0RL, England
Penguin Group Ireland, 25 St. Stephen's Green, Dublin 2, Ireland (a division of Penguin Books Ltd.)
Penguin Group (Australia), 250 Camberwell Road, Camberwell, Victoria 3124, Australia
(a division of Pearson Australia Group Pty. Ltd.)
Penguin Books India Pvt. Ltd., 11 Community Centre, Panchsheel Park, New Delhi—110 017, India
Penguin Group (NZ), 67 Apollo Drive, Mairangi Bay, Auckland 1311, New Zealand
(a division of Pearson New Zealand Ltd.)
Penguin Books (South Africa) (Pty.) Ltd., 24 Sturdee Avenue, Rosebank, Johannesburg 2196,
South Africa

Penguin Books Ltd., Registered Offices: 80 Strand, London WC2R 0RL, England

This is a work of fiction. Names, characters, places, and incidents either are the product of the author's imagination or are used fictitiously, and any resemblance to actual persons, living or dead, business establishments, events, or locales is entirely coincidental.

THE LAWMAN

A Berkley Book / published by arrangement with the author

PRINTING HISTORY
Berkley edition / March 2007

Copyright © 2007 by Michael Newton.
Cover design by Bruce Emmett.

ISBN: 978-0-425-21465-7

BERKLEY®
Berkley Books are published by The Berkley Publishing Group,
a division of Penguin Group (USA) Inc.,
375 Hudson Street, New York, New York 10014.
BERKLEY is a registered trademark of Penguin Group (USA) Inc.
The "B" design is a trademark belonging to Penguin Group (USA) Inc.

PRINTED IN THE UNITED STATES OF AMERICA

10 9 8 7 6 5 4 3 2 1

For Al and Lennie

1

"You gonna play them cards, or what?" the dealer asked.

Jack Slade considered it. He held a pair of jacks and garbage on the side, though any card he threw away might theoretically match one he drew as a replacement. With four opponents at the table, it was doubtful that he'd draw another jack, much less another pair. And yet—

"We're waitin', mister."

Slade glanced up and pinned the dealer with his eyes. The other man was five feet eight or nine, compared to Slade's six-one, but heavier, maybe 220 pounds, with solid muscle underneath a layer of fat that could've used a bath. The dealer hadn't shaved this week, or washed his face, as far as Slade could tell. Long hair protruded from beneath his weathered hat, resembling strands of moldy hay.

"I'm thinking," Slade replied. "You have an early date?"

"I might." The dealer grinned. "I might at that."

"Go on and fold then if you're in a hurry."

"Fold the winning hand?" The dealer snorted. "I don't think so."

That was trash talk, Slade decided—or it *might* be. There was no way to be positive until the dealer made his discards, but Slade had played the game often enough with strangers facing him to judge most circumstances pretty well.

Slade took his time, as much to irritate the dealer as to help himself decide what he should do. He sipped his beer and fought the urge to grimace, noting that the drink had lost its chill while he was otherwise engaged.

Two jacks and nothing. Even if he drew three cards as miserable as the ones he held, the pair would stand.

But would it win?

Eleven dollars in the pot so far. It wasn't much, and he had twenty more in front of him, but that could vanish easily enough if Slade grew careless.

"Mister?"

"Three," Slade said, and pitched his discards toward the center of the table.

It was getting on toward supper time, and Slade's eyes smarted from the haze of smoke that filled the Southern Cross saloon. He didn't use tobacco personally, but it hardly mattered in the present circumstances. Everybody was a smoker in the Southern Cross, like it or not.

"Three cards," the dealer echoed, dealing them with thick, blunt fingers that were black around the nails. Slade watched him, making sure all three came off the top, although he didn't think the unwashed man was slick enough to cheat effectively.

He could be wrong, of course. It never hurt to watch.

Slade felt the others watching *him* as he received his cards. Immediately on his left, a dandy with a bowler hat drew deeply on a thin cheroot, cards stacked facedown in front of him and covered with both hands. The player's face showed nothing Slade could use, but if he drew and managed to improve his hand, there'd be a small tic at the corner of his mouth as if a grin was trying to break free.

Beyond the dandy, moving clockwise, sat an older man, his gray hair nearly gone on top, with muttonchop sideburns to compensate. He wore a vest over a long-sleeved shirt with fraying at the cuffs. His nose was long and narrow, holding up a pair of spectacles with metal rims. His upper lip was scarred, either from surgery to mend a harelip or from being cut when he was younger. Either way, long years after the fact, it made him slow to smile.

The dealer sat across from Slade, his broad back to the painted windows. Daylight made its way around the batwing doors, but it was late enough and they were far enough inside the room that Slade's view of the dealer wasn't hampered by the glare.

Between them, on Slade's right, the final player was a cowboy with a face carved out of saddle leather, shaded by a rolled-brim Stetson. He chewed tobacco in an absent-minded way, leaning occasionally toward the cuspidor beside his chair, and didn't seem to mind that he'd been losing slowly, steadily, throughout the past two hours. He had drawn a single card this hand, and grimaced when he failed to fill his flush or straight.

Slade lifted his three cards and fanned them out beside the jacks, keeping his face expressionless. He had worked hard for years on end to rid himself of tells, the quirks that told opponents whether he was pleased or irritated by a deal, if he was bluffing or had what it took to win a hand.

Against the odds, he'd drawn another pair. Deuces, but it improved the jacks. Slade felt a tingle of excitement at his nape, knowing he had a chance, but didn't let it reach his eyes. Two pair would lose to seven other hands, and three more men still had to draw their cards, but everyone was waiting for his bet.

"Three dollars," Slade announced, and dropped his coins into the pot.

The dealer blinked at him, then turned to face the bowler hat. "What'll it be?" he asked the dandy.

"Two cards, if you please."

"The man takes two."

Slade watched the dandy claim his cards, slot them into the middle of his hand, and fan them just enough to read their faces. The tic told Slade his hand had not improved.

"Three bucks to you," the dealer said

"Too rich for me," the dandy said. "I fold."

"One down," the dealer said, rubbing it in, then turned to face the player on his right. "How many cards, old-timer?"

"One should do."

"One card it is."

The old man palmed his card and studied it. He blinked twice, which might be the smoky air or a reaction to his draw, but Slade couldn't interpret it.

"Your bet, " the dealer prodded.

"I'll stay for three."

The bet told Slade his hand hadn't improved, but he was staying in the game. Guessing the cards he held was something else. If he'd been trying for a full house, Slade supposed the old man hadn't drawn the card he needed. On the other hand, if he had blown a straight or flush, he should've folded. That told Slade that he was likely sitting on two pair, maybe three of a kind, but lacked the confidence to raise Slade's bet.

"I'm taking two," the dealer said, which cast a shadow on his boast about the winning hand. He dealt himself two cards, examined them, and flashed a dingy smile. Eyes meeting Slade's, he said, "I'll see your three and raise you one."

Could be a bluff, Slade thought. Or maybe not.

The cowboy on Slade's right drew three cards, cursed at them, and folded. When he shot his next brown bullet at the cuspidor, it seemed to be a commentary on the game.

"Another buck for you to stay," the dealer said to Slade.

Eighteen dollars in front of him. Maybe two hands, if he kept losing. Slade was down almost two hundred dollars since he'd stepped off the train in Holbrook, Arizona, three days earlier, but he kept thinking that his luck was bound to change.

Please, God.

"Raise two," he said, and slid his coins across the table-top.

The dandy, out of it, sat smoking his cheroot and watched the old man to his left. A frown crinkled the bald man's scar. He clenched his teeth, making his sideburns ripple. "No," he said at last. "I'm done."

"That's two to me," the dealer said. "I'll see the bet and raise you two."

There was a fine line between confidence and foolishness, Slade realized, but knew the dealer wouldn't run. Not this time. "Call," he said. "Let's see your hand."

"Two pair," the dealer said, smiling. "Tens over treys." The cards fanned out in front of him, a stray queen seeming out of place and lonely in the hand.

"Jacks over deuces," Slade replied, facing his cards. "My pot."

He raked the money in and left the dealer glaring at him, while the deck passed to the man's left. The cowboy shuffled twice and let Slade cut the deck before he called the next game.

"Ante up for five-card stud."

Five dollars in the pot to start, before the cowboy started dealing to his left. The first card went facedown, a nine of hearts to Slade. He concentrated on the other faces at the table, watching them for signs of pain or pleasure as they eyed their hole cards, gaining little from the exercise.

The cowboy started on his second round, dealing the cards faceup. Slade drew a six of spades and bet a dollar, watching as the deal moved on. The dandy on Slade's left received the ace of spades and matched his dollar bet. The old man drew the five of hearts and put his dollar in the pot. Across from Slade, his unwashed adversary pulled the four of hearts and bet a dollar. When the cowboy dealt himself a queen of hearts, he made the bet unanimous.

"Round three," the dealer said, and turned another card faceup for Slade. "We got a five of clubs, possible straight."

Slade thought about his hole card and decided it was worth another dollar. "One to stay," he said.

The dandy caught a king of clubs and smiled, putting another dollar in the pot without comment. The dealer filled in for him, saying, "Another possible straight."

The next card, to the old man, was the jack of clubs. It didn't fit the five of hearts already showing, but he put another dollar in the pot. No one would fold this early, Slade supposed, when they had two cards left to go.

Across from Slade, the former dealer drew a four of clubs to match the heart already showing. "First pair of the game," the dealer said, as yet another dollar crossed the tabletop.

The cowboy dealt himself a jack of spades, against the showing queen, and put two dollars in the pot. "Raise one," he said before continuing the deal.

Slade reckoned that he wouldn't raise without a fair card in the hole. Something to make a pair, most likely, or a straight still two cards short. At least Slade knew it couldn't be a straight flush, with the mismatched heart and spade. They went around the table, each matching the raise, which made it twenty dollars in the pot.

Slade's next card was the eight of hearts. He had to fight to keep the smile off of his face, hearing the dealer say, "Still working on that straight."

"Two dollars more," Slade said, and put his money in the pot. He would've liked to raise, but filling inside straights was always tricky, and he didn't want to spook the others into folding yet. They couldn't know his hole card was a nine, and he was saving it for a surprise.

Depending on the last card, though, the joke might be on him.

The dandy drew an ace of hearts, showing the best pair on the table. No facial tics this time, only a smile as he doubled the dealer's bet. "Let's make it four dollars," he said.

The old man caught a five of spades, his pair the smaller of the two revealed so far. Instead of folding, though, he matched the dandy's bet and turned to face the player on his left.

Slade's adversary scanned the table, waiting for his card. When it came up the four of spades, he beamed and clapped his grimy hands together, mimicking a pistol shot.

"Three of a kind," the dealer said, sounding depressed.

"I'll see that four and raise it two," the happy man said. Six dollars went into the pot.

The cowboy dealt himself a three of clubs and folded, thereby telling Slade that nothing in the deck would let him beat three fours. His straight was broken, and his hole card couldn't be a jack or queen.

Slade owed four dollars on the round. The dandy and the old man owed two each to call the standing bet. They paid up and the deal continued clockwise, Slade holding his breath for the final card he would receive. As hopeful as he was, he almost didn't recognize the bright seven of hearts that made his straight.

It was the best he could've hoped for, but he dared not let the sudden rush of pleasure surface. While the dealer said, "*Still* working on that straight," Slade eased back in his chair, forcing a frown and hoping that he hadn't overplayed the moment. It came down to acting now, his best hand of the week, but if he tipped his hand by *over*acting, he could chase the others out.

Or maybe one of them would beat him yet.

"I'll stay for six," Slade said, trying to make it sound like stubbornness, instead of confidence.

The dandy's last card was a deuce of spades. It should've been a letdown, but he didn't flinch and matched the standing bet without a whimper. That told Slade that either he had something in the hole to give him courage—meaning that it had to be another ace—or he'd decided on a bluff to buy the hand.

It didn't matter either way to Slade. Three aces couldn't beat his straight, and he was in no mood to quit.

The old man drew a jack of hearts for his last card, and that made two pair showing. The grim expression on his face told Slade his hole card wouldn't make it a full house, no five or jack in hiding to complete the hand.

"I fold," he said disgustedly.

"Last card," the dealer said, and slid a deuce of hearts faceup across the table toward Slade's unwashed opponent. Undismayed, the grizzled player spent a moment studying the coins and bills in front of him, then pushed a handful toward the center of the table.

"I bet ten more dollars," he declared. "Who wants to call?"

"I'll see your ten," Slade said, "and raise the same."

The would-be hardcase blinked at him across the table, glaring hard. The dandy to Slade's left slumped in his chair and said, "It's too damned rich for me."

"That makes it just the two of us, mister." The unwashed man leaned forward, elbows on the table, glowering.

"And it'll cost you ten to see what's in the hole," Slade answered.

It occurred to him that he had never learned the other players' names. That wasn't terribly unusual, but it had set a tone that militated against friendly play.

So what?

Slade hadn't stopped in town to make new friends. He'd needed money and the cards had run against him more than for him, until now. It was past time for him to catch a break and ride it to the winner's circle.

"Ten it is," his adversary grunted. Dirty fingers sorted cash and scrabbled forward to deposit ten more dollars in the pot. "So, show me what you got."

Slade faced the nine of hearts and heard the dandy mutter, "Damn!" The old man shook his head and reached into his pocket for the makings of a cigarette. Their dealer found the grace to smile.

Slade waited for his adversary to reveal the four of diamonds, cackling as he claimed the pot, but what he saw turned up instead was a completely useless ace of clubs. Slade's straight steamrolled three of a kind into the dirt.

"Looks like you win, mister," the dealer said.

"Looks like." Slade raked in the pot and spent a moment sorting, counting. Two hands in a row, with eighty dollars on the second round, had brought him halfway back toward breaking even. He could either test his luck or walk away, be satisfied for now with what he had.

The cowboy turned to Slade and pushed the deck in his direction. "Your deal, mister."

"I don't think so."

An unwashed face leaned closer to him from across the table, reddening. "You don't think *what*?"

Slade met the gimlet gaze without flinching and said, "I'm out. That plain enough?"

"Out, hell! You gotta let us have a chance to win our money back!"

"Says who?"

"*I'm* sayin' it."

"Show me the rule," Slade said

"The *rule*? Hell, ever'body knows—"

"That losers want to win," Slade interrupted him. "I get that part. Show me the rule that makes *you* special. Where's it say I have to sit here all night long and let you pick me clean?"

"Fair's fair, dammit!"

"Uh-huh. That's what I thought." Slade rose, sliding the money deep into his pocket. "Gentlemen, good day to you."

Slade felt the move before he heard the other player's chair scrape back across the sawdust-littered floor. It might have been inevitable from the moment he sat down to play and saw the stocky stranger glaring at him, as if they were longtime enemies. There was no reason for it, but—

"He's got a knife!" somebody said. Maybe the dandy in the bowler hat, hunched forward in his seat to shield himself from injury.

Slade grabbed his beer mug, still one-quarter-filled with tepid ale, and flung its contents in the face of his attacker as the loser lurched around the table, blade in hand. It stung the other's eyes and left him blinking, cursing, flailing blindly for a moment with the wicked-looking knife.

Slade took the opportunity to step closer and smash the empty mug into his adversary's face. Brass knuckles were a common weapon used in barroom fights, but *glass* knuckles possessed a cutting edge second to none. Slade felt the shattered mug slice deeply into a flabby, bristled cheek, and dodged a jet of blood erupting from the wound.

His enemy released the knife, raised both hands to his bloody face. Wet, croaking sounds replaced the stream of curses that had issued from his lips a moment earlier. He wasn't falling, though, so Slade stepped in to help the thing along.

He hooked a left into the stout man's gut, ducked low beneath a backhand slap that sprayed the room with blood, and drove his right fist hard into the other's face. Slade couldn't swear his adversary's nose was broken, but it gave a satisfying *crunch*. The impact staggered his opponent, dropped the big man to one knee.

Would he get up again?

Slade watched him trying, little rat eyes glaring dizzy

hatred, and he knew he had to finish it. Flexing his sore right hand, Slade made a choice and stepped in close, slamming a kick into his enemy's forehead. There was no anger in the glazed eyes any longer as the kneeling man fell backward, sprawling supine in the sawdust with his face a bloody mask.

Slade took two dollars from his pocket, dropped them on his adversary's chest, and told the room at large, "Somebody get the sawbones over here to stitch him up."

Outside, the air was fresh and clean. After the smoky atmosphere inside the Southern Cross, Slade didn't even mind an errant breeze that stirred dust devils in the street.

It would be nice to have his outfit cleaned and pressed, but Slade supposed he might be running out of time. He was a stranger in Holbrook, a gambler with no ties to the community, whose latest game had wound up spilling blood. The fight wasn't his fault, but Slade's experience told him that he was likely to receive a visit from the local lawman, probably before the night was out. There would be questions, maybe a suggestion that he find another town in which to ply his trade.

So be it.

Holbrook hadn't been that lucky for him anyway. As towns went, it had been a loser almost from the moment he arrived. He had enough cash in his pocket now to settle up at the hotel, purchase a ticket on the next train out of town, and stake himself to a piece of the action in some other dusty hamlet somewhere down the line.

It was a gambler's life, the life he'd chosen for himself.

But it was getting old.

Slade passed a restaurant, considered stopping in to have a steak, then changed his mind and kept on walking back to his hotel. The place was one of two that faced each other from opposing sides of Main Street, monuments to progress or the dream of progress yet to come. Slade hadn't noticed patrons overrunning either place, but he'd secured a small, clean room at decent rates.

The desk clerk met him with a smile, then reconsidered it and eyed Slade curiously as he crossed the lobby. Slade ignored him, moving toward the stairs, until the man's voice called him back.

"Um . . . Mr. Slade?"

"What is it?"

"Sir, you have a telegram. I wasn't sure . . . that is . . . the boy came just a while ago, and . . ."

Slade came back to stand before the counter. "Where's the wire?" he asked.

The clerk gaped at him. "Wire. Yes, sir. Right here."

Slade took the flimsy Western Union envelope and turned back toward the stairs, climbing to reach the second floor, palming his key as he approached the door labeled 2D. Once he was safe inside, Slade locked the door behind him, dropped his key beside the washbasin, and caught a glimpse of his reflection in the upright mirror.

"Damn."

He knew then why the clerk had eyed him so strangely. Blood was spattered on the right side of his face, perhaps a dozen droplets from his barroom adversary that he hadn't noticed. Glancing down, Slade saw the hand that had received his telegram was also smeared with blood, across the knuckles, with a few flecks on the thumb.

He washed up quickly, checking again to make sure his shirt and jacket bore no crimson stains. If they were there, Slade couldn't spot them, and they could wait for cleaning until he found himself another place to rest.

Holbrook was done.

They had a sundown train, he knew that much, since it had brought him into town. Slade checked his watch and started packing, not that there was much to put in his valise. He owned a razor, shaving mug, a comb, two extra shirts, another pair of pants, two slender ties.

And one Colt Peacemaker in tie-down leather, with the gunbelt coiled around it like a snake.

Slade took the hardware from his bag, considered it, then strapped the belt around his waist. He told himself that it was just to make more room, but Holbrook had gone sour on him in a hurry, and he feared there still might be more trouble waiting for him as he took his leave.

The telegram.

Seeing the blood spray on his face had pushed the envelope out of his conscious thoughts. Now Slade retrieved it from the dresser, slit it open, and removed the yellow sheet it held. Unfolding it, he read the message once, then started over from the top.

> *John Slade—regret to inform you of your brother's death on April 7 stop Investigation of particulars continues stop For further information and personal effects contact clerk of US Court Lawton Oklahoma territory stop Sincere condolence stop—Harmon Ford US Deputy Marshal*

Slade settled in the room's one straight-backed chair to keep himself from falling. He felt short of breath, as if a hard fist had connected with his solar plexus, emptying his lungs.

Regret to inform you of your brother's death.

It was incredible, the crippling power that resided in a string of printed words. Mere symbols etched on paper, but they robbed Slade of his strength, put a lump in his throat, stung his eyes.

It had been close to four years since he'd last set eyes on James, but it was always in Slade's mind to make the journey, seek out his brother, and spend a few days on Jim's ranch, catching up on old times. Slade had delayed the trip a hundred times, telling himself he'd go when he was better off financially. Wanting to make a splash, impress Jim that the black sheep of the family had finally made good.

Now he would never have that chance.

Slade smoothed the crumpled telegram against his knee and checked the date again. According to the message, Jim had died on April 7, nearly two months earlier. The news had taken that long to catch up with Slade, chasing his tracks across New Mexico and into Arizona.

"Damn."

Investigation of particulars continues.

What in hell did *that* mean anyway? If Jim's death had been due to accident or illness, there'd be no need for investigation by a U.S. marshal. That spelled murder, or suspicion of it at the very least.

What were the personal effects referred to in the telegram? Why hadn't they been shipped back to his parents in St. Louis? Those were questions Slade would have to answer for himself.

In Oklahoma.

"Damn it all to hell."

Slade took his time folding the telegram and placed it in the inside pocket of his coat. He had a destination now, although it wasn't one he had anticipated when he left the Southern Cross saloon. He was too late to see his brother, much less help him, but at least he could find out what happened.

Maybe he could even make it right.

Too late for that, Slade thought. *Too late and then some.*

Slade donned his hat, picked up his worn valise, and gave the room another look to make sure nothing that he valued had been left behind. It was as empty and anonymous as on the day when he'd arrived, a space that fairly symbolized Slade's life.

Nobody home.

No home, in fact.

He left the door ajar and went downstairs. The clerk stood frowning, checking out his face, apparently relieved to find no bloodstains on his cheek this time.

"I'm leaving," Slade told him.

"Now, sir?"

"Now."

"Um . . . I'm afraid that we must charge you for the night. You understand, sir, with the hour—"

"That's fine," Slade said. "Just add it in."

The clerk bent to his ledger, made some scratches on a small notepad, and spoke a number. Slade took out his winnings from the afternoon and paid the bill, declining a receipt.

He still had time to get that steak before the sundown train arrived, but Slade had lost his appetite. The finest gourmet fare would only taste like ashes to him now.

He left the hotel lobby, turned right toward the railroad depot, and had covered half a block before the gruff voice hailed him from behind.

"You, there! The gamblin' man! Wait up!"

Slade turned to find his adversary from the Southern Cross advancing down the wooden sidewalk, boot heels clomping on the dusty boards. Someone had wrapped his face in rags, apparently without the benefit of stitches, since his blood was leaking through the cloth.

"See what you did to me?" the stout man challenged him.

"You got off easy," Slade replied.

"Think so? Let's see how *you* get off!"

The bearded gambler hadn't worn a gun in the saloon, but he had found one somewhere since their scuffle. It was tucked inside his belt, behind the buckle, angled for a right-hand draw.

"You're making a mistake," Slade said.

"Oh, yeah? It wouldn't be the first time."

"I believe that," Slade replied.

The man stopped six or seven paces distant, scowling from behind the cloth that wreathed his face. His right hand twitched, anxious to clasp the pistol.

"Think you're smart, I bet," he said. "We'll see how smart you are here in a minute."

"This is how you judge intelligence?" Slade asked.

"It's how I judge a man," his enemy replied.

"Too bad." Slade dropped the bag from his left hand and heard it strike the boards beside his foot.

Slade couldn't smell the liquor on his adversary's breath, but he'd have bet the money in his pocket that the man had downed at least four shots of courage while his face was being wrapped. Slade hoped the firewater would spoil his aim.

"You wanna walk away from this," the stout man said, "just give my money back and get on out of town."

"I'm leaving anyway, if that's a help," Slade said.

"My money first."

"You lost the hand. If you can't swallow that, you shouldn't play at all."

"You cheated me!"

"I wasn't dealing," Slade reminded him.

"Regardless."

Slade gave up. "You want the money, take it."

"What, you think I can't?" the other challenged him.

"Let's see."

The stout man made his move, tugging the six gun from his belt. The front sight caught up for a heartbeat on the leather, giving Slade the time he needed and a little more. He drew, aimed, fired, and watched red mist explode from one of his opponent's knees.

His would-be killer fell, the second time that Slade had put him down. He lost his pistol in the fall, hands groping for the ruin of his left knee while the long-barreled revolver spun away, beyond his reach.

Slade stepped around the weeping, cursing man, retrieved the piece, and brought it back. It was a Smith & Wesson, showing signs of rust, but still a killing tool. Slade thumbed the hammer back and bent to press its muzzle tight against the other man's forehead. Eyes filled with pain crossed as they tried to focus on the gun.

"Third time's the charm," Slade said. "Next time I see you, you're a dead man. Understand me? Are we clear?"

"I hear you, mister."

"Right. But are you *listening*?"

"I am! I swear to God!"

A crowd was gathering, but Slade still took his time. "Tell me your name," he said.

"Tom Whitman."

"Do we understand each other, Tom?"

"We do."

"Be sure. Next time I see your face, I take you down. No warnings, no discussion. Right?"

"That's right."

"I'll leave your pistol at the railway depot. Pick it up when you can walk. And then think twice before you follow me."

"Ain't doin' that," Whitman replied. "I swear!"

"Maybe you're smarter than you look."

"I hope so, mister."

"So do I."

Slade turned and left him sitting on the sidewalk. Halfway to the railway depot, he stopped at an alley's mouth, opened the captured weapon's cylinder, and spilled its load of death into the dust. The empty gun he carried with him to the station, three blocks farther west.

The ticket clerk was twenty-odd years old and obviously bored. "How do I get from here to Lawton, Oklahoma?" Slade inquired.

The young man checked his schedules, made some notes, then read them back to Slade. "Train out of here tonight will take you into Lubbock, Texas. There, you switch and take the Katie Flyer into Oklahoma Territory. Lawton's on the line."

"How much?"

"Two dollars into Lubbock, three more to your destination."

Slade retrieved his roll of cash. "Let's set it up."

"Yes, sir!"

The youth seemed happy now, a chore to do before he settled into tedium once more. Slade waited for his tickets, checked the information printed on them, and secured them in a pocket of his vest.

"How long until the train gets in?" he asked.

"Another twenty minutes, give or take."

He wondered if the marshal would arrive before the train, deciding that it didn't matter. He was leaving Holbrook, leaving Arizona. That should satisfy the law for now.

And if it didn't, there'd be hell to pay.

2

The train arrived and left on time, no badges to delay it. Slade supposed that Holbrook's marshal must have questioned witnesses and satisfied himself that Whitman had earned his wounds. Or maybe he was one of those lawmen who simply didn't care.

Slade was the only passenger who went aboard at Holbrook, and the car he chose was nearly empty. Seated toward the front, a man and woman in their early thirties traveled with a girl Slade pegged as being three or four years old. Mother and daughter both had flaxen hair done up in curls that spilled around their faces like a mass of golden Christmas ornaments. The father wore his dark hair parted in the middle, and observed Slade with a cautious eye.

Smart man.

In other circumstances, Slade might have approached the woman—would have, more than likely—but his mind was elsewhere at the moment, and he never trespassed underneath a husband's very nose.

He didn't need another brawl or shooting. Slade would save his rage for now and spend it later, where he reckoned it might do some good.

The car's last passenger sat halfway back, on the left side. He was an older man, whose gray hair and mustache echoed the fabric of his suit. The clothes he wore had been expensive in their day, but were a trifle shabby now, though fairly well maintained. Slade took him for a drummer, likely hauling samples of his merchandise in one or both of his old carpetbags.

Slade found a seat near the back of the car and settled in to let his thoughts unwind. Night overtook them on the rails, sweeping along behind them from the east on silent wings, but Slade felt no immediate desire for sleep. He had too much to think about, too many images and questions roiling in his head.

His first thought: Jim was dead, some kind of mystery surrounding it, and if a U.S. marshal couldn't solve it, Slade felt honor-bound to try. He didn't know what that investigation would entail, where it would lead him, but he'd find out once he got to Oklahoma and heard the circumstances of his brother's death.

The telegram itself was odd. Slade thought the law would reach out for his parents first, well settled in St. Louis, pillars of the church and mercantile community. Perhaps a wire had gone to them as well, and how would they have taken it? They obviously hadn't claimed their son's effects from Lawton. Had they fetched the body home for burial, or would that be too much to ask?

Two sons, two disappointments, but at least Jim had been business-minded, even if he wouldn't stay at home and study law, the way their father always wanted. Jim had longed to be a rancher and was making it, the last Slade heard. Building a home and herd, earning a reputation that inspired respect.

Slade's dreams had never been that clear or that constructive. He'd always wanted to be *going* somewhere, never thinking of a final destination or a plot of land to call his own. What was the point in having legs, he asked himself, if he was only standing still? Why was he born with eyes, if there was nothing to be seen beyond the city streets where he was born and raised?

He was the black sheep of the family, and then some. Disinherited for starters, when he wouldn't toe the line, cut off from any contact with his folks at home, unless he showed up at their door with hat in hand and an apology that ran too hard against the grain. They would've managed to forgive him somehow, Slade supposed, but neither of his parents would forget. He'd always be the son who shamed them and defied their plans for how his life should run.

So be it.

Slade couldn't turn back the clock, and wouldn't if he'd had the power. He was more or less contented with his life so far, gambling and going where the spirit moved him, asking nothing of the next town down the road except a poker table and a place to sleep.

Slade won more than he lost, and rarely had to fight for what he'd won. Tom Whitman was the first loser who'd tried to kill him in a year or so, the first time he'd spilled blood since Christmas 1888.

That thought took Slade back to a dive in Pueblo, Colorado, and a knife fight that had left his body scarred. The first time he had killed a man. There'd been some talk of lynching, but the sheriff was a stalwart sort who wouldn't let a mob tarnish his star. He judged the killing self-defense and saw Slade safely out of town, as soon as Slade was well enough to travel.

Slade brought his mind back from the realm of ancient history to here and now. The telegram from Lawton still confused him. It was no surprise his parents hadn't told him Jim was dead. Not speaking meant they wouldn't tip him off if Judgment Day was scheduled for next Tuesday, and Slade guessed they'd have no way to find him, even if they changed their minds.

So, how had Marshal Harmon Ford located him?

Slade guessed the information must've come from Jim somehow. He hadn't written Jim from Holbrook, but he'd dropped a line from Tucson some weeks earlier. The pickings had been sweeter there, likewise the women, but he'd overstayed his welcome when a certain lady's husband took offense at Slade's close friendship with his wife. Slade guessed it hadn't been their dining out, so much as what was on the menu for dessert.

That mental image almost won a smile from Slade, but then his brother's face came back to haunt him. Not the grinning, suntanned face he knew, but slack and pale, with eyes that had a dead man's dusty look.

Too late to make things right perhaps, but he could try.

"I'm coming," whispered Slade. "I'm on my way."

Five hundred miles of track stretched out between Holbrook and Lubbock, with a mountain range to cross when they were halfway through New Mexico. The train clocked thirty miles an hour, more or less, on open desert, slowing down to five or six when it was climbing, and it made a couple dozen stops along the way for water, fuel, cargo, and passengers. A trip that should've taken sixteen hours, nonstop over level ground, thus stretched to twenty-eight.

Slade slept in fits and starts along the way, but got no rest to speak of. When he dozed, Jim came to him in haunting dreams, not speaking, just his pale face hovering, his dead eyes staring with intensity enough to pierce Slade's soul.

Jarred from his sleep, Slade woke to guilt that made no sense. He hadn't murdered Jim, hadn't abandoned him.

They'd gone their separate ways years earlier but had kept in touch, unlike some other members of the family.

It's not my fault, Slade told himself.

Why couldn't he believe it?

Slade normally enjoyed traveling by rail. He didn't have to think about the weather, finding forage for a horse or water for the two of them. His progress was unlikely to be interrupted, whether by some act of God, a hungry cougar, or distempered rattlesnake, and other humans who he met along the way were likely to ignore him. Slade enjoyed his solitude, the feeling of security that came with rattling across the landscape in a steel box, sealed off from the outside world. It made him feel immune to danger in between depots along the way.

Slade had been riding trains in one way or another for the best part of a decade, stealing rides at first, then buying tickets with the money earned from cards. In all that time, he had been robbed exactly twice—once as a stowaway, and six years later, when a team of bandits came aboard his train midway between Denver and Colorado City. That job had cost Slade two hundred dollars and a watch that marked his last link with his kinfolk in Missouri.

He had let both go without a fight, deciding he could always win more money, buy himself another watch, but pride could never plug a bullet hole.

Some fights were unavoidable, while others could be sidestepped by a man willing to bend a little. Avoiding trouble when he could did not make Slade a coward—in his own mind anyway. He thought of men who courted trouble day and night as fools, not worth the lead and powder that would send most of them on to early graves.

Survival was an art in the West, and Slade was a survivor.

As for Jim . . .

He had no way of learning what had happened to his brother, not until he spoke with the authorities in Lawton. Speculation prior to that was wasted effort, but Slade couldn't help himself. What else was he supposed to think about while counting off the empty miles?

Somewhere east of Gallup, waking in the middle of the night, Slade spied a fire outside his window, lighting up the pitch-black desert. It was half a mile north of the tracks at least, but he could still make out the rough shape of a house engulfed by flames. His fellow passengers slept through the show, but Slade kept watching while the fire receded and at last winked out, smothered by darkness.

Settling back into his seat, he idly wondered what had caused the fire, what kind of tragedy it had visited upon the home's inhabitants. Had they escaped in time? Were Indians or outlaws waiting in the night outside to cut them down as they emerged? Was it a simple accident, somebody's candle or cigar stub unattended while they dozed, made love, or boozed the night away?

That was the way of things, in Slade's experience. A man or woman who ignored details, rushed through the hours of their lives without a care, often woke up to find those lives in flames, collapsing into ruins while they stood by, helpless. He supposed something like that had happened to his brother, though the Jim he knew had always been meticulous. A risk taker, of course, but they were always *calculated* risks, never a blind leap from the precipice with no idea of what lay down below.

Slade's train reached Lubbock shortly after two A.M. The Katie Flyer wasn't due for seven hours yet, so Slade went looking for a place to sleep. The first hotel he found had one room left, a fourth floor corner with a window overlooking garbage in a narrow alley. Slade wasn't particular and paid the full night's rate, leaving instructions to be awakened at five A.M.

Inside the boxlike room, Slade checked the window latch, then took the room's lone chair and wedged it underneath the doorknob. Having secured the room within his limited ability, Slade stripped and hung his clothing in the open cupboard designated as a closet, then crawled into bed, sliding the Peacemaker beneath his pillow.

All he needed now was sleep.

And chasing it, Slade hoped he wouldn't dream.

A knock woke Slade five minutes late, by his watch, but it gave him ample time. He washed his face and shaved, seeing no changes in the mirror that he could've specified, pointing to this or that new wrinkle as a sign that he had lost the only kin who'd been on speaking terms with him for years.

Maybe those marks showed on the soul, and not the flesh.

Slade dressed, closed his valise, and made his way downstairs. The drowsy clerk who'd signed him in was still on duty, managing a nod and half smile as he took Slade's key.

"Will you be staying with us any longer, sir?" he asked.

Slade shook his head. "I'm done."

"Well, if you're ever back in Lubbock, please—"

Slade walked out on the rest of it, spotting the restaurant he'd seen the night before, closed then, but open for the early breakfast trade as daylight drove the shadows back from sidewalks to the alleys where they lived. Slade crossed the street, went in, and found a window seat that let him watch day breaking over Lubbock.

There was nothing much to see, in fact. Nothing to match the red-haired waitress who appeared and took Slade's order for a steak and eggs, with fried potatoes on the side. She had her hands full, wasn't in the mood for talk, and Slade could sympathize. He wasn't on his best game either, staring at the street as shops began to open, wondering about the urge that made folks settle in one place and bet their futures on a dream.

He'd never understood the urge that made Jim want to

wrangle cows, for instance. Slade had known his share of cowboys, nearly all of them ill-educated drifters with a killing thirst for alcohol. They spent half their time eating trail dust, the rest of it flirting with jail. If pressed, Slade couldn't name one cowboy who had risen far above the grit he carried on his clothes and underneath his finger-nails.

That hadn't been his brother's dream, however. Jim was bent on *owning* steers, not simply chasing them around between railheads. He saw a future in the land and in the trade, telling himself and anyone who'd listen that he meant to carve an empire from the prairie.

Empire, hell.

Regardless of a man's size when he was alive, no mat-ter what his reach, the ground he occupied on crossing over still came down to roughly three feet wide and six feet deep.

But what about the rest? Slade asked himself.

Jim was a man of property, or had been, and the pass-ing reference to personal effects didn't explain what had become of all his land, his stock, his home.

Slade wondered if there'd been a will, unmentioned in the telegram. By rights, Jim's property should all go to his family, since he had never married, but the thought of Joshua and Maris Slade owning a cattle ranch in Okla-homa Territory was enough to spark a smile.

Slade lost it when he thought about the land and the re-sponsibility passing to him. Panic enveloped him for something like two heartbeats; then he shrugged it off. Jim wouldn't be that foolish, trusting him with anything that must be nurtured and sustained.

Slade cleaned his plate and drank his coffee, paid his bill and left the redhead a generous tip. She flashed him a smile on his way out the door, making Slade stop and wonder who'd care if he missed the day's train heading north.

No one.

He was already too late to help Jim, and the marshal in Lawton would be there tomorrow, next week, or whenever. A short stay in Lubbock would cost Slade no more than a piece of his soul.

He decided against it, moved on toward the depot, exchanging a nod here and there with the early birds sweeping off sidewalks in front of their stores. Settled people whose futures were bounded by walls, inventory, and books filled with numbers detailing their profit or loss. Slade wondered how they stood it, what was lacking from his makeup that he never felt the urge to put down roots.

No matter. He supposed it was too late for him to change.

Slade reached the depot with time to spare, picked up a day-old newspaper someone had left behind, and smoothed the wrinkles out of it before he started reading. Its news was timely but routine, a litany of crimes and celebrations, gains and losses, dreams come true and nightmares realized. Slade tired of it after the second page and put the paper back where he had found it, waiting empty-handed for the train.

The Katie Flyer was ten minutes late, which made no difference in the scheme of things. Slade had another ride ahead of him. Two hundred miles, say seven hours minimum, with stops along the way. It still beat riding horseback, which would probably have taken him a week, if he encountered no real problems on the trail.

Slade wished he had a book to pass the time, but he was traveling light, no excess baggage other than his thoughts of Jim. Their paths had separated years ago, but they had always stayed in touch, and Slade had never seriously thought about a world without his brother in it. Now he found the thought unsettling in a fundamental way, but there was nothing he could do about it.

Too damned late.

Slade knew there wasn't anything he could've done to save Jim, short of moving in with him and watching him around the clock, and even that would be no guarantee of safety. Slade wasn't his brother's keeper, but he couldn't shake the feeling that he should have been.

The Flyer made up some of its lost time, only a handful of departing passengers and minor cargo swiftly loaded in the boxcars farther back. Their path lay over open country, mostly flat and dry, but gaining color as they traveled farther east. They passed a dozen dusty towns that seemed nearly identical to Slade. Church steeples moved from one end to another, faded colors varied on the shops and houses, but their look was all the same—sun-bleached and tired, as if the very buildings had been worked almost to death.

The settled life, Slade thought. *No, thanks.*

He watched the land unfold before him, giving way from state to territory as they crossed the Red River, leaving Texas and civilization behind. Law was sparse in Oklahoma Territory, frequently challenged by wide ranging bandits and renegades who'd jumped one of the region's several native reservations. Slade had glimpsed a double lynching from the train, last time he'd come to visit Jim, but that was on another route, riding the southbound rails from Wichita.

He saw no bodies dangling from the trees this time, no homesteads scarred by smoke and flames. The Katie Flyer rolled past herds of cattle, grazing free on open land, with scattered riders posted to protect them.

Here, a man owned that which he could hold and guard by force. Jim had explained the losses he sustained to rustlers, renegades, and Mother Nature. In a case of theft, most ranchers tried to settle it themselves, but Jim had been the law-abiding sort, preferring charges on the books to corpses swinging in the breeze.

Slade wondered whether it had been that attitude that cost his brother's life.

Not that he sanctioned killing in the course of normal day to day events. Slade carried two ghosts on his conscience, both of men he'd slain in clear-cut self-defense. He didn't go looking for trouble, sidestepped it whenever he could, but on those two occasions at least there had been no escape.

What would he do now that his brother had been killed?

First, learn the facts. No one was served by going off half-cocked and jumping to conclusions. Slade knew nothing of Jim's neighbors, any other people who had been part of his life—or death. He counted on the marshal, Harmon Ford, to fill those gaps and help him learn what had become of Jim.

And when he knew, what then?

If Slade got information that his parents didn't have, should he approach them with it? Share his findings and solicit their advice? In this extremity, would they relax their rigid rules enough to speak with him?

Considering that question, Slade discovered that he didn't care. He could address a letter to them, make the reading of it their choice, then forget about the whole damned thing.

Unless there were accounts to settle first.

In that case, Slade knew he would have to see what happened, how events played out. There might be nothing he could do. But then again . . .

No hurry, Slade reminded himself. Whatever had happened to Jim, he was already two months late getting the news. If it was murder, those responsible could be in North Dakota or relaxing on the California coast by now. Without their names and physical descriptions, Slade would likely never find them. Never track them to whatever hideaway they'd found.

If it was murder. If the marshal's choice of language wasn't just deliberately mysterious.

Relax, he thought. *You'll find out soon enough.*

And then the payback could begin.

A young conductor came around near dusk, announcing that they were five miles outside of Lawton. Slade stayed put, his satchel on the seat beside him, nothing to be packed before he left the train. Throughout the car he occupied, some of his fellow passengers prepared to disembark, while others kept their faces to the windows, weary, apathetic, bound for who knows where.

Lawton was just another town, albeit half again as large as any other they had passed since leaving Lubbock. From the depot, Slade passed on to the main thoroughfare, pausing to scan the downtown layout and assess its possibilities.

From where he stood, Slade counted three saloons, all going strong, with two hotels that he could see and several dozen shops just closing for the night. Foot traffic vied with horses and a few buckboards. The tall, obligatory church spire stood directly opposite the railway depot, at the far end of the street. God might have noticed what was happening in Lawton's western sector, but so far He hadn't intervened.

Slade had a deck of cards in his coat pocket, but he didn't feel like playing at the moment. It was late to see the marshal, he supposed, so he set off to find a room instead. The morning would be soon enough to speak of death and mystery. Another night of grim dreams wouldn't kill him, most particularly if he took a bottle to his bed.

Or something else.

Slade felt the urge, passing the first saloon and glancing in past batwing doors, but he was put off by the sight of working girls. They'd lend a sympathetic ear if he required it, even weep with him for money, but the need for comfort was already fading as he stood there on the sidewalk.

Slade decided that he didn't want to feel better. Not yet, not for an hour or a night. He'd wait and listen to the marshal first, ask any questions he could think of, and decide what should be done—if anything—about his brother's death.

And personal effects, he thought. *Remember those.*

Whatever Slade found out, whatever he decided, he would make his choices in the cold, hard light of day. There'd be no blundering around in haste, on unfamiliar ground, to sabotage whatever plan he made.

Food first, then sleep. Tomorrow he would meet the law, assuming Harmon Ford was still in town, and Slade would figure out what ought to happen next. If Ford was unavailable, he'd ask around, find out who else had known his brother and could sketch in the circumstances of his death.

Dusk followed Slade along the street until he reached the first hotel, then passed him by as he entered the lobby. They'd begun to look alike, these transient homes away from home, most featuring some kind of artwork on the lobby walls and registration clerks who either looked like children or Methuselah.

Slade reckoned he fell somewhere in between.

This was a young one, smiling as he said, "Good evening, sir. Do you require a room?"

"I do."

"How long will you be staying with us, sir?"

"A few days," Slade replied. "I'm not sure yet."

The clerk explained the hotel's rates. It cost less by the week, and Slade paid half down in advance. He palmed the key to Room 4A, facing the street in front.

"We have a laundry service," said the clerk, as if reluctant to release him. "Other services can also be arranged, depending on the purpose of your visit, sir. Business? Pleasure?"

"I'll let you know," Slade said, and left the young man staring after him as he proceeded toward the stairs.

3

Slade woke at dawn with the uneasy feeling that a new place often gave him, amplified by the oppressive knowledge that his brother had been killed, if not in Lawton, then at least nearby. He'd slept the night through with his Peacemaker beneath the lumpy pillow, more tired than he would've guessed from simply riding on a train. If he had dreamed, the images were lost, and that was fine with Slade.

His view of Lawton's main street showed him early risers on their way to operate or patronize the local stores. He'd seen the same in Lubbock, in Holbrook, and in a hundred other towns, where nerves or habit roused him at ungodly hours to observe the Other Half. Each time, he felt a nagging mix of longing and relief.

No steady job for Slade, watching the clock while someone else watched him, demanding that he sweep floors, restock shelves, or jot down calculations in a ledger. He was free to travel where and when he wished, pleasing nobody but himself. The downside was that no one gave a second thought to him beyond a poker table.

Now that Jim was gone, no one on Earth cared if he lived or died.

Slade guessed that wasn't literally true, but he'd have bet good money that he could predict his family's reaction to a telegram announcement of his death. Slade's mother might weep briefly, quietly in private, while his old man fussed over the lighting of his pipe.

"I tried to warn him," Joshua Slade would say. "Time and again, I tried. Whelp should've seen it coming. Threw his life away to spite me. And for what, I ask you? All for what?"

The old man never changed. Some found it charming, but they hadn't lived full-time beneath the old man's roof, hadn't experienced the numbing sense of *always* being wrong.

Slade had escaped at age sixteen, while Jim hung on another eighteen months or so before he made the break. They'd talked about that lag time later, Slade surprised to hear that Jim hadn't been punished for his brother's flight. The old man hadn't blamed him, but neither had he drawn Jim any closer.

Some things—and some people—never changed.

Slade took his time shaving and dressing, calculating that the marshal's office would be closed for several hours yet. He buckled on his gunbelt, no point taking chances, and locked up before he went downstairs.

The clerk was reading a dime novel about Wild Bill Hickock when he saw Slade coming down the stairs. He set the little book aside and plastered on a smile.

"Good morning, sir!"

Slade nodded. "Where's the nearest halfway decent restaurant?"

"Across the street and four doors north, sir. Geraldine's."

"And after that, the U.S. marshal's office?"

That produced a blink. "Another two blocks north, sir. On your left."

Outside, the morning had begun to simmer. It would be a long, hot day. Slade's stomach rumbled, spurring him along the sidewalk to the bright façade of Geraldine's, painted a startling red with white trim, two large windows facing on the street that let the diners eye pasersby and vice versa.

Slade entered on a wave of succulent aromas, found a corner table set for two, and read the menu written on a six-foot slate with yellow chalk. A dark-haired waitress found him several minutes later, carrying a cast-iron coffeepot. She filled Slade's cup without waiting for him to ask.

"You Geraldine?" Slade asked.

"I wish. What will you have?"

"Fried eggs, potatoes, ham. What's Texas toast?"

"Big bread."

"I'll have that too."

She didn't write his order down. A smile flicked on and off before she turned away.

The place was nearly full, most of the diners locals by their look. Some of the men wore guns, but they were a minority. It told Slade that the town was fairly settled, even if the countryside at large was plagued with rogues and renegades of every race and color. Lawton's folk were civilized—or putting up a front at least.

The food came quickly, pleasantly surprising Slade with both its quality and quantity. Not knowing when he'd have a chance to eat again, Slade took his time and finished every bite. He used his chewing time to watch the other customers, and found some of them watching him as well.

It was another way to pick out the locals, noting who paid close attention to a stranger in their midst. They didn't have to stare, but little flicking glances cast in Slade's direction had the same effect. A few of them engaged in whispered conversation, not always discreet enough to keep their eyes away from Slade while they were talking.

He was used to it; a drifter learned to read the signs, but some of those around him showed more interest than he had anticipated. A few of them *were* staring by the time Slade cleaned his plate, the women blushing when he caught them at it, men inclined to simply frown.

Slade felt eyes following him when he rose and went to pay his bill. He let them track him to the register, then to the door, where he abruptly turned and faced the room. A couple of the women gasped at that, then busily attacked their breakfasts, while the rest mumbled a resumption of their conversations.

Strange.

Slade moved along the sidewalk toward his second destination, half expecting other townsfolk to be gawking at him on the street, but no one seemed to notice him. He reached the U.S. marshal's office, smaller than the shops on either side of it, and tried the door. It opened to his touch and Slade entered.

A man roughly his own height, twenty-odd pounds heavier, was tacking wanted posters on a corkboard near the room's lone desk, back turned to Slade. He heard the door and swiveled, blinked twice at the new arrival, then declared, "I'll be goddamned and go to hell!"

"Is something wrong?" Slade asked.

"Not wrong." The lawman dropped his extra posters on the desk, moving to meet Slade in the middle of the room. "I wasn't sure if you'd be coming, Mr. Slade. Whether the telegrams I sent would reach you, or—"

"You know me, Marshal?"

"Hell, who wouldn't? I knew you were Jim Slade's brother, but nobody told me you were *twins*."

"Identical, in fact."

"I see that. Harmon Ford." The marshal offered Slade a large, rough hand. "I'm glad you're here."

"One of your wires caught up with me in Arizona. I'd have been here sooner, but I didn't know. . . ."

Slade suddenly ran out of words. His shoulders slumped. The breakfast he'd just eaten felt like lead weights in his stomach.

"Have a seat, why don't you?" Ford suggested.

"Thanks."

Slade settled into one of two chairs set before the marshal's desk. Ford walked around the other side and slowly nestled in a seat that rocked and creaked beneath him.

"My condolences about your brother, Mr. Slade. I would've told you sooner if there'd been a forwarding address, but as it was—"

"No problem," Slade replied. "I never know exactly where I'll be myself from one week to the next."

"Guess Lawton wasn't on your list."

"Not recently."

"Well, family falls out of touch sometimes," Ford said. "Been there myself."

"Your wire said Jim was killed on April seventh."

"Right. I hate to break it to you this way, Mr. Slade, but—"

"He was murdered."

"That's a fact. Yes, sir."

"I got that from your wire. 'Investigation of particulars continues.' "

"Sorry. There's no smooth way to say it in a telegram."

"What happened, Marshal?"

Ford answered with a question of his own. "Were you familiar with your brother's business, Mr. Slade?"

"Familiar? He was raising cattle when I saw him last, building a spread."

"How long ago was that, if I may ask?"

"Almost four years. The spring of '87."

"Well, he built that spread, I'll tell you. It took nerve and then some, but your brother had a couple thousand acres and a sound herd when he passed. Good breeding stock, plenty of water. He'd done well, and there was better yet in store. Of course, achievement on that scale comes with a price."

"You're saying he had enemies."

"Who doesn't, when you think about it?" answered Ford. "The question is, do we have anything our enemies want bad enough to take away by force?"

"Somebody killed Jim for his land and livestock?"

"When you say it plain like that, I can't make out a case," Ford said. "That's why I'm still investigating, see?"

"But you believe it."

"Mr. Slade, we've got all kinds of bad men here in Oklahoma. Some bad women too, don't kid yourself. The gentle sex, my ass. *Somebody* shot your brother in the back, from ambush, riding on his own land in the middle of a Sunday afternoon. They shot him off his horse, then gave him two more out of meanness, making sure he stayed down. That's the bitter truth of it."

"Do you have any suspects?"

"Now you're hitting on my problem," Ford replied. A frown carved furrows in his long, tanned face. "Stockmen in Oklahoma have to deal with rustlers. That's a fact of life. Some thieves are independent operators. Self-employed, like. Steal a herd of cattle, maybe horses, and they change the brands. Light out for Mexico or Kansas with 'em, who knows where."

"And others?"

"Well, some think—and I won't say they're wrong, but I can't prove it—some think certain rustlers go another way. Some think they hire out to a man or group of men who want more land themselves. Steal from the neighbors maybe, hoping they'll get sick of it and sell out to the highest bidder. If they *don't* sell, maybe stealing's not enough. Maybe a stubborn man gets taken out some other way."

"You've given this some thought," said Slade.

"It's what they pay me for. Not much, I grant you, but I try to earn it just the same."

"And if you've thought about it that much, you must have a name in mind."

"Suspicion isn't proof," Ford said. "And even if it *was,* we've got procedures hereabouts. I'd have to make a case that satisfies Judge Dennison, file charges in the normal way, make an arrest, see how the trial goes. We don't hold with private justice in the territory, Mr. Slade."

"Meaning you won't give me that name."

"Meaning exactly that, if there was any name to give."

Slade didn't push it. "In your wire, you mentioned Jim's effects."

"Yes, sir. I haven't got 'em here, but you can see your brother's lawyer for the details."

"Who would that be?"

"Amos Whitaker. Best lawyer in the territory, if he does say so himself." A mirthless smile from Ford.

"He's here in Lawton?"

"One block south. You would've passed his office, coming up here from the railroad depot."

"Well, then, Marshal, if there's nothing more that you can tell me . . . ?"

"Nothing you could hang your hat on, I'm afraid." Ford rose and stood behind his desk, arms crossed. "There's nothing I'd like better than to file charges on those responsible, but that takes evidence. I just don't have it yet."

"And maybe never will."

Ford's nod was solemn. "That's a possibility I won't deny. But if I get the proof I need—"

"I'll be the first to know?"

"No, sir. Judge Dennison comes first, then Tom Bodeen,

the prosecutor. Third would be the fellows I arrest. Afraid you're somewhere further down the line."

"As long as it gets done," Slade told him, rising from his chair.

"It's always my intent to do the job. Helps some when people don't get in my way."

"I'm not a manhunter."

"That's good to hear. I reckon everyone should stick to what he knows."

"If there's a choice," Slade said. "That lawyer's name was Whitaker?"

"Just down the street and on your right. Can't miss it."

Slade shook hands with Ford again and left the marshal's office. He had much to think about, but it could wait until he'd seen the lawyer. Maybe Whitaker could fill in some of what Ford hadn't said and make Slade understand why justice in his brother's case had been so long delayed.

Slade wanted answers, and his patience was already wearing thin.

The lawyer was a short man, bald but for a fringe of ginger-colored hair above his ears and a stray tuft on top that gave him the appearance of a quail. His beakish nose and small eyes heightened the resemblance, further heightened by the way he had of standing with his hands tucked in the pockets of his vest, arms bent like wings.

Slade found the office easily enough from Marshal Ford's directions, and walked in without a knock. A cowbell mounted on the door frame clanked announcement of his entry, and the lawyer came at once from a back room to see who might require his services. At the sight of Slade, he stopped dead in his tracks, blinked twice, and made a little *humphing* sound.

"Would you be Amos Whitaker?" Slade asked.

"Indeed. And you are . . . ?"

"John Slade. Most folks call me Jack."

"Of course!" A hint of color crept into the lawyer's pallid cheeks as he came forward, hand outstretched. "I must say, the resemblance to your brother is remarkable."

Whitaker's hand felt fragile, wrapped in Slade's. He pumped it twice and let it go, permitting Whitaker to take a short step backward. "I presume you're here about the will?"

Slade frowned. "I don't know anything about a will. The wire I got from Marshal Ford said I could fetch Jim's personal effects. I spoke to him just now, and he sent me to you."

"And rightly too. Please, follow me."

Slade trailed the lawyer through an open doorway to his private office. They were suddenly surrounded by bookshelves, all packed with volumes bound in leather, titles etched in fine gold leaf. Whitaker's desk was polished to a mirror shine, more law books stacked at two corners, as if to pin it down.

"Please, have a seat," said Whitaker, already circling the desk. Slade found a chair and settled in, feeling a sense of déjà vu.

"I understand," said Whitaker, "that you and James have not seen one another for some time?"

Slade nodded. "Four years, give or take."

"Your brother was a man of property. *Substantial* property, in fact. In terms of real estate, he owned two thousand, one hundred, and sixty-five acres, most of it prime grazing land. Then, there's the house and outbuildings, of course. His stock included some eleven hundred cattle, three stout breeding bulls among them, and about one dozen horses."

"I had no idea he'd done so well," Slade said.

"Oh, yes indeed." The lawyer flashed a smile, then reconsidered it. "Unfortunately, um, from your perspective, I suppose, your brother's will leaves nearly all his property to his fiancée."

Now it was Slade's turn to blink, surprised. "Fiancée?"

"Ah." Whitaker shifted in his seat, seeking a comfort that eluded him. "I take it that you didn't know he was engaged?"

"First thing I've heard of it," said Slade.

"I can assure you, Mr. Slade, that everything surrounding the engagement and the will is perfectly aboveboard. If you wish to see—"

"You've got me wrong," Slade interrupted him. "I'm not here to dispute the will. I didn't know there *was* one till you broke the news just now. I'm not a farmer, Mr. Whitaker, and I don't want to be. If Jim found someone who could make him happy near the end, I'm happy for him. Both of them, that is."

It was a minor marvel, watching Whitaker relax. He lost another inch or so of height, without the stiff defensive posture, and without the pinched expression on his face he seemed a younger man. No more than forty-five perhaps, and someone Slade could share a drink with if they hadn't lived in different worlds.

"Sir, I congratulate you on your wisdom and humanity," said Whitaker. "If I but had a dollar for each time some spiteful relative has crawled out of the woodwork to contest an honest will . . . But never mind all that. There are, as Marshal Ford informed you, certain items of your brother's that he's handed down to you."

"Before we get to that," said Slade, "the marshal hinted that he has a fair idea about who might've murdered Jim. He wouldn't give me any names, something about a court case and the evidence, but I suspect he may have spoken more directly on the subject when he talked to you."

"As to that subject, Mr. Slade—"

"Jack's fine."

"As to that subject, Jack, our marshal tends to be a tight-lipped man. There *was* a group of miscreants whom he suspected for a time, I understand—the Mathers gang, I think it was, pure villains to the core—but as for evidence . . . well . . ."

"Mathers, you say?"

"Dred Mathers is, or was, the leader of that group, I think. He's well known in the territory as a thief and cutthroat."

"But nobody's done a thing about it?"

"Well, now, *knowing* something's not the same as *proving* it in court, you understand. And *catching* outlaws in the territory is entirely something else again."

"Truth is," Slade said, "I'm more concerned right now with Marshal Ford's idea that certain wealthy folks might be behind Jim's death. Not shooters necessarily, but those who hire it done."

Whitaker's face went pale again. "I'm sure I couldn't speak to that with any confidence," he said, his voice sounding cracked and dry. "If Marshal Ford has any such ideas, he's not shared them with me."

"Because I'd pay to learn that name," Slade said.

"In which case, Jack, I'm doubly pained to tell you I have no such information. If I did, of course . . . well, then . . ."

"All right then," Slade relented. "What about those personal effects?"

"Of course." Whitaker rummaged through a bottom drawer, produced a blue-backed document some fifteen pages long, and opened it around the halfway point. He quickly found what he sought.

"Your brother noted a proclivity for travel on your part," said Whitaker. Brief smile. "He's left you your choice of the horses from his ranch—two of the dozen, that would be—together with his prize saddle and matching gear, a Winchester rifle, and two hundred dollars in cash. The money's on deposit at our local bank, where it's been drawing interest since your brother passed. The rest is waiting for you at his home. We can go out and see Miss Faith—"

"The fiancée?"

"That's right. Faith Connover. They had a June wedding in mind, but now, of course . . . well . . ."

"Can we go this afternoon?"

"Today? Well, I suppose . . . I mean, I'll look at my appointment book and see . . . Of course, why not!"

"Say one o'clock then?"

"One it is."

"I'll meet you here," Slade said.

"And in the meantime, if you need—"

Already up and moving toward the exit, Slade said, "Let's just take it one step at a time."

Slade needed whiskey after talking to the lawyer. It was early yet for drinking, but he didn't care. He stepped into the first saloon he found on his side of the street and drank two shots straight up, before retiring with a cold beer to a corner table.

There was so much that he hadn't known about Jim's life, and now so much about his death that had to be resolved. It was bizarre to think of Jim being engaged, but Slade had told no lies to Whitaker. If Jim had found someone who pleased him, made his life a little happier, then more power to them both. Slade didn't want the ranch or livestock, wasn't even sure he wanted one horse from the spread, when he considered it.

But there was something else he *did* want.

Slade wanted the names of those who'd killed his brother, and the man or men who'd paid to have it done, if any such existed.

Names.

Dred Mathers was the first, apparently some kind of

long-term fugitive the marshal either couldn't catch or couldn't build a solid case against. Slade didn't give a damn about the legal niceties. If he could find this Mathers, Slade would make him talk—and make him pay.

Maybe he'd need those horses Jim had left him after all. Maybe the rifle too.

When Slade was halfway through his beer, a shadow fell across his table. He glanced up to find a tall, thick-bodied man standing before him, well dressed for the time and place, a gray suit and a matching hat set squarely on his head.

"May I join you?" the stranger asked.

Slade glanced around the nearly empty barroom. "I see lots of other tables, mister."

"As do I. However, we have business to discuss."

"What business would that be?"

"If I may sit . . . ?"

Slade nodded silently. The stranger sat across from him, the empty tabletop between them. All they needed was another hand or two for poker.

"You're Jack Slade," the stranger said. "The spitting image of your brother, whom I knew quite well. I'm Douglas Freeman. Doug to friends."

It was a stretch, reaching the offered hand across the table, but Slade held the grip a moment, felt his own strength briefly tested.

"Now we're introduced," Slade said, "how did you know my brother?"

"Why, we're neighbors. *Were,* that is, until the tragedy. I own the Rocking Y, adjacent to your brother's spread. Three thousand acres, and we're growing all the time. I hope that you'll accept my most sincere condolences."

Instead of answering that plea, Slade prodded him. "The business . . . ?"

"Direct and to the point. I like that in a man." Freeman delayed his answer while he flagged a waitress, ordered whiskey from his private stock, and poured a dark shot from the bottle that she brought him. "May I tempt you?" he inquired.

"I'm good with this," Slade said, hoisting his mug.

"Right. Well, then. Before his terrible, untimely death, I was negotiating with your brother for the purchase of his property. He had a view toward marriage, as you may have heard, and ranching in the territory is a grim life for a woman. Grim, and then some. We were haggling over price when . . . well, you know the rest."

"I'm getting bits and pieces as I go along," Slade said.

"Your brother had been plagued with rustlers lately, as we all are, but he'd suffered more than most. It wasn't just the loss, of course. There'd been some shooting incidents around the spread, I understand. His fiancée was naturally upset and pressing him to find a place in town."

"As what?" Slade asked.

"Excuse me?"

"Find a place *as what*? Jim was a rancher. What was he supposed to do in town?"

"Well, now, I wasn't privy to their conversations—"

"But you're telling me about them all the same."

"In our discussions, Jim related certain information as to why he looked with favor on the sale. I didn't press beyond that point, not wanting to invade his privacy."

"What brings you round to me?" asked Slade. "How did you even know I was in Lawton?"

"Oh, my. You've created quite a stir, if I may say so. The resemblance to your brother, who was well known in these parts . . . Remarkable! There's no way you could pass along the street without exciting comment."

"And the word got back to you this fast?"

Freeman sipped whiskey, careful not to break eye contact. "It's no secret I had dealings with your brother, that we had a bargain in the works. Word gets around."

"Apparently. But you've been misdirected."

"Sir?"

"I just spoke to my brother's lawyer," Slade replied. "Turns out I've got no legal interest in the spread. You'll have to deal with Miss—"

"Faith Connover. I know the lady."

"Well, then . . ."

"And my problem is that she's declined to sell."

"You've lost me now," said Slade. "If she was set against ranching with Jim, seems like she'd cut a deal in nothing flat."

"Women, my friend, surpass all understanding."

"Still, I don't see what you want from me."

"It crossed my mind that you might have some dealings with Miss Connover while you're in Lawton. Paying your respects, if nothing else."

"I might."

"And when she meets you—when she *sees* you—it occurred to me that you might reason with her. Help remind her of the reservations she expressed to Jim, and all the hardships that she'll face, trying to run the place alone."

"Just talk her into selling out."

"All in her own best interest naturally."

"And if I manage that . . . ?"

A shrug from Freeman. "I'd expect to pay you for your time, of course. Call it a finder's fee, shall we? How does five hundred dollars sound?"

"Sounds like you're hungry for my brother's land."

"You wouldn't try to hold me up now, would you?" Smiling with a nervous edge.

Slade matched that smile, without the nerves.

"I'm going out to Jim's place later on today. The lawyer's taking me."

"That Whitaker. Watch out for him," said Freeman.

"I watch out for everybody."

"As do I." Freeman finished the whiskey in his glass and

capped the bottle, rising from his chair. "Perhaps we'll speak again before too long?"

Slade raised his mug, a parting toast.

"I wouldn't be surprised," he said.

4

Slade didn't have much appetite for lunch, but forced himself to eat it anyway. It was his habit to take meals when they were readily available, not knowing when he might fall short of food or cash. He tried another restaurant, but got the same result, with darting sidelong glances and occasional frank stares from other diners in the crowded room.

At least Slade knew his brother was a man well recognized. But was that good, or bad?

He understood the spook factor all right, how people might recoil from a dead man's identical twin. To the best of Slade's knowledge, most Lawton inhabitants wouldn't have known Jim had a brother, much less a living double of himself. The differences between Slade brothers had been miniscule—a mole on Jim's neck, nowhere seen on Jack; a few divergent scars they had picked up along the road of life—but most who met Slade casually, knowing Jim was dead, could be forgiven a degree of shock.

What had they *really* thought of Jim? Between the marshal and his lawyer, Slade had been presented with a rosy picture of his brother, thriving in the world of cattle commerce, trusted and respected by his neighbors.

Most of them at least.

That Douglas Freeman was an oily character, too glib by half. Slade didn't like him, wouldn't trust the man as far as he could throw an anvil. Something in his story of the pained fiancée hanging onto land she hated, just for old times' sake, rang hollow.

Slade would solve that riddle soon enough, when he met Faith Connover. In the meantime . . .

How had other residents of Lawton and the Oklahoma Territory viewed his brother? If Slade had misjudged Freeman, who else was a likely suspect in Jim's death?

Dred Mathers.

It came back to him, no matter how Slade tried to make the pieces fit another way. If Jim was killed by Mathers or some member of his gang, the outlaw was his best source for details of what had happened, *why* it had happened. Mathers could explain if he had killed Jim to protect a local rustling operation, or if someone bigger, richer, had paid money for the job. And if Jim's murder was a contract killing, Mathers could supply the name of his employer.

Could. But *would* he?

Yes.

Slade didn't plan on giving him a choice.

Finding the gang could be a problem, most particularly if they'd scattered after Jim was killed. Slade didn't mind the effort, though. He felt he owed his brother something for the years apart, the things he'd missed about Jim's life that came clear to him only now.

Too late.

A home, two thousand acres, and a fiancée. Jim had achieved the life most Western ranchers dreamed about while they were breaking sod behind a plow or tracking strays through driving rain and sandstorms. Jim had been a bona fide success, but someone couldn't stand to see the dream played out in daily life. They'd snatched it from him, killed Jim in the process. Now, perhaps, they wanted to cash in on what he'd built, at bargain rates.

But Jim's assassins had forgotten one thing that might come around and bite them when they least expected it.

They hadn't counted on a brother's wrath.

From lunch, Slade walked back to the lawyer's office for their one o'clock appointment. He arrived five minutes early and found Amos Whitaker already waiting on the sidewalk. They proceeded to the livery stable, where a buckboard had been readied for their journey.

Whitaker rose unassisted to the driver's seat and clutched the buggy whip, while Slade mounted to sit beside him, on the lawyer's right. The seating left his gun hand unencumbered, just in case they met some kind of trouble on the road.

When they had cleared the stable, turning north on Main Street, Whitaker remarked, "I take it that you've never seen your brother's ranch?"

"He didn't have two thousand acres when I saw him last. More like a hundred, I believe it was."

"Four years of work can make a striking difference," said Whitaker. "James—that is, Mr. Slade—was certainly a man of action."

"Call him James, if that was how you knew him." Slade was wondering if he'd known Jim at all, how they'd lost the connection that had bound them closely during childhood.

"We were friends, I think," the lawyer said. "At least, I felt so."

"Then you'd want to see his killers punished."

"Certainly!"

Nothing but open land around them, now that they were clear of Lawton. Nowhere for the lawyer to escape.

"I had the feeling, when we spoke this morning, that you might be holding something back," Slade said.

Whitaker's face had settled back into its pinched expression. "Mr. Slade, I can assure you—"

"Do you know a Douglas Freeman, Mr. Whitaker?"

The lawyer stiffened. "Anyone who deals in property or stock around these parts knows Mr. Freeman. May I ask—?"

"He looked me up this morning," Slade pressed on. "Ten minutes after I left you, he tracked me down. That's some coincidence, me being new in town and all."

"If you're suggesting that I—"

"Freeman tells me Jim was on the verge of selling out. He claims the bride-to-be was pushing Jim to find a place in town, stay off the range with all its troubles, but she's changed her mind now that he's dead. Does any of that ring a bell with you?"

After a silent moment, Whitaker replied, "No, sir. I can't say that it does. If James was planning to unload his spread, he never said as much to me."

"So, you're surprised."

"Indeed I am, sir."

"Would you say Freeman was lying then?"

Whitaker swallowed hard. "I couldn't make that judgment, Mr. Slade. There may have been negotiations that I wasn't privy to, in which case—"

"Wouldn't that run against the grain for Jim, making a deal that big without his lawyer standing by to check the p's and q's?"

Less hesitation this time as the lawyer said, "I think it would. Yes, sir."

"And if I told you Freeman offered me five hundred dollars to persuade the almost-widow she should sell, what would you say?"

"I'd say, 'Be careful,'" Whitaker replied.

"That sounds like good advice."

They rode in somber silence for the next few miles, a narrow rut of road unscrolling through the flatlands toward a speck on the horizon that resolved itself, by slow degrees, into a house and barn, surrounded by outbuildings and corrals.

"Jim's place?" asked Slade.

"We've been on James's property—that is, Miss Connover's—for something like an hour now. This was his home."

Slade scanned the prairie that surrounded him. It felt strange, knowing his brother, younger by five minutes, had owned everything as far as he could see. The house looked solid, well constructed, standing off some sixty paces from the tall, broad barn. Slade saw a bunkhouse, storage sheds, a chicken coop. Horses moved restlessly in one corral; the other stood empty. No cattle anywhere in sight, but Slade supposed they must be grazing somewhere else, beyond his range of vision.

"Don't tell me that she works this place alone," Slade said.

"Oh, no." Whitaker frowned at the idea. "Some of your brother's hands remain, out of respect for him as much as anything. That's caused some talk, as you'll imagine, but I give no credence to it."

Frowning with the lawyer, Slade approached the last home of the brother he had lost.

Slade wasn't sure what he'd expected, but the woman who came out to meet them on the wide front porch was slender, five feet six or seven inches tall, with hair almost the color of her mourning dress. She didn't wear a veil, thus granting Slade a clear view of her perfect oval face and blue eyes that were surprising with the backdrop of that raven hair. Her lips were full, coral-pink beneath a fine, straight nose. The color in her cheeks suggested that she didn't keep herself shut up inside the house.

Slade had no trouble seeing what attracted Jim to Faith Connover, and he noted her reaction as he stepped down from the buckboard. Startled didn't cover it. She looked as if she'd seen a ghost—which, in a way, she had.

Whitaker introduced them, and her handshake was another nice surprise. She gripped Slade's hand with solid strength, hung on a moment longer than was absolutely necessary as she said, "For some reason, I thought that you and James must be fraternal twins."

"No, ma'am."

"I see my error. Please, won't you come in?"

Slade hesitated, turned to face the lawyer. "Mr. Whitaker, I wonder if you'd mind us speaking privately. Miss Connover and I, that is."

Whitaker fumbled for an answer, glancing back and forth between them. "Well . . . I don't . . . I mean . . ."

"With your permission naturally," Slade said to Faith. "No impropriety intended, I assure you, ma'am. If you'd prefer that Mr. Whitaker remain, by all means—"

"No," she said, deciding on the spot. "I don't believe that's necessary. Mr. Whitaker, thank you for bringing John to see me. I've no doubt that you have work awaiting you in town."

"But when he needs to leave—"

"He's come to claim his things," Faith told the lawyer, "which include horses, if I recall correctly. You can ride, John, I assume?"

"Yes, ma'am."

"Well, there you have it, Mr. Whitaker."

"But Miss—"

"And we have half-a-dozen hands for company, if you're concerned about a chaperone." Her smile had shifted to the brittle side.

"Of course," said Whitaker. "I'll just be going then."

"I'll see you later, back in town," Slade said. "We'll talk about that bank account."

"Whenever it's convenient, Mr. Slade."

They stood and watched the buckboard pull away, Slade half-expecting Whitaker to glance back toward the house, but he sat rigidly on the driver's seat and focused on the track in front of him. The thoughts inside his head were anybody's guess.

"We may have caused a scandal, I'm afraid." Faith's smile had lost its cutting edge. "Of course, it wouldn't be my first."

Slade followed her inside and joined her in a parlor furnished with a woman's touch, yet masculine enough to let a man relax. It wasn't how he would've pictured Jim's abode, but Slade could see his brother living there and liking it.

Especially with Faith.

He'd warmed to her immediately, no surprise in that. She was an eyeful, but her attitude impressed Slade more than her appearance. If required to judge, Slade would've said that she was grieving without breaking; he'd have called her strong, determined, but still vulnerable. As for whether she could run the spread and boss its crew indefinitely on her own, Slade wasn't sure.

"Coffee?" she asked when they were seated in a pair of armchairs set before a fireplace, facing one another.

"No, ma'am. Thank you."

"Please don't call me 'ma'am,' John. I feel old enough already."

"As you wish—if you'll call me Jack."

"I love your brother very much," she told him. "It's important to me that you know."

"I'm glad to hear it." Noting that she used the present tense, as if forgetting Jim was gone. "I'd say he was a lucky man."

"You think so? After all that's happened?"

"Well—"

"Some people think I jinxed him. Did you know that?"

"No, ma— No."

"Sometimes, I swear, it seems that way to me."

"I don't believe in jinxes. Someone murdered Jim. It wasn't hoodoo magic."

"No? Perhaps then, I distracted him. If he'd paid more attention to his enemies than to our wedding plans, maybe he'd be alive." Bright tears welled in her eyes. "Each day I wonder if his death was my fault somehow. Whether I—"

"Did you conspire with someone to assassinate him?" Slade asked bluntly.

Faith drew back as if he'd raised a hand to strike her. Angry color flushed her cheeks. "I certainly *did not*! If you think—"

"I think nothing of the kind," Slade interrupted her. "But someone planned his killing, and it's them I mean to find."

After a silent moment, Faith asked Slade, "What would you do to them?"

"I don't know yet," he answered frankly. "I suppose it would depend on who they are, how many, and how well connected."

"Yes, of course." Was that a hint of disappointment in her voice?

Slade changed the subject for a moment, feeling he had gotten off on the wrong foot. He said, "I haven't kept in touch with Jim the way I should have. It's been four years, pretty near, since I saw him last. If I'd known it would really be the last time . . . well I would've tried harder."

"You called him Jim?"

"Always."

"I called him James."

It had a ripe sound, coming off her tongue. Slade told her, "Jim's a kid's name, I suppose. Never grew out of it."

"I didn't mean—"

Slade talked over the start of what sounded like an apology. "I don't know how much James explained about our childhood. I was first to leave the nest, you might say, and we had some trouble keeping in contact after that."

Faith smiled. "He said you were a wild one."

"Too wild for our folks at least. They may forgive me for it when I'm dead." Slade instantly regretted saying it, the ancient bitterness he couldn't hide. His "Sorry" sounded lame, even to him.

"Please, don't apologize for being honest. I could use a dose of truth these days."

"Who's lying to you, Faith?"

She frowned. " 'Lying' may not be quite the word—at least for most of them. It's more a feeling that they're holding back, won't tell me things I have the right to know."

"I got the same sense from your lawyer, and from Marshal Ford in town," Slade said.

Faith leaned a little closer to him, blue eyes sparkling like gems. "What were you told?"

"By Lawyer Whitaker, not much of anything beyond the bare terms of the will. He blames some outfit called the Mathers gang for killing Jim, but Marshal Ford can't find them. Then again, he hints that someone else may've arranged for Mathers and his bunch to do the job."

Her face looked stricken. "So, Ford's told you more in one day's time than I've learned in two months. I guess it really *is* a man's world after all."

"Not necessarily. He wouldn't trust me with the name or names he's sitting on."

"Afraid you might go after them, I'd bet."

"And you might win," said Slade. "But first I need more names."

"Dred Mathers?"

"It's a start, but hunting him appears to be a local sport.

Without a decent lead, I'll wind up eating Ford's dust all the way, with naught to show for it."

"I'll help in any way I can, of course. But as it stands—"

"There's one more name I'd like to try on you," Slade said.

"Which is?"

"Freeman."

Her face turned hard, gaze chilled. "Oh, *him*."

"You know him then?" asked Slade.

"Only too well—but not as well as he'd enjoy."

"It's like that then."

"Don't let me overstate it, Jack. It goes back to the land. If I speak honestly, I guess I'm only incidental."

"He's been after Jim's land for a while, I take it?"

"Longer than I knew James, which would be a year next month. He swept me off my feet, you see. Our relatively short engagement was the scandal of the county, never mind what we supposedly got up to when the busybodies weren't around to watch."

Faith didn't seem embarrassed by the new course of their conversation. Quite the opposite, in fact. Defiance brought the life back into her.

"About this Freeman character . . ."

"'Friends call me Doug,'" Faith said, mimicking him, a fair impersonation. "James was not among those friends, I can assure you. He rejected each and every one of Freeman's offers for the land."

"How many offers would that be?" asked Slade.

"At least four in the time that I knew James. He may have kept some others from me, but I doubt it."

Looking at her, Slade didn't think he would've. "Were the offers fair?"

"I gathered they were on the low side, although not an outright steal. James simply didn't care to sell, and when the other trouble started . . ."

"Other trouble?"

"Rustling mainly," Faith replied. "There's always some of that out here, a fact of life for ranchers, but it almost seemed that James was singled out. And then a barn fire too. The barn you see today is only four months old."

"Shooting?" asked Slade.

She nodded. "Twice I'm sure of. Once, the hands ran into trouble on their nightly rounds. George Meeks was wounded here." A slim hand touched her left shoulder, close to her breast.

"The second time?"

"A bullet came in through the upstairs bedroom window. We were . . . sleeping."

"Once again at night," Slade said.

"The vermin favor darkness."

"Freeman told me Jim was of a mind to sell, for your sake, when he died. Now you've surprised him, changed your mind about leaving the ranch. Claims not to understand the turnaround when he's come to you with an offer."

Faith surprised him with a laugh. It had a razor's edge. "The offer's true enough," she said. "As for the rest, if you want fresh manure, go out to the corral."

"He's lying then?"

"James wouldn't sell this place to *anyone,* but once the trouble started, he blamed Freeman for it. After that, if he was forced to sell somehow, it would've gone to anyone on Earth *but* Douglas Freeman. Satan could've bid a dollar, and James would've picked him first."

"Jim made no secret of suspecting Freeman, I suppose?"

"He definitely spoke to Amos Whitaker about it. I went with him to the office that morning, two weeks before he died. From what James told me, and the gist of their discussion, it was plain he'd also had a word with Marshal Ford."

"Ford wouldn't give me Freeman's name," Slade said.

"That's no surprise. Without sufficient evidence to

charge the man, Ford would be asking for a slander suit. He could lose everything he has, and that's not much."

"You think him honest then? The marshal?"

"I'd say yes," Faith answered. "But he puts his faith in laws and regulations. He may *think* Freeman is guilty, but he can't—or won't—do anything without the proper evidence."

"Which brings us back to Mathers," Slade remarked. "I need to have a word with him."

"For that," Faith said, "I'm guessing that you'll need a horse."

They bypassed the corrals and walked out to the barn. The sunlight glimmered on Faith's hair, but made her mourning dress seem darker than an open grave.

Two ranch hands watched them from the yard outside the bunkhouse, scowling in their hat shade until Faith waved to them, letting them know she was all right. The men still stared at Slade, perhaps seeing their late boss come alive, or maybe wondering what Slade would do about his brother's death.

He had been wondering that very thing himself.

"We keep the best horses in here," Faith said. She started pulling on the heavy door, then stood aside and let Slade finish it.

The barn was shady, cooler than the outer yard. Slade smelled the horses, heard them shifting in their stalls before he saw them. Lined up on his right, four were poking their heads over wooden gates to catch a glimpse of visitors.

"This one is Hercules," Faith said, introducing Slade to a Thoroughbred stallion, jet black. "James hoped to breed, maybe race his foals. . . ."

The stallion shied from Slade, regarding him with warrior's eyes. Slade kept his hands well clear.

"Zoë's the next in line," Faith said. "My favorite. Of course," she added quickly, "you're at liberty to choose whichever pair you want."

Slade knew he wouldn't pick the piebald mare. He guessed Faith knew it too.

A roan stallion was third in line. It stood impassively, regarding Slade with something short of curiosity. "And this is Mercury," Faith said.

"Jim never lost his fondness for mythology, I guess."

"Never. He would've been so good with children."

Slade had no response to that, but Faith moved on, as if none was expected. In the last occupied stall, an Appaloosa sidled forward, snuffling cautiously at Slade.

"We called him Jack," Faith said.

"A gelding?"

Laughing, she replied, "It's nothing personal."

"Maybe to him."

"He likes you," Faith observed as Jack let Slade reach out and stroke his face.

"He's broken, I suppose?"

"James never *broke* a horse," said Faith. "All four of these are saddle-trained."

Jim would've made the same distinction, Slade supposed. "I'll take this one, if you have no objection."

"And the second?"

"I'll have enough trouble caring for one horse," Slade replied. "Might change my mind if I lose this one while I'm in the neighborhood, but if that happens, I'll pick one of those outside."

"James wanted you to have the best," said Faith.

"He beat me to it," Slade replied. Before she had a chance to blush, he said, "The lawyer led me to believe there'd be a saddle and some other gear."

"Of course. This way."

The saddle was a beauty. Dark brown, hand tooled leather, with a silver pommel cap and brass stirrups. It came with blanket, bit and bridle, empty rifle scabbard, and a set of saddlebags.

"It's all great," he told Faith.

"There's one more thing."

She led him to a workbench, where a longish object wrapped in burlap lay. Faith carefully uncovered it, revealing a Winchester Model 1873 lever-action rifle in .44-40 caliber. The weapon wasn't new, but it had obviously been maintained with loving care.

"James gave up hunting," Faith explained, "but he still loved that Winchester. I see you wear a gun yourself."

"I've never been a hunter," Slade informed her. "But it may be time to start."

"Where will you go?" she asked him.

"Back to Lawton, for a start. They know Dred Mathers there, even if no one's seen him lately, and I'm betting Freeman won't be far away."

"What will you tell him when he asks about our conversation?

"I see two ways we can go on that," Slade said. "First is, I take his money, then use it against him, but he won't be happy when he finds out that I've lied about your willingness to sell the ranch. I don't mind facing him, but I've no wish to make things worse for you."

"That leaves the truth. He won't like that much better."

"No, but he can't claim we tried to cheat him. Maybe that'll slow him down a bit, instead of throwing more fuel on the fire."

"He won't stop trying for the land. If I don't sell, he'll pull the same tricks that he did with James."

"At least you'll be expecting it," Slade said. "How many hands have you got on the place?"

"Six left when James was killed. I've still got five, plus Ming, the cook."

"Spread thin, are they?"

"They don't get lots of sleep."

"And less to come," Slade told her. "I won't lie to you. It's likely to get worse, before we come to daylight on the other side."

"Have you done this kind of thing before?" Faith asked. "Fought range wars?"

"No, but fighting's pretty much the same, no matter where it's done. If you're outnumbered, use whatever weapons and advantages you have to shave the odds."

"Meaning?"

"I'm not sure yet," Slade said. "The quick way is to bushwhack Freeman and be done with it. Cut off the snake's head, and the body dies. Of course, there's still that one chance in a thousand that we're wrong about him, and I'd rather not hang for a dumb mistake if I can help it."

"Hang?"

"It's murder if he doesn't start the shooting, right? Suppose I try for him and miss, which is another possibility. Then *I'm* a fugitive, along with Mathers, and you're still no better off."

"So, what? We sit and wait?"

"I didn't say that," Slade replied. "In poker, you can raise and force the other man to show his hand."

"It's not a game, Jack," Faith reminded him.

Slade smiled. "You'd be surprised."

5

Faith wouldn't let Slade leave without a meal under his belt, and he obliged her with mixed motives. It was plain to Slade that she could use the company, and that she wanted him around a little longer for the memories of Jim his face evoked.

On Slade's side of the deal, he found Faith charming, physically attractive, vulnerable in a way that made him want to hold her—and irrevocably out of reach.

She was his brother's fiancée, for one thing. Even now that Jim was dead, it would've felt like stealing something precious from his brother, and Slade knew he'd have a hard time living with it if he crossed that line.

Besides which, Faith Connover occupied a world remote and unapproachable from Slade's. She obviously came from money, as had Slade, but he'd rejected family and fortune, burned his bridges most emphatically, and turned his back on anything that smacked of roots, white picket fences, children playing in the yard. Jim would've given her all that, and more, but Slade believed it wasn't in his makeup. He could offer nothing but a wild ride, with a crushing letdown at the end.

That wasn't good enough for Faith by half, Slade making up his mind that they would never pass beyond the point of being friends.

And if he wasn't careful, even that might get her killed.

They made small talk, mostly about his early life with Jim, the kind of antics twins got up to when their parents weren't around to crack the whip. Slade chose his stories carefully, making his childhood brighter than it was, and glossing over his decision to escape at age sixteen.

Someone had said, *Go West, young man,* but no one bothered to explain what happened after that. Slade kept it light, with some of his poker stories where no bloodshed was involved, then brought it safely back to Jim. It saddened Faith that the brothers had fallen out of touch, but there was nothing anyone could do about it now.

After dessert—a wedge of apple pie with cream—Slade offered his excuses and prepared to leave. Faith walked him to the barn again and waited while he saddled Jack. Slade didn't mind the Appaloosa's name, supposing it would never come up in his conversation with a stranger. He could almost see Jim smiling as he named the horse, could almost hear Jim's laughter if he cocked his head just so.

It had been six or seven months since Slade last put a saddle on a horse, but he remembered how. He'd been expecting some resistance from the Appaloosa, since he was a total stranger, but Jack didn't give him any grief. Instead, the gelding seemed almost impatient to be out of there, as if the place had soured for him and he craved fresh air.

Slade took the saddlebags, though he had nothing to put in them at the moment, and went back to fetch the Winchester. This time, he found a box of cartridges beside it on the workbench, where there'd been none earlier.

"I thought you might be needing those," Faith said. "James always said an empty gun's no good to anyone."

"You may be needing them yourself," Slade answered.

"I've got more. Guns in the house, and all the hands are armed. I hope it doesn't come to that."

Slade wasn't much on hoping, but he kept that to himself. He took his time loading the rifle, slipping fifteen rounds into the magazine beneath its barrel, while the hammer rested on an empty chamber. When he was finished, it went in the saddle scabbard, and the partial box of shells fit nicely in his saddlebag.

"All set," he told her.

"Can you find Lawton alone?" Faith asked.

"I memorized the landmarks."

"Good. I hope that you'll be careful."

"That's my best advice to *you*," Slade said.

"Both of us then. And I suppose you'll let me know what's happening?"

"As best I can."

"You won't just . . . disappear?"

"I've never been much good at magic tricks," he answered.

"Only card tricks."

"That's my game."

Mounted, he bent down from the saddle, gave Faith's hand a parting squeeze, and left her standing in the barnyard. It was hard, not looking back, but Slade used every ounce of self-control he had. A backward glance meant more than saying a thank-you for a plate of stew, or even for a horse and rifle. It betrayed a feeling Slade couldn't acknowledge, for a woman whom he couldn't claim.

The Appaloosa was as well behaved as any horse Slade had encountered. Some horses were skittish of him, maybe sensing that he trusted two legs over four, while others saw it as a point of pride to test his strength. Jack seemed, if not excited by their pairing, at least content. The gelding didn't need a rough hand, answered to a nudge as well as any voice command, and had enough pep in his stride to be mistaken for a colt.

The ride back from Jim's spread gave Slade more time to think. Faith had referred to busybodies spreading tales, and Slade supposed he knew what those were all about. He didn't know if Faith had occupied the ranch while Jim was living, and he'd never ask, but there were some who looked for *sin and evil* every time young lovers met.

Slade's parents would've understood that, would've been among the first to cut Faith down behind her back. Another reason why he'd run away from home, to rid himself of the backbiting and hypocrisy.

As if a change of scene could conquer that.

Before he reached the Lawton city limits, Slade had hatched a battle plan of sorts. He had its phases mapped out in his mind, all neatly labeled and coordinated, but he knew that wasn't how things went in daily life.

If he succeeded, even partially, there'd be an element of chaos he could not control. But even knowing that gave Slade an edge. To some extent, he could expect the unexpected and be ready—please, God!—when it came.

Slade passed the bank and found it closed, likewise the lawyer's office. Neither came as a surprise, and he rode on until he reached the livery stable, where he introduced himself and booked a stall for Jack. The hostler would safeguard his saddle, but Slade took the saddlebags and rifle back to his hotel.

"Good evening, sir," the clerk called out to Slade as he passed through the lobby.

"It just might be," Slade said, and started up the stairs.

Slade launched phase one of his plan in the saloon nearest to his hotel. The Dry Gulch was anything but, overflowing with whiskey and beer, boasting barmaids who might go upstairs with a man who asked nicely and had enough money to spend. The house games included roulette, faro, poker, and blackjack.

Slade downed a shot of red-eye at the bar, then took a mug of beer back to the nearest poker table with an empty chair. "May I?" he asked the four men holding cards.

"More money's good for everyone," the house dealer responded. "Have a seat."

Slade watched them play the hand, looking for tells, then put his ante in the pot for the next hand. "I'm wondering," he said to no one in particular, "if you can help me find a friend of mine. Dred Mathers is his name."

The other players at his table stared at Slade as if he'd just announced he had consumption, with a side order of smallpox. Three of them said nothing, while the fourth declared, "We come to play cards, mister, not to talk."

"Some law against mixing the two?" asked Slade.

"There's laws, and then there's common sense," another cautioned.

Slade sat through a hand of five-card draw, folding a pair of jacks to keep it sociable. During the shuffle for the next hand, he remarked, "If somebody could help me find old Dred, I'd make it worth his while."

No one replied to that, and Slade decided sociability should only go so far. His full house swept the table, adding fifteen dollars to his stake, and left the dealer with a frown.

By then, Slade had begun to learn which players blinked or snuffled when a new card disappointed them, who shifted in their seats to show approval of a deal, and who would bluff with next to nothing in his hand. He drew a pair of queens, improved it with a third one on the second round, and took that hand as well.

"You got the Devil's luck, mister," the player on Slade's left suggested. He was gaunt and pale enough to pose for advertisements for the mortuary trade, though Slade couldn't decide if he'd do better as an undertaker or a corpse.

"What's that supposed to mean?" Slade asked, putting the barest edge to it.

"Just what I said," the pale man answered. "Nothing more."

"You wouldn't know Dred Mathers, I suppose?"

"Know *of* him. That's enough for me right there."

"I take it then that he's been seen around these parts."

The dealer interrupted him, announcing, "Five-card stud."

Slade concentrated on his cards, wound up with eights and aces showing, what they called the dead man's hand since Wild Bill Hickock took his full house on to heaven years ago. Slade bet the cards that he had showing and the others lacked sufficient confidence to call his bluff, folding without a clue that Slade's hole card was a pathetic deuce of clubs. The hand gave him another twenty-seven dollars and a fair excuse to quit.

"Looks like I'm done."

"Just passing through, I guess?" the pale man asked.

"Until I find what I've been looking for," Slade said.

He walked back to the bar and bought another beer, then nursed it while he watched the other games. Roulette was strictly for the gamblers who would bet on anything—a random choice of numbers, red or black, the double zero waiting to annihilate them all. It was a sucker's game, even supposing that the table wasn't rigged in favor of the house.

Blackjack was better, but it still required more luck than poker. First time around, a player either got the money cards or didn't. Trying to improve a poor hand while the dealer stood on seventeen was nerve-racking at best. A coin toss gave the players better odds.

Poker, by contrast, was a science. If a man could read the opposition and recall the basic odds, there was no reason short of outright cheating why he couldn't win consistently. Not every hand, of course. Not every game. But a professional could pay his bills and have a stake left over, maybe even taste the fabled good life now and then.

Slade had begun to wonder what the good life *was* exactly. Clearly, Jim's ideal had differed from his own, but which of them was right? Jim had the spread, the stock, the fiancée—and he was dead. Slade had a new horse, a new rifle, and a growing list of enemies he'd never met.

Maybe there *was* no good life, Slade decided.

Maybe there was only life, and what one made of it.

Slade had a third beer warming up in front of him, and was about to try the Gay Paree across the street, when someone sidled up beside him at the bar. The undertaker's corpse ordered whiskey, paid in coin, and drained his shot glass in a single gulp.

"How much do you allow for someone who can help you find your friend?" the gaunt man asked, keeping his eyes fixed on the mirror set behind the bar.

"Depends on how much help they give me," Slade replied.

"Suppose I put you next to one of Mathers's bunch, right here, right now."

"Five dollars down," Slade said. "Another twenty if it gets me where I need to go."

"I'll take the five and call it quits," the other said. "Look down the far end of the bar. Red shirt and blue bandanna there. You see 'im?"

"Yes."

"He rides with Mathers. Whether he'll admit it to a stranger, now, that's something else."

"My problem," Slade acknowledged as he laid five dollars on the bar. The gaunt man made it disappear, then turned back toward the gaming tables, looking for a place to lose it.

Slade let him find a place, then pushed off from the bar

and made his way past steady drinkers to the other end. His target was a man of average height, whose rust-red shirt and blue bandanna clashed beneath a low-crowned hat. His face had alcoholic color in the cheeks and wore a two-day growth of beard. The pouches underneath his eyes were dark enough to pass for bruises.

Slade stepped in beside him, one foot on the rail. Fed up with wasting time, he said, "I'm told you know Dred Mathers."

The drinker half-turned, eyeing Slade, and nearly jumped. He said, "Somebody told you wrong."

"That so?"

"I'm telling you it is." A tremor in his voice.

"Because I'd really like to find him."

"Then I g-guess," the other said, "that you're shit out of luck."

With that, he drained his glass, then turned and left Slade standing at the bar. Out through the batwing doors into the night he went, and disappeared.

That's one, Slade thought, and left his beer unfinished as he followed toward the street. Next stop, the Gay Paree.

Slade was waiting on the street next morning when the lawyer came to work. Whitaker seemed a bit surprised to see him, or it simply may have been the puckered-up expression he usually had. Either way, he offered greetings, used a brass key on the door, and led Slade back into his office.

"So, if I may ask, sir, did you find Miss Connover . . . accommodating?"

Slade considered the inquiry, trying to decide if he should take offense on Faith's behalf, then said, "I got my brother's things. We talked a bit."

"Oh, yes?"

The lawyer seemed to be expecting details, but Slade's

silence left him disappointed. The moment stretched between them, causing Whitaker to fidget at his desk, straightening pencils and the like, until he finally broke down and asked, "What can I do for you this morning, Mr. Slade?"

"There's still the matter of that money waiting in the bank," Slade said.

"Of course. When did you want to claim it?"

"Now's as good a time as any, I suppose."

"You mean *right now*?"

"Is that a problem?"

"No. Well . . . no, I mean . . . of course not." Whitaker seemed flustered now. "I have appointments later in the morning, but if we proceed directly to the bank—"

"Sounds good to me," said Slade.

He trailed the lawyer back outside and waited while the door was locked again. That done, they traveled two blocks south and crossed the street to reach the Lawton Bank of Commerce. Once they were inside, a man of middle age, dressed in a charcoal-colored suit, came up to Whitaker and pumped his hand, smiling so broadly that it almost seemed the top half of his head would fall away.

"Good morning, Amos. Can I help—" The banker caught a glimpse of Slade and stopped in mid-sentence. "Oh, my!"

"Indeed," said Whitaker. "If you'll allow me?"

"By all means," the banker said.

"John Slade, meet Charles McLain, president of the Lawton Bank of Commerce and sundry other enterprises in the territory."

They shook hands solemnly, the banker offering, "I'll wager you're related to James Slade."

"His brother," Slade replied.

"*Twin* brother," Whitaker amended, just in case McLain was slow. "He's here to settle the escrow account."

"I see." The banker nodded, frowning slightly, as if he'd

just been informed of tragedy befalling some forgotten, distant relative. "Escrow account. You'll want to change the name presumably. Perhaps make a deposit?"

"I'll just take the money, thanks."

"Ah. Well, in that case, if you'd kindly see the second teller, I'm sure everything's in order. There'll be paperwork for both of you to sign. If you'll excuse me . . ."

With no prospect for deposits, Slade had lost McLain's interest. He didn't mind a bit. In fact, he'd found the banker's fawning attitude repulsive, though he guessed it was a necessary trait for one who lived by talking others into giving up their money to a stranger's care.

They got in line behind a fortyish woman with a wilted feather in her hat, and waited while the teller sorted through a mess of coins to give her currency. When it was their turn, Whitaker described their errand and the teller gave them forms to sign, seeming to share his master's personal reluctance to let go of any cash. At last, the teller took Slade's money from a drawer, counted it twice, and placed the stack of bills in front of him.

Two hundred dollars richer, Slade said his farewell to Whitaker outside the bank and walked back to the marshal's office. Harmon Ford was still adjusting wanted flyers on the notice board when Slade entered.

"You do that all the time?" he asked.

"We have a lot of bad men in the territory, Mr. Slade."

"I gathered that. You reckon Douglas Freeman may be one of them?"

Ford turned to face him, posters gripped in one hand, thumbtacks in the other. "Where'd you hear that name?"

"All over town," Slade answered. "Yesterday, he braced me in the restaurant, asking if I'd persuade my brother's fiancée to sell their land. Would you agree that's passing strange?"

Ford shrugged, setting the tacks on the corner of his desk. "It's not for me to say. Bad timing maybe. Insensitive might cover it." A frown. "I'm not sure what you're asking me."

"When we spoke yesterday, you hinted that there might be more behind my brother's death than simple rustling. Someone bigger, plotting with the shooters."

"I don't *hint* around at things," the marshal answered gruffly. "I related a suspicion which, at present, has no evidence supporting it."

"Suspicion. Fine, let's go with that."

"I told you yesterday, suspicion isn't proof."

"I'm not a lawyer or a judge," Slade said. "Just tell me what name comes to mind when you're considering my brother's death."

"I don't have any—"

"Mathers is a name I'm hearing, Marshal. Does it ring a bell?"

"Dred Mathers has a record, and he's wanted on suspicion of assorted felonies. That's true."

"Jim's death among them?"

"I've explained to you already, Mr. Slade, if I had any evidence—"

Slade interrupted Ford again. "And when you think about the man behind Dred Mathers, what's *his* name? Freeman?"

"For all I know," said Ford, "he's just a rancher and a businessman. Done better than most others hereabouts, Doug Freeman has, but that's the way life goes."

"You *don't* suspect him then?"

Ford sighed. "Without some kind of evidence—"

"All right. I hear you, Marshal."

"Do you, Mr. Slade? Because I get the feeling you're not listening."

"I hear you saying that you can't do anything about my brother's murder."

"If I had the—"

"Evidence," Slade finished for him. "Fine. What will it take?"

"I've warned you once about pursuing any kind of private action in this matter."

"I'd be more impressed with that if you were taking some *official* action."

"Mr. Slade . . ."

"Forget it, Marshal. Fix your posters there, and see if something comes to you. Meanwhile, I take it there's no law against me asking questions?"

"No law I'm aware of," Ford replied.

"Right then," Slade said. "I'll be in touch."

Slade didn't have to go in search of Douglas Freeman. He was walking back to his hotel from lunch, same restaurant, when a familiar voice addressed him from behind.

"Jack Slade! A moment of your time?"

Slade turned to find Freeman advancing on him, seeming stern and energized despite the smile that he kept plastered on his face. Slade focused on his eyes, deciding that the smile was a disguise, as phony as an actor's stick-on whiskers.

"Mr. Freeman."

"Doug, please." The rancher pumped Slade's hand three times and let it go. "I trust you kept your date with Miss Connover?"

"I wouldn't label it a date."

"Appointment then."

"We spoke."

"About?"

"My brother's death."

"Of course, it was a tragedy. I had in mind—"

"It's strange, don't you agree, that no one's been arrested yet?"

Freeman considered that, clearly annoyed that Slade

kept steering him off track. "Frankly, there are so many outlaws in the territory, and so many places they can hide, it's something of a miracle that we solve any crimes at all."

"When you say 'we'—"

"I mean the law, of course."

"Of course. Would it surprise you, Doug, to hear that Marshal Ford suspects my brother's death may not be just an ordinary killing?"

"I'm not sure I follow you."

Slade reckoned it was time to stir the pot. "He's got some hardcase by the name of Mathers down as the most likely shooter, but that's not the end of it."

"Indeed?" One of Doug Freeman's eyebrows seemed intent on crawling up his forehead, like a caterpillar.

"No. The marshal figures there was big money behind the guns. Somebody hoping he'd find Jim's spread on the auction block at bargain rates, if Jim was gone."

The smile on Freeman's face narrowed a little, showing fewer teeth. "Is that a fact?"

Slade shrugged. "You know how lawmen are. One of them gets a notion in his head, next thing he's hounding some poor devil all the way to Mexico. Your marshal strikes me as a man who doesn't let things go."

"I'd say that's fair."

"A bulldog with a bone, I'd say. Once he gets hold of Mathers, it'll all fall into place."

"You're confident of that?" asked Freeman.

"Well, I'm looking into things myself," Slade said. "I don't like sitting still and waiting while somebody else does all the work, you know?"

"I'm sure I'd feel the same myself. As for your visit with Miss Connover—"

"She won't be selling, Doug."

The smile winked out. "How's that?"

"Apparently," Slade said, "Jim never told her anything about plans to sell the ranch. Does that strike you as odd?"

"I'm not sure—"

"After he made all those promises to you, I mean."
Slade shook his head. "It's too bad none of what you two
discussed was ever put in writing. When I raised the subject with Jim's lawyer—"

"Whitaker. I warned you about *him*."

"You did, Doug, for a fact. Seems like he never heard
about the sale arrangements either."

"We were still in the preliminary stage, but—"

"Anyway, I guess you're out of luck, Doug. Sorry. I suppose that means no finder's fee."

The twist in Freeman's lip wasn't a smile this time.
"Well, Jack, you didn't *find* much, did you?"

"No," Slade said. "But I'm still looking."

"That can be a risky occupation in a place like this.
Hunting for killers when you've got no badge, no warrant,
no authority of any kind."

"That's what the marshal said."

"Smart man."

"I hope so," Slade replied. "I'm giving him some time
to find Jim's killers, while I ask around in private, all po-
litelike. But if he can't help me . . ."

Slade left it unfinished, hanging there between them.
Freeman couldn't seem to let it go. "Then what?" he asked.

Slade shrugged. "It's hard to say. Depends on what I
find out for myself, I guess. I've got one name already.
When I find the man belongs to it, smart money says I'll
get some more."

"And give them to the marshal?"

"Names may not be good enough for him. He talks a lot
about the need for evidence and such. That's what he's
looking for."

"But maybe you don't care so much about the rules?"

"I've never been a stickler," Slade admitted.

"It's a reckless way to live," Freeman suggested.

"Well, it hasn't killed me yet."

"Why take the chance?"

"My brother's dead. Somebody needs to pay for that."

"No matter what it costs?"

"That's how I see it," Slade replied.

"In that case," Freeman said, "I wish you luck."

Slade watched the man's retreating back and wondered whether he had said too much, for Faith's sake. *Never mind,* he thought at last. *I have to start somewhere.*

And if his hunch was right, he would be starting at the top.

6

Mack Riley could've used a drink. In fact, he'd been consuming alcohol for several hours back in Lawton, but the fright and the ride that followed it had sobered him unpleasantly. Now, he had bad news to deliver—unbelievable bad news—and he would have to do it dry.

He sat and fidgeted outside the cabin where Dred Mathers hung his spurs when he was stopping in the area. Inside, the moans and loud bed-squeaking told him Mathers hadn't finished up with Jenny Acton yet. Riley was moved to wonder how Dred kept it up so long, but then he lost that train of thought, returning to the problem that weighed heavy on his mind.

Bad news was one thing. Mathers never took it well, and he'd been known on rare occasions literally to kill the messenger.

Bad news wrapped in a fairy tale was something else entirely, but how could Riley shade it otherwise?

No way at all.

He either had to tell exactly what he'd seen or keep his mouth shut altogether, and the fear was gnawing at his vitals, giving him the cramps like when he ate too many chili peppers.

"Oh, God! Oh, Jesus!" Coming from the cabin.

Squeeeak-squeak-squeeeak-squeak-squeeeak.

The symphony of love, or something like it.

Riley sat and listened, crossed his legs to ease the pain, then bit his lip as Mathers started working up to a crescendo. Dred himself was silent, but the bed and Jenny said it all.

"Oh, God! Oh, God! Oh, God!"

SqueakSqueakSqueakSqueakSqueakSqueakSqueak.

"Oh, Gooooooood!"

Riley sat waiting for another moment, trying to ignore the men around him with their gloating smiles, poking each other in the ribs and snickering. If they'd seen what *he* had, no hint of laughter would've passed their lips.

Someone was off the bed and moving in the cabin now. Clomping around in boots, which made it Mathers. Riley hoped he wouldn't stop for coffee or a smoke before he came outside. The news was eating Riley up inside, making him grimace as if someone had a tight grip on his family jewels.

The door opened and Mathers stepped onto the porch. He wore a wide-brimmed hat, gunbelt, and boots over long underwear that could've used a washing. Maybe two. He hadn't shaved in several days, and Riley saw a smudge on his left cheek, below the eye, as if Mathers had smeared a bit of ash there, after cleaning out a fireplace.

"Boys," he said to no one in particular. "How long you all been here?"

" 'Bout long enough," said Wiley Grace, smirking.

"I hope so," Mathers said. " 'Cause next time I might haveta charge you for the lesson."

"If you charge," Frank Lugar asked him, "does it mean we get to watch?"

"You can't afford that kinda lesson, Frank," said Mathers. "All of you together couldn't raise that kinda money."

"Maybe Jenny'd let us have a discount, bein' friends of yours and all," said Corey Chapman.

"Corey, hush!" warned his brother, Quinn.

Too late.

Mathers had turned in Corey's general direction, peering at him from the hat brim's shade. "I don't believe I heard that, Corey," he said evenly. "Repeat it for me, would you?"

The color had drained out of Corey's face. "It wasn't nothin', Dred."

"Sounded like something. Are you tellin' me my ears have gone bad now?"

"I didn't *mean* nothin'," Corey amended, standing with his eyes downcast.

"I didn't ask you what you *meant*," Mathers replied. "Just tell me what you *said*."

"Dred, hell," Quinn Chapman interrupted. "He's half-drunk and just about three-quarters stupid. Don't pay no attention to him there."

"The two of you together in it now," Mathers observed. "Is that about the size of it?"

"No, sir," Quinn answered. "Ain't no two of us in *anything*. Ain't nothin' happening at all."

"Somebody gets a rowdy mouth," Mathers observed, "I just might haveta shut it with a .45 slug."

"There's no need for that," Quinn Chapman said, then rounded on his younger brother. "*Is* there, Corey?"

"Nope. No need for that at all."

Mack Riley mouthed a silent curse. Bad news was churning in his gut, and now the idjit Chapman brothers had put Dred in a foul mood. Riley was wishing he could shrink away to nothing and become invisible when Mathers spotted him.

"You're back from Lawton early, Mack," he said. "What's going on?"

"I got something to tell you," Riley said.

"All right."

"It's . . . odd."

"Why don't you spit it out?"

"Last night, while I was drinking at the Dry Gulch, comes a stranger walking up beside me, asking if I knew you."

"Me? By name?" asked Mathers.

"Said somebody told him you and I might know each other."

"Which somebody?"

Riley frowned. "I didn't ask him. When I turned around to face him, he . . . he was . . ."

Mathers stepped closer. "Are you choking on a bone or what? Out with it!"

"Jesus, Dred, he looked just like that rancher. You know who I mean."

"Guess not," Mathers replied.

"The one we kilt, back around Easter time. Remember now?"

In other circumstances, Mathers might've kicked him off the porch and then around the yard for sassing back, but now he seemed intrigued.

"What do you mean, he looked just like him?"

"What I said. His face, his build. The clothes were different, but otherwise a mother couldn't tell the two of 'em apart."

"Sounds like you drank a bit too much before this stranger started asking questions," Mathers said. "You're known to love that whiskey, Mack. Isn't that right?"

"I wasn't drunk enough to see no ghost, unless—"

Damn it!

He hadn't meant to let that slip, and now he couldn't take it back.

Mathers was staring at him, crouching down at Riley's side to get a better look. "Did you say *ghost*? Is that what I just heard you say?"

"Um . . . well . . ."

"You're telling us the ghost of somebody we killed two months ago walked up to you in a saloon and asked where he could find us?"

"You," Riley corrected him. "He asked me about *you*."

"I see." Mathers glared at him for a moment, then rose from his crouch—and burst out laughing. The assembled rustlers hesitated long enough to make sure that it wasn't just some kind of trap, then followed suit.

When the hilarity subsided, Mathers prodded Riley with his toe and said, "I'll tell you what, Mack. You can be my ghost hunter. Go back to Lawton, find this spook if he's around, and find out what the hell he wants with me. Take Bran along, in case you lose your nerve."

"Why me?" Bran Huffman asked.

"Because I said so!" Mathers snapped. "Any more stupid questions? No? All right then. Saddle up and ride!"

The Gay Paree saloon had been a dry hole on his first go-round, but Slade gave it another try on his third afternoon in Lawton. It resembled the Dry Gulch in layout, though the owner's halfhearted attempt at French decor gave Slade something to smile about.

In place of a roulette wheel, the Paree had two dice tables and a wheel-of-fortune that would fleece the bettors ninety times out of a hundred. Slade ignored them, left the sheep to find their own way through the slaughterhouse, and homed in on a poker table short one player. The house dealer was a fat man, with three wobbling chins and a stomach that held him well back from the table, stretching his arms as he shuffled and dealt. He smoked skinny cigars and had combed red hair straight back from his round suet face. The other three players matched Slade's mental image of farmers, ranging in age from late twenties to fifty or so.

The dealer favored five-card draw, Slade's game of choice if he had any say about it. On the first hand after he sat down, Slade won twelve dollars with a pair of queens. He lost eight dollars on the next two hands, then came back strong with a full house, tens over treys, recouping his losses and making four dollars to spare.

So far, so good.

While the dealer was shuffling and letting the man on his left cut the deck, Slade inquired of the table at large, "Do any of you know a fellow called Dred Mathers?"

One, the oldest player, shook his head, a solid negative. The other three eyed Slade with frank suspicion, darting glances from his face down to his vest and jacket. Looking for a badge perhaps?

"We try'n concentrate on poker at the table," said the dealer, smiling just to keep it friendly, though his tone belied such cordiality.

"I wasn't asking for an address," Slade replied. "Just trying to find out if anybody knows my friend."

"This one's a friend of yours?" the middle farmer asked.

Slade didn't mind lying in a good cause. "We met a couple years ago," he answered. "Dred said I could likely find him hereabouts, if I was ever passing through the territory."

"Hmm."

"Is that a yes or no?" Slade pressed.

"We're playing five-card draw," the dealer interrupted. "You in, mister?"

"You bet." Slade put a dollar in the pot.

"Sometimes it's wise," the dealer said, "to let folks have their privacy."

"In which case," Slade replied, "I'd have to ask how you know Mr. Mathers doesn't want to hear from me."

"He doesn't wanna hear from anybody," said the youngest of the three.

"Now, Clete," the dealer cautioned, leaving it at that.

"Sorry," the young man said.

Slade concentrated on his cards. He held two jacks, the ace of spades, a four of clubs, and a deuce of hearts. After a round of bets, he ditched the smallest cards and drew two more: a ten of diamonds and a jack of hearts, to match his clubs and spades.

Slade watched the other faces, bet with quiet confidence, and saw two of them fold. Only the rancher in his fifties still remained. He called Slade's final raise and faced a solid pair of kings.

"Three jacks," Slade countered, showing him, then raked in twenty-seven dollars.

"I hate to leave you in the lurch," he told them, "but if none of you can help me find my friend, I'm bound to try my luck elsewhere."

"Luck's what you'll need," the dealer said, shuffling as Slade got up to leave.

Slade went back to the bar. A different bartender was working, younger and thinner than the one he'd met the night before. He bought a beer and asked about Dred Mathers, got a simple head shake in return.

"You don't know if he's in the area?" Slade prodded.

"Don't know him at all," the barkeep answered. "Wouldn't recognize him if he rode in on a horse right now."

"You'd notice, though, I bet."

"Might do."

Slade climbed out a little farther on the limb. "What would it cost to find someone who *does* know Mathers?"

That elicited a shrug. "Can't say, not knowing him myself."

"Well, then, for you to ask around?"

"Good way to lose my job, sounds like." The bartender was young, but not a fool.

"I wouldn't want you to be obvious about it," Slade explained.

"You said he was your friend."

Touché.

"That's right," Slade said, "but there's no point in spooking him before I get a chance to see him and explain."

"Uh-huh. So, what's it worth to you?"

"Depends on the result," said Slade. "A dollar, just for asking. Call it five, if something you deliver leads me to my friend."

"Five dollars."

"Right."

"In gold?"

"If that's the way you want it."

"Awright then." Wiping the bar, the young man said, "I'll ask some people, find out what they got to say. You'll be around Lawton a day or two, I guess?"

"Long as it takes."

"Come in tomorrow or the next day then, round this same time. I'll let you know if I hear anything."

"Sounds good." Slade left a dollar on the bar, beyond what his beer cost, and left the Gay Paree.

Doug Freeman watched the rider drawing closer, pale dust rising from his horse's hooves. A pair of Freeman's men escorted him, keeping their distance on the flanks, but staying close enough to use their Winchesters if there was any need.

There wouldn't be. Freeman was well acquainted with his visitor, and while he didn't like the rider, they had business to discuss.

When he was close enough to make out scowling fea-

tures, Freeman rose from his hand-carved rocking chair
and moved to the edge of the porch, still careful to stay in
the shade.

His home lay two miles east of Lawton, and his ranch—
the Rocking Y—sprawled over some three thousand acres.
It was land Freeman had purchased with his money, sweat,
and blood. Of late, however, others did most of the sweating for him, and the blood wasn't his own.

Dred Mathers reined in as he reached the yard, walking
his horse until it nosed the line made by the roofline
shadow of Doug Freeman's house. It was a funny point of
pride with Mathers, each and every time, to stay outside
the comfort zone until he was specifically invited. Freeman
wasn't sure what that suggested, but he took it for a quirk
of a disordered mind.

"It's good to see you," Freeman lied. "Come on and try
some shade, why don't you?"

Mathers gave a facial twitch in place of a response, dismounted, tied his reins to the porch railing, and joined
Freeman in the shade. A straight-backed chair was placed
beside the rocker, waiting for a visitor whose comfort was
no great concern of Freeman's. Someone who was not expected to remain for supper, much less spend the night.

When Mathers was seated, Freeman waved his riders
off, watched them turn in the direction of the bunkhouse,
casting sidelong glances at his guest before they left.

"Your boys don't like me much," said Mathers.

"They don't have to like you. I'm the only one with an
opinion on the Rocking Y," Freeman replied.

"Big man."

"And getting bigger all the time."

"I hear Slade's woman still won't sell."

"We're in negotiations."

"Right."

"It's Slade we need to talk about," said Freeman. "He's
the reason why I called you here."

"You want to talk about his ghost?" Mathers inquired.

"Say what?"

Mathers spat brown tobacco juice out toward the yard. He nearly missed the porch. "That's what I'm hearing out of Lawton. Friend of mine tells me he saw the man's own ghost, having a cold one at the Dry Gulch yesterday. The spook was talking to him, if you can believe it. Funny thing is that he mentioned me."

"And you *believe* that crap?"

"I'll tell you something, Douglas. I've been scaring people all my life. I know what fear looks like, and I can promise you, this friend of mine was shaking in his boots. I don't know who or what he saw—"

"I do," the rancher interrupted.

"Oh?"

"Slade has—or had—a brother. They were twins. Identical. Name's Jack. He's staying at the Lawton Arms so far."

"And asking questions," Mathers said.

"Seems so."

"How in the hell'd he get my name?"

"You know *I* didn't give it to him. He'd already talked to Marshal Ford and Amos Whitaker before I spoke with him."

"You think Ford's onto us?" asked Mathers.

"Not unless you've told your boys more than they need to know, and one of them's been gossiping."

"No way."

"We should be all right then," said Freeman. "Anyway, as far as Ford's concerned."

"What's that supposed to mean?"

"Slade's brother may turn out to be a problem on his own. We spoke again this afternoon, and he's not happy with the progress Ford's been making."

"Meaning none at all."

"He dropped your name, then mentioned rumors that

you may have killed his brother on behalf of someone else."

"Saying all that right to your face." Mathers was smiling now. "Is he a fox, or just an idjit?"

"My opinion," Freeman said, "you would be making a mistake to sell him short."

"I'll make a note. Meanwhile, I don't like Ford still sniffing after this. He oughta let it go."

"It's only been two months," Freeman replied. "You killed one of the best known ranchers in the western territory."

"*We* did," Mathers said, correcting him.

"That's right."

"Don't be forgetting it."

I won't, thought Freeman. *And when you're no further use to me . . .*

"Maybe I ought to have a talk with him," said Mathers.

"Talk with who?"

"That lawman."

Frowning, Freeman said, "That may not be the wisest course of action."

"Hell, he's just one man."

"A U.S. marshal, Dred. You *do* remember that he works directly for Judge Dennison?"

"So what?"

Incredible. "So, if you kill him, Dennison may ask for reinforcements, launch a full investigation. By the time he's made one, some of us may be standing on a scaffold."

"Thanks for the concern," sneered Mathers. "But you hadn't ought to worry, Mr. Freeman. I don't squeal."

"Not even for your life?"

"Nobody's gonna put a rope around my neck. Long time ago, I made my mind up on that score."

Freeman admired a man with principles. "It doesn't always work out like we plan," he cautioned.

Mathers stroked the grip of his revolver, rolled his

thumb across the hammer spur. "You want a safe bet," he replied, "go on and put your money on the fact that no one's taking me to prison or the gallows. Period."

"Consider that you're not the only one involved in this," said Freeman.

"I've considered it, all right." When Mathers smiled this time, it had a predatory gleam that raised the hairs on Freeman's neck. "I think about it every time somebody mentions Slade."

"Perhaps it would be better if you left the territory for a while. Let things cool down."

"Better for who?"

"For all concerned," Freeman replied. "You wouldn't have Slade's brother and the marshal breathing down your neck. And if you're not around to keep them hunting, then there's nothing that can lead them back to me."

"Where would you have me go?"

"The world's your oyster, Dred. Go on to San Francisco or New Orleans. Maybe Mexico. It's not for me to dictate where you travel."

"No, you're right. It's not for you to say." Mathers considered it a little longer, then remarked, "A trip like you're describing would cost money. If I take the boys along—"

"You definitely should," said Freeman. "While I'm sure they're fine young men, I don't know if they share your . . . scruples in respect to silence."

"'Fraid they'll spill the beans, is that it?" Mathers laughed. "Relax, why don't you. I already told you, they don't know who paid the tab on Slade."

"Still . . ."

Mathers bolted upright from his chair, a sudden lurching movement. "I'll consider what you say, Doug. Sure I will. And I'll get back to you if I decide to go somewhere. Make the arrangements for my traveling expenses. In the meantime, you should just relax."

Freeman sat watching as the gunman rode away.

"Oh, I'll relax, all right," he told the breeze. "When certain folks are dead and gone."

Dred Mathers took a sip of whiskey, waiting for the burn. When it had spread from gut to gullet, he opened his eyes to find Bran Huffman and Mack Riley staring at him.

"So, you're back," he said. "Let's hear it."

"Well, he's there, jus' like Mack said," Huffman reported. Riley nodded right along with him, for emphasis.

"The ghost," said Mathers.

"I'm not sayin' that," Huffman replied. "But he's a cold dead ringer for that Slade, all right. Like lookin' in a mirror. And he's definitely askin' questions about you."

"What kind of questions?" Mathers prodded.

"Nothin' special that we heard of. Just does anybody know you, where can you be found, that kinda thing. Tells people he's a friend of yours."

"Does he?" Mathers managed a smile. "What sort of answers is he getting?"

"None that I saw." Huffman turned to Riley. "What about you, Mack?"

"Nothin'," Riley agreed. "The ones we seen 'im talkin' to all put him off. Mostly just shake their heads and walk away."

"The ones you saw." Mathers had trouble keeping up the smile. "But what about the ones you *didn't* see?" he asked.

"Well, Dred," said Huffman, "I can't hardly vouch for them, now can I?"

"No, you can't. And that's my point."

The gunmen looked confused. "What point was that, Dred?" Huffman asked.

"The point about not leaving anything to chance," Mathers answered. "It only takes one loose-lipped fool to pin a bull's-eye on our backs."

"You reckon that this spook or whatever he is will try'n find us?" Huffman's face had lost some of its color.

"Let's drop this shit about a *ghost*," Mathers declared. "While you were watching him ask questions, I found out exactly who this stranger is." He let the silence stretch between them, finally demanding, "Well? Who wants to know?"

"I do!" said Huffman, hand raised like a child in school who needs to use the privy.

"Me too!" Riley echoed.

"He's the rancher's *brother*, boys. Not just a brother neither. They were *twins*. No spooks, you see?"

"I didn't know Slade had a brother," Huffrnan said.

"We live and learn," Mathers replied. "And if he's not a ghost . . ."

The shooters saw where he was going with it. "Then we make him one?" Riley suggested.

"That's a thought," Mathers agreed. "But first, we've got another problem. Seems like Marshal Ford's still sniffing round Slade's grave, trying to figure out who put him there."

"You wanna take off for a while?" asked Huffman. "Let him sweat?"

"It's been suggested," Mathers said, "but I don't like loose ends. They have a way of coming back together, either trip a fellow up or hang him."

"Whadda you wanna do?" asked Riley.

"I'm inclined to think the marshal needs a lesson. We could teach him to leave well enough alone."

"Kill 'im, you mean?" The thought seemed to disturb Bran Huffman.

"We're just talking here," Mathers replied. "But it's a way to go."

"Risky. That kinda thing can backfire if it ain't done right," said Riley.

"Meaning that it should be done right, if we do it," Mathers said.

"Well, yeah."

"Or not do it at all," Mathers suggested. "This is Harmon Ford."

"He's just a man, like any other."

"He's the law."

"The law ain't bulletproof," Huffman remarked. "I kilt a deputy one time, in Texas. There warn't nothin' to it."

"That's the spirit," Mathers said. "But I don't want you getting cocky. Ford's a fair hand with a gun. He's killed some."

"Some, and *then* some," Riley interjected, looking glum.

"Don't fret yourself, Mack. No one's asking you to pull the trigger by your lonesome."

"Anyway, there's still Judge Dennison to think about," said Huffman. "Kill Ford, and he'll raise hell from here to Sunday week."

"Let him. He still needs proof to file a charge, and he won't have it," Mathers said.

"And after Ford, we do this twin?" Huffman inquired.

"We'll get around to him," said Mathers, "if he's still in town. Could be he'll lose his nerve and run back home, wherever that is."

"Maybe we should just take him," Riley proposed, "and leave Ford be."

"Too dangerous," Mathers explained. "If we kill off the brother, but the marshal's still alive, it gets him all fired up to hunt us twice as hard."

"I didn't know the job was gonna be this kinda trouble," Riley groused. "It was supposed to be one man, but now we're killin' brothers, marshals. Damn it, Dred, what's next?"

"If I could tell you that, Mack, I could run the world. We'll have to wait and see, unless . . ."

"Unless what?" Riley asked him warily.

"Unless you'd rather cut and run," Mathers replied. "I'd hate to think the strain was wearing on your nerves."

"My nerves?"

"You know. They do things to a man, his nerves. Make him all jumpy sometimes. Or they make him talk too much."

"You know me better, Dred. Hell, if I talk, my neck's the first one in a noose."

"You'd best remember that, and who your friends are. Right?"

"I'm not forgettin' anything," said Riley.

"Good. Then you won't mind if we need help with tying up a few loose ends."

"You know I'll help. Hell, yes!"

"So, we're in business then. Bran, you go fetch the other boys, and we'll decide what's to be done about the marshal's nose."

7

The note had come as a surprise to Harmon Ford, slipped underneath his office door when he arrived at half-past seven in the morning. Almost stepped on it, he had, before the little *swishing* noise of paper dragging over floorboards made him glance down, thinking that a snake had found its way inside somehow.

Instead, it was a piece of foolscap paper, folded once across and clumsily addressed to him in pencil: "Marshel Foard." He'd checked the sidewalk, up and down, from force of habit, though he'd known the person who deposited the note most likely wouldn't hang around to watch him read it. If they did, there were a hundred places they could hide or merge with foot traffic along the street and easily escape his notice.

More curious than irritated, Ford had closed the door, opened the note, and read: "I no who kilt Jim Slayd. If you want no come Cripple Crick at nune."

Ford had to puzzle on the last word, thinking that his correspondent obviously was no genius. It could be "nine" misspelled, or a phonetic stab at "noon." Considering the fact that Cripple Creek was a two hour ride from town, and anyone who knew him had to realize he couldn't make it from a seven-thirty start, Ford put his bet on noon and let it ride.

If he was wrong, too bad. The person who had scrawled the note could make another date, or they could go to hell.

Experience told Ford that it was probably someone's odd notion of a joke, say fifty-fifty odds, but there were still two other possibilities. One was that someone finally intended to come clean about Slade's murder, maybe motivated that his brother was in town and asking questions. If it took a meddling amateur to break the case, Ford didn't mind.

The other possibility, of course, was bait.

The rendezvous could be a trap.

Ford considered it, and then decided that he had to go regardless. Joke or trap, it was his duty to pursue all leads in crimes that fell within his jurisdiction. He would be prepared for anything, however. No mistake about it.

Getting ready for the ride to Cripple Creek, he'd packed a sandwich, filled his traveling canteen with water, checked his rifle's load, and slipped an extra box of cartridges into his saddlebag. Ford also took an extra pistol from his desk and slipped it through his belt around in back. Lastly, as he was leaving, he went back and took a sawed-off shotgun from the wall rack, just in case.

Too much?

In Harmon Ford's opinion, there was no such thing as being overcautious when the stakes were life and death.

He spent his time in transit wondering who might've penned the note, and why they'd waited until now. No matter how he viewed the problem, turned it inside out or stood it on its head, he came back to the twin. Slade's brother had had the impact of a rock tossed in a pond. Ripples were spreading, and it just might be that he'd spooked someone into spilling evidence that would allow Ford to arrest the murderers.

Or else . . .

As he drew nearer to the meeting place, Ford took the shotgun from its scabbard, resting it across his saddle horn. It was no good for shooting at a distance, but if someone rushed him from the undergrowth along the creek, the scattergun would drop them without any need to aim. Buckshot at close range was the world's great leveler.

The stream known locally as Cripple Creek, because it broke at one point and jogged sideways over stony steps, ran for three quarters of a mile from the northwest to the southeast. The note had failed to specify a certain meeting place, and since he couldn't cover the whole creek at noon precisely, Ford decided he would simply let himself be seen and see if anything happened at the appointed time.

If not, at least he would've had a day out from the town, away from people wanting to talk about things that were typically none of his business—or theirs.

Ford had covered half the creek's length by the time the sun above told him that it was noon. He would go on and ride the other half, then double back and do it all again before he gave up and returned to town. He'd stop somewhere along the homeward journey, well away from Cripple Creek, and eat his lunch in peace, cursing the trickster who had lured him this far for nothing.

Ford had barely formulated that plan, when a bullet struck him in the left shoulder and punched him from his saddle. He was airborne when he heard the rifle shot, clutching the shotgun in a death grip with his right hand as he fell.

His impact with the ground stunned Ford and made him fire one barrel of the shotgun. That blast spooked his mare and sent her racing back along the creek, in the direction they'd just come from. Cursing, painfully aware that now his rifle and spare ammunition were beyond his reach,

Ford struggled from the spot where he had landed, worming through tall weeds to seek the cover of an old oak tree.

A second rifle shot rang out, somewhere above him, to his right now, and the bullet peeled bark from the tree he'd picked as cover. Ford didn't return fire, knowing that his twelve gauge couldn't match a rifle's range. He couldn't tell yet, from the sounds of gunfire, if his enemy was close or far away. Until he knew that and could make his first shot count, Ford wasn't wasting any ammo.

Pain and blood loss sapped his strength. Ford dug a handkerchief out of his pocket, teeth clenched tightly around a scream, and used it as a compress for the wound in front. It cost him too much, feeling for an exit wound in back, so he quit trying. It was time to concentrate on getting out alive, now that the trap had sprung.

Damned fool, Ford cursed himself. *You never should've come out in the first place. Serves you right.*

He was surrounded by a world of scuffling movements, unsure whether sounds he heard were made by men or rodents in the grass. Waiting for targets to reveal themselves, Ford focused on remaining conscious and alert. He had to fight now, or the bastards who had ambushed him would win.

Harsh sounds of someone rushing toward him, through the cattails, made Ford raise the scattergun and fire its second barrel. Buckshot pellets cut the reeds and wrung a squeal of pain from someone, thirty yards or so from where Ford sat.

"Take that," he said, drawing his Colt.

"And Marshal," said a gloating voice behind him, " *you* take *this.*"

Supper with Faith, a second time, told Slade that she enjoyed his company. They talked at first about his progress on Jim's case, but since there really wasn't any, they were soon forced to digress.

Faith told him more about the ranch, how Jim had built it in the years when he and Slade were mostly out of touch. Jim had stood firm against the rustlers, reservation-jumpers, and assorted trash who drifted through the territory with an eye for easy profit based on someone else's sorrow. There had even been a pitched fight at the house, when horse thieves tried to make off with Jim's stock, about two years before. Faith showed him bullet scars he hadn't seen on his first visit, mostly patched and painted over now.

"It must've been a hard time for you, knowing all of that was going on," Slade said.

Faith smiled. "Well, some of it happened before we met, of course. But James made me feel safe, no matter what. I always knew—well, *thought*—that we'd be here for one another."

"And you're still not letting go."

"How can I? When you have a dream within your grasp, you don't just give it up."

"Dreams change," Slade told her. "People too. You planned to work this place with Jim, not on your own. It's different today."

She met his level gaze. "You're saying now that I should sell? Because I—"

"No," he interrupted. "Selling now would only give the men who killed Jim what they wanted all along. But afterward, when everything's been sorted out . . . maybe . . ."

"Would *you* be interested?" Faith asked him. "If I meant to sell the land, I know Jim would prefer—"

Slade shook his head. "I'm not a rancher, Faith. I don't know anything about the business, what it takes to make a go of things. I'd run this place into the ground before a year was out."

"But you could *learn*," she said. "I know you could."

"It isn't in me. Honestly."

Slade's answer seemed to disappoint her more than any lack of progress in his brother's case. He felt compelled to offer an apology, but Faith stopped him, raising a hand between them.

"No," she said. "You're right. Each person knows what's right for him or her. I thought . . . well, never mind. I'll make my own decision later, when we've settled with the bastards who killed James.'"

Her language startled Slade, then made him laugh. Faith joined him in it, and they wound up holding hands, until Slade noticed and withdrew his, feeling heat rush to his cheeks.

The menu was a kind of blur for Slade. He knew that there was steak and baked potatoes, with some kind of greens, a fresh pie for dessert, but most of what he carried with him on the slow ride back to Lawton would be images of Faith Connover, echoes of her voice without specific words to spoil the way it made him feel.

And all the way, Slade told himself that there could be nothing between them. Nothing more, that is, than finding out who'd murdered Jim and seeing justice done by any means available.

He'd let the marshal and his friend, Judge Dennison, mete out that punishment if they were equal to the task. But if they didn't make some progress soon, Slade reckoned that he'd have to do the job himself, without the law's trappings.

One way to tackle it, he thought, might be to switch his method right around. Instead of searching for Dred Mathers, hoping that the rustler would expose Doug Freeman, Slade could tackle Freeman first. Force him to name the gunmen he had hired, say where they could be found.

And then?

Gunpoint confessions weren't admissible in court, but if it went that way, Slade knew Freeman would never go to trial. He'd face a higher court instead, and Slade would send him there.

Lawton was reasonably quiet, save for the neighborhood around the Dry Gulch and the Gay Paree. Slade didn't feel like playing cards, so he rode past the two saloons, down to the livery, and waited while the hostler put his Appaloosa in a stall, dispensing ample feed. Walking along Main Street to his hotel, Slade reconsidered stopping for a drink or two—no poker, not tonight—but didn't want to spoil his mood.

If he went into one of the saloons, he'd be obliged to ask again about the Mathers gang, would feel delinquent if he didn't, and Slade thought he'd plowed that ground sufficiently already. He could haunt the dives from now until Doomsday and gain no further information, if the locals wouldn't talk.

His one lead was the Gay Paree's young bartender, but Slade could only meet him on the day shift. He would try tomorrow, find out what he'd purchased for his dollar with a promise of five more behind it, and give up if there was nothing to be learned.

Doug Freeman next.

He made that solemn promise to himself.

Crossing the hotel lobby, Slade noticed a grim-faced man slouched in one of the easy chairs, off to his right. The stranger held a newspaper but wasn't reading it. Slade watched him from the corner of his eye, but saw no hostile move before he reached the stairs.

Inside his room, Slade locked the door and reached into his vest pocket for matches, moving toward the nearby lamp. When he was halfway there, a pistol's muzzle touched his neck, behind one ear. Slade froze, hearing the hammer cocked.

"One move," a gruff voice said, "and you're a dead man."

• • •

Someone to Slade's left struck a match and lit the lamp, revealing two men in the room besides the one who held a gun against Slade's head. Slade thought at once of Mathers and his gang, then noticed that the two men he could see wore badges pinned to their lapels. Grim faces glowered at him over guns.

"What's this about?" he asked all three of them at once.

The pistol nudged his skull a little harder. "Keep your mouth shut," said the first voice that had spoken, "and your hands raised shoulder-high."

Slade did as he was told, standing immobile while the stranger on his right moved in and took the Colt Peacemaker from his holster. "What about the gunbelt?" he inquired.

"We'll get it in a minute," said the first man. "Check him over first. Make sure that's all he's carrying."

The man on Slade's right shrugged, raising both hands to show that they were filled with six guns. On his left, the lamp-lighter holstered his weapon, edging forward with his hands outstretched.

"Don't shoot me now," he said, "if anything goes wrong."

"Just get it done!" the leader snapped.

"Awright, for heaven's sake."

It wasn't the most thorough frisk Slade had endured, but his captor found the knife sheathed in his boot and pulled it free. When he had turned Slade's pockets inside out and palmed the roll of cash he found, the deputy stepped back and said, "He's clean."

The leader stepped away as well, no longer needing pistol contact with Slade's skull. Taking a chance, Slade turned to glance at him and saw another face he didn't recognize.

"You've got my money now," he said. "If that's what this is all about, you didn't need the badges."

With a snarl, the leader of the trio swung his weapon

hard against Slade's cheek. The room tilted dramatically and Slade was on the floor before he knew it, grimacing against the bolts of pain that radiated through his head. A jolt of nausea came right behind the shock, but Slade stopped short of tossing up his dinner on the boots planted before his face.

"You got a smart mouth, mister," said the pistol-whipper. "Now you've found out what it gets you. Is there any more you want to say?"

In for a penny, Slade decided. "Well, if you're not here to rob me, then I'll ask again: What in the *hell* is this about?"

"You see the badges," his assailant answered. "We're arresting you."

"For what?"

"Murder, as if you didn't know."

That put another twist in Slade's unhappy stomach, but he didn't let it freeze his tongue. "Who is it you suppose I've killed?" he asked.

"Play dumb if you've a mind to," said the man off to his left. "But it ain't gonna help."

"All right," Slade said. "No names then. Let me see your warrant."

"What the hell?" one of them blurted out. "You knocked his brains loose, Curtis."

"Hey, don't tell me you forgot it, in a law-abiding town like this," Slade chided them. "I can't believe it, with your judge and all keeping a close eye on the local riffraff."

"What's this warrant business?" asked the deputy who held Slade's gun.

"Shut up!" the one called Curtis warned.

"He's got a valid question," Slade replied. "Real deputies would know that if you haven't seen me do a crime with your own eyes, you need a warrant to arrest me. That's the law. Of course, if you *saw* me commit a murder,

I assume you would've done something about it at the time, being lawmen and all. If not—"

"Get up, you bastard!" Curtis raged.

He drew a foot back, primed to kick, but he was interrupted by a rapping on the door. Reluctantly, he turned to open it. Slade peered between his legs and had an upside down view of the stranger from the lobby, now sporting a badge on his gray jacket.

"What's the holdup?" he inquired.

"Holdup is right," Slade answered from the floor. "These *deputies* have got no papers, and they just relieved me of my cash. Are you part of the gang?"

"What does he mean, Curtis?"

"Forget it." Turning back to Slade, Curtis demanded, "Are you getting up, or do we drag you through the streets?"

"I'm not sure I can help you," Slade replied. "I feel a little scrambled at the moment."

Curtis rounded on the others. "Stand him up, goddammit! Drag him, if he won't walk on his own."

The flanking deputies closed in, holstered their guns, and hauled Slade upright by his armpits. Standing drove another railroad spike of agony into his head, and Slade might well have fallen but for strong hands boosting him on either side.

"We're going to the jailhouse now," said Curtis. He stood close, letting Slade smell the onions on his breath. "If you've a mind to run, you'll have your last chance on the street." His weapon prodded Slade beneath his chin. "Fact is, I hope you do."

"Guess you'll be disappointed then," Slade said.

"We'll see."

The stairs were awkward, dizziness returning in a rush, but Slade managed with rough help from the captors bracing him on either side. It was a tight fit in the stairwell, three abreast, with shoulders rubbing wallpaper. Curtis went first and slowed them further, backing down the stairs, keeping his six-gun trained on Slade. The late arrival came along behind, playing caboose.

They reached the lobby somehow, and it got a little better after that, traversing level ground. Slade's escorts powered him across the lobby, while the clerk stood gaping at them in astonishment. Slade reckoned the reaction was an act—someone had clearly let the men into his room—but at the moment, it held no importance for him.

On the sidewalk, townsfolk stopped to watch the five-man party pass, eyeing Slade, perhaps debating what he'd done to rate the escort. Then again, from the expressions on some of their faces, maybe they already knew about the crime of which he stood accused.

Murder.

It was the worst out here, right up with stealing horses. Either one could get him hanged by order of the court—or lynched, if folks in town got restless, didn't feel like waiting for a trial.

Slade understood the charge and its potential repercussions. All he didn't know, at this point, was the victim's name.

Who had been killed in Lawton recently, besides his brother? Had Doug Freeman somehow bribed or tricked the marshal into blaming Slade for Jim's death back in April?

Anger at the very thought gave Slade the strength to walk without assistance, but his flankers kept a firm grip on his arms regardless.

If it went to trial, Slade knew that he could prove he wasn't in the Oklahoma Territory when his brother died. Dozens of witnesses could place him in New Mexico, if anybody cared and took the time to ask.

But if they *didn't* listen, *didn't* ask . . .

They reached the jailhouse. Curtis entered first, then held the door for Slade and his bookends. They marched him through another door, behind the marshal's vacant desk, and lodged him in an empty cell.

"I want to see the marshal," Slade demanded as the door slammed shut.

"Maybe you'll see him in your nightmares," Curtis said, "since it was him you killed."

"These wounds look bad," Dred Mathers said. "What were you doing that he shot you in the ass?"

"Tryin' to dodge that shotgun, dammit!" said Frank Lugar. "What'n hell you think?"

"I think you did a piss-poor job of it," Mathers replied. "You're short the best part of a cheek back here, and if I had to guess, I'd say your hip was busted."

"Jesus Christ, it hurts!"

"I reckon so."

The others stood around them in the line shack where they sometimes gathered to talk business, before a hard night's work. It wasn't sundown yet, but Mathers reckoned Frank was on the fade.

"I need a sawbones," Lugar whined.

"See, that's a problem, Frank." Mathers put all the sympathy that he could muster in his voice, admitting to himself it wasn't much. "We got the marshal lying dead by Cripple Creek, and he's still got that sawed-off with him. If we take you to a doctor with his buckshot in your ass, how long you reckon it'll be before somebody knows you had a hand in it?"

"I didn't kill nobody!" Lugar said.

"And that's the *other* problem," Mathers said. "You being an accomplice makes you guilty under law, but if you can persuade Judge Dennison you didn't pull a trigger, then he might just slap you with a little bit of jail time. If you named who did the killing and repeated it in court."

Through clenched teeth, Lugar said, "You know me,

Dred. I'd never squeal on anybody. Never have, and never will."

"I trust you, Frank. I do. But once a doctor gets ahold of you, there's just no stopping it. They'd either hang you or convince you that a deal's in order. And I reckon either one would break my heart."

"You can't just leave me, Dred!"

"No way I'd do that, Frank. What do you take me for?"

"But none a you can patch a wound this bad. You just ain't trained for it."

"You're right again." Rising, he towered over Lugar, lying huddled on the ground. "That's why I figure that the best thing I can do is ease your misery."

"Dred? What the—?"

Mathers drew his six-gun, cocked it, aimed, and fired into the rising scream. His bullet silenced Lugar instantly, but didn't stop the little tremors running through Lugar's body while the nerves and muscles got belated news that he was dead.

"We got no shovels," Corey Chapman said.

"Don't need 'em," said his brother, Quinn. "We got coyotes."

"Coyotes," Corey echoed. "That's a good one."

"It's a shit-ass thing to say, is what that is," Bran Huffman growled.

"Listen, you—"

Mathers broke into the argument before it could explode. "We've got *matches*," he reminded him. "I aim to burn the line shack. Give old Frank a sendoff like the Injuns used to do it in the day."

"That's smart," Mack Riley said. "Somebody finds 'im later, let 'em sift the ashes, guessin' who it was."

"And pick the buckshot from his roasted ass," said Corey Chapman with a grin. "Maybe keep it for a souvenir."

"Show some respect," Mathers commanded. "Just

because he's dead, you don't have leave to mock him. Frank saved my ass once or twice, and I recall a time he helped you out in Texarkana, when your brother didn't lift a finger."

"Jeez, Dred, I was only jokin'."

"Keep it to your goddamn self, and fetch dry brush we can use for kindling. Double quick now! All of you!"

They spent ten minutes piling tumbleweeds and such around the shack. Then Mathers set the kindling on fire at several points and they stood back to watch it burn. The line shack caught in nothing flat, was totally consumed by flame within two minutes, and its roof caved in after another five. Soon after that, the watchers had to duck and run as cartridges on Lugar's gunbelt started cooking off, their bullets whining aimlessly into the dusk.

"He'll bag us yet!" cried Corey Chapman, running for his horse.

"Shoots better now than when he was alive," crowed his brother, Quinn.

Mathers was last to ride away and leave the line shack smoldering, with Lugar's last remains inside. He was already thinking past the marshal and their loss, deciding what he ought to do about Slade's brother.

And Doug Freeman.

Don't forget about that two-faced piece of—

"Dred!" Mack Riley hailed him from the shadows, drawing closer on his pinto. "Now we done the marshal, what's the next move? Are we leavin'? Goin' somewhere else?"

"I'm working on it, Mack," he said. "Give me some time. You'll be among the first to know."

8

Slade's cell contained a metal bed frame bolted to the wall, some kind of straw-filled bag or pad to serve him as a mattress, and a threadbare blanket that smelled strongly of the stable. There was nothing else resembling furniture, and no slop bucket for emergencies.

The last omission was a conscious choice, Slade reckoned, meant to spare the jailers being doused with filth whenever prisoners got rowdy. On the downside, that meant inmates had to be escorted to an outdoor privy when they felt the need, or else risk dirtying the cells.

Slade filed the information in his aching head for future reference, but felt no urge to stretch his legs just yet. He found enough discomfort in the simple act of lying still and trying to make sense of what had happened.

He was being held on the suspicion that he'd murdered Harmon Ford. He wondered when and where the marshal had been slain, with less attention to the *how* of it. If Ford was killed while Slade was dining with Faith Connover, he had a solid alibi.

If not . . .

It did no good for him to guess who might've killed the
lawman, but Slade had a few ideas. Could it be mere coincidence that Ford was murdered one day after Slade confronted the marshal with his suspicions about Douglas
Freeman and the Mathers gang? Had Ford begun to nose
around more energetically, and thereby sealed his doom?

Of course, Slade realized, a U.S. marshal in the Oklahoma Territory might have enemies to spare. There'd be a
list of wanted fugitives for starters, followed by the rela-
tives and friends of criminals Ford had arrested, men confined to prison or condemned to hang. There might be
hundreds who would cheer news of the marshal's death,
but Slade thought he could narrow down the search dramatically by focusing on Lawton and his brother's case.

Barely twenty-four hours earlier, Slade had braced
Ford, challenged his authority in no uncertain terms, and
might've left the marshal thinking it was time to give Jim's
case a closer look. Within moments of that terse exchange,
Slade had spoken to Freeman, delivered Faith's rejection
of the rancher's bid, and taunted Freeman with his own
plans to investigate Jim's death, letting the chips fall where
they may. Pairing those conversations with the news of
Ford's murder led Slade to think he might've lit the fuse.

It troubled him, because he sensed the marshal was—
had been—a good man in his way, if not a dynamo where
manhunts were concerned. Slade hadn't wished Ford any
harm, and he regretted any part he might've had in carrying the marshal to an early grave. There was a certain irony
in charges being filed against him for the murder, when his
personal inquiries might have spurred the killers into striking when they did.

Or maybe not.

Slade's head was throbbing. Sickly waves of pain prevented him from pacing nervously around his cell. Instead,
he took the handkerchief that had been left to him, mois-

tened one corner with his own saliva, and began to dab
blood from a shallow cut along his hairline. It was painful,
but it helped him focus on the task at hand.

Step one was getting out of jail.

Slade hoped to do it legally, thereby avoiding further
charges and a trigger-happy posse breathing down his
neck, but in the last analysis he knew he could accomplish
nothing from his cell. Without assistance from outside, he
could mount no serious defense to any charges filed
against him, and he would remain an easy target for lynch-
ers while he was confined. Ford might've stopped a mob
from entering the jail, but Slade had no faith in the deputy
named Curtis or his pals.

He didn't want to think about escape just yet, but Slade
would keep the possibility in mind. His cell contained
nothing to serve him as a weapon, but the privy might be
useful yet. A walk outside, perhaps with only one guard to
accompany him, and—

Never mind that now.

Where would he go if he was freed by hook or crook?
What would his first stop be?

It irritated Slade to realize he didn't know where Freeman lived, or even if the rancher had a place in town. That
information could be ascertained, but it would be of little
value to him if his captors kept his money and his horse.
Mobility was paramount.

Slade didn't fret about a weapon. Once he had the target in his sights, and within striking range, some handy object would suggest itself. If it came to that, he'd face Doug
Freeman empty-handed, teach him what a beating really
was, and keep it up until Freeman identified his triggermen
or died defending them.

Slade didn't think the rancher had that kind of sand. He
might be cold enough to hire assassins, but Slade guessed
he'd try to keep his own hands clean. There might've been
a time when Freeman fought wild beasts and men to win

his land, but now the animals were on his payroll, and the only dirt beneath his fingernails was rusty flakes of blood rubbed off while shaking hands with murderers.

That didn't mean Doug Freeman would be soft. He had a reputation and position to maintain, an empire in the making that he would defend with every weapon he could find. But being civilized, even if it was only superficial, just cosmetic, dulled a killer's edge.

Slade had been civilized himself, or nearly so, but he could feel it sloughing from him like the caked blood on his scalp.

A sound of voices from the outer office drew Slade from his reverie. He sat up on the bunk, head swimming for a moment, then relaxing into the familiar throb. A moment later, the connecting door swung open and a man of middle age stepped through it, Curtis close behind him, almost treading on his heels.

"What happened to his head?" the older man inquired.

"Resisting," Curtis answered, hard eyes daring Slade to challenge his report.

Slade took the bait. "He means resisting three men without warrants when they broke into my room and took my money."

"Shut it, you—"

"Curtis."

The stranger didn't raise his voice. He didn't need to. Curtis shut his mouth without another word, face darkening until Slade thought his head might burst.

"I want this man's belongings on the desk out front when I get finished here," the older man instructed. "Anything goes missing, you're responsible. Hear me?"

"Yes, sir."

"Give me the key and leave us now."

"But, sir—"

"Don't make me say it twice."

Curtis retreated, keyless. The connecting door clicked

softly shut. Slade's visitor unlocked his cell and stepped inside.

"John Slade?"

"That's me."

"Judge Isaac Dennison."

"I recognize the name," Slade said.

"May I sit down?"

"It's your jail."

Dennison sat at the far end of the bunk, arm's length away from Slade. If he was worried about Slade attacking him, it didn't show.

"Do you require a doctor's care?" the judge asked Slade.

"I doubt it. No."

"The men who picked you up exceeded their authority," said Dennison. "They were supposed to find you and report to me. They had no orders to arrest you, or . . ."

Judge Dennison reached up and drew a fingertip along his own hairline, where steel gray framed a suntanned face.

"I'll live," Slade said, "unless you plan to hang me."

"Are you planning to confess a hanging crime?"

"Not likely."

"Then you're reasonably safe," the judge replied.

"That Curtis told me I was charged with killing Marshal Ford."

"Curtis. How should I put this? He's a sober man, and mostly well intentioned, but he soaks up too much hellfire of a Sunday and it keeps him burning through the week. He wasn't the best choice to serve as deputy, even in an emergency. That's my fault. If you want to file a charge of battery against him, I will put it on the docket."

Slade frowned, suddenly confused. "But he's your own man."

"He's an amateur who can't control himself," said Dennison. "My man was Harmon Ford. He was my senior deputy and one of only three I've got patrolling half the territory. I don't even want to think about the mischief that'll come to pass before I manage to replace him."

Getting back to urgent business, Slade inquired, "So you don't think I killed the marshal?"

"Why on Earth would I think that?"

"I got the notion from your deputies."

"Damned fools. They're back to being shopkeepers tomorrow, after breakfast. I've no time for bunglers."

"Well, Judge, if I'm not a suspect, why exactly did you want to see me?"

"To discuss your brother's case and learn what bearing it may have on Marshal Ford's assassination."

"You probably know more about my brother's death than I do," Slade replied. "He'd already been nearly two months in the ground before I found out he was dead."

"But you discussed the case with Marshal Ford?" asked Dennison.

Slade nodded, instantly regretting it. "We talked about it twice. First time, he told me Jim was killed from ambush, shot three times. He started out by blaming rustlers, then suggested someone else might be behind it. I asked him for names. He didn't offer any."

"And the second time you spoke?"

"Yesterday afternoon. I told him what I'd heard, talking to certain folks in town. Gave *him* some names, and asked him if they rang a bell. He didn't want to go out on a limb. Next thing I know, that Curtis claims I murdered him."

"From what I gather, you've been asking questions here and there," said Dennison.

"That's right. And I told Ford I planned to keep on asking, if he couldn't find the killers."

"You're entitled, heaven knows, but it's a risky way to go. You see that now?" asked Dennison.

"I'm used to taking risks. My brother's life was worth it."

Dennison sat watching him in silence for a moment.

When he spoke again, his voice was grave. "I need to know those names," he said.

Why not? Slade thought. "Jim's lawyer, Amos Whitaker, mentioned Dred Mathers and his gang. Nobody seems to have a clue where they might be. And then, my first day here in town, one of your business types stopped by to see if I could make Faith Connover sell off my brother's land. He offered me a finder's fee if I could swing it."

"And this 'business type' would be . . . ?"

"Doug Freeman."

"Ah."

"So you're familiar with him."

"Everyone in this part of the territory knows him, one way or another," Dennison replied. "You spoke to him once only?"

"No. He came back for an answer yesterday, right after I saw Marshal Ford the second time."

"And I assume Miss Connover's determined not to sell?"

"That's right."

"How did he take that news?" asked Dennison.

"He wasn't happy. Then, I went and pissed him off myself."

"Meaning?"

"I may've led him to believe that Marshal Ford suspected him of some involvement in Jim's death."

"May have, or did?"

"I did. Told him, while I was at it, that I meant to keep digging until I had some solid answers of my own. As I recall, he told me asking questions could be dangerous."

"A threat?"

"Nothing that I could prove."

"Well, Mr. Slade, you've given me some food for thought. I'll have to sleep on this and see what comes to me. Meanwhile, you're free to go. Without trying to parrot anybody else, I'm bound to say you may, in fact, be jeopardized by making further inquiries."

"My choice," Slade said.

"Just so you know, I can't protect you if that's how you choose to go, unless . . . No, never mind."

"Say it."

"Well, I was thinking that you might acquire some measure of security, however slight, if you agreed to work for me."

"As what?" Slade asked.

"I only have one job available," said Dennison. "You'd be replacing Harmon Ford."

"That knock I took has got me hearing things," Slade said.

"No, I believe you heard me right."

"In that case, Judge, maybe it's *you* that took the beating."

Dennison pinned Slade with gimlet eyes. "Are you a wanted man?" he asked.

Slade had to smile at that. "No, sir. I don't believe I'm wanted anywhere. But—"

"I don't ask much of my deputies," the judge pressed on. "Just total dedication, honesty, devotion, and a dash of courage."

Slade reminded him, "I'm not a lawman."

"No one is, until he takes that badge and pins it on his shirt."

"I mean to say that I've got no experience."

"I wish there was some kind of training school for U.S. marshals," Dennison replied. "Maybe there *will* be someday, but I don't expect to see it in my lifetime. As it is, you do your learning on the job. I'll tell you what the law says. You arrest the ones who break it, if there's evidence."

"Why me?" asked Slade.

The judge sat staring at his dusty boots for half a minute before answering. At last, he said, "I've spent half my life judging men. It's what I do and who I am. Looking at you, I see a man who wouldn't cut and run when trouble's coming. I believe you have a measure of determination and intelligence. How *much* of those you have is something that we'll have to test. And you're a gambler."

"Is that good?"

"Depends. Some gamblers are degenerates, no self-control. They'd bet their family's last penny that the sun won't rise tomorrow, if some other joker bets it will. Your kind of gambler studies odds and angles, learns the game before he antes up, and wins more than he loses. Am I right?"

Slade nodded, suffering a little less that time.

"That's part of law enforcement," Dennison observed. "The rules are written down or stored up here." He tapped his temple with an index finger. "How you play the game depends on who you're up against, the odds against you, and the stakes you're playing for. But one way or another, Mr. Slade, you always play to win."

"Within the rules," Slade said.

"Oh, yes. That's paramount. Bring me a prisoner all beat to hell, who's put his mark on a confession that he couldn't read, I guarantee *you'll* be the one who lands in prison. Kill an unarmed man—or *any* man who isn't threatening somebody's life or property—and I may have to hang you."

"Judge, I never stay in one place very long."

A shrug from Dennison. "Maybe you'll like it here and change your mind," he said. "Or maybe you'll stay long enough to find your brother's killers, then go off and leave me high and dry. Right now, I'll take what I can get." He nodded toward the outer office. "And I don't have much."

"You'd let me work on Jim's case?"

"Mr. Slade, before this afternoon I had three deputies patrolling thirty-four thousand square miles. Now I've got two, not counting those who brought you in. Luke Walker

hangs his hat in Catesby. Aaron Price works out of Enid.
We communicate by telegraph and only see each other in
the flesh when they come down to testify in court."

"Must make it hard," Slade said, "for you to know exactly what they're doing."

"They're veterans," said Dennison. "I'd trust them with
my life—or with my grandchildren, if it came down to
that. You, on the other hand, would operate from Lawton,
under my perpetually watchful eye."

"So, this would be my office?" Slade inquired. "I mean,
out there?"

"It would."

"And there'd be long days in the saddle, chasing folks
who'd kill me just like they were stepping on a bug, bringing them back to you for trial."

"If we have evidence and they're indicted. That's about
the size of it," said Dennison.

"You haven't mentioned what this dream job pays."

"The princely sum of fifty dollars each and every
month, plus reimbursement of expenses if I deem them
job-related."

"Food and water basically," said Slade.

"I might throw in a cold beer every now and then."

"And if I don't accept your proposition?"

"Mr. Slade, it's been a quarter century since we dis-
pensed with slavery in this nation. You are free to go, whatever you decide. I'd strongly caution you, however, against
meddling in your brother's case without proper authority.
Obstructing justice is a serious offense all by itself. If you
got careless, say, and killed someone you thought had
harmed your brother—well, that's just plain murder."

"Ford already warned me that you don't like vigilantes," Slade replied.

"And I hope you were listening."

"I pay attention when it counts."

"I'm glad to hear it."

It was Slade's turn to inspect his boots, as if the answer to his problem might be written there, in dust and leather creases. He could take the badge that Dennison had offered him, with all its strings and rules attached, or he could risk a hangman's noose for dealing with Jim's killers privately.

Assuming he could find them.

And assuming that they didn't get him first.

"I want Jim's killers punished," he told Dennison. "I mean to see it done. And what the hell, I may as well get paid."

"You've made an old man happy," Dennison replied. "Let's see how long that lasts."

Slade followed Dennison out of the cell, through the connecting door to Marshal Ford's office. *His* office now, or shortly.

Curtis and the other three stood watching as he entered with the judge. They wore no badges now. Their tin stars had been lined up on the desk, beside Slade's gunbelt, bankroll, and the knife they'd taken from his boot.

"You'll want to count that money, I expect," said Dennison.

Slade took his time about it, finally announcing, "It's all here."

"A damned good thing too." Turning to his cashiered deputies, the judge said, "You boys won't be needed any longer. Go and sin no more." Then, as an afterthought, "You hear me, Curtis?"

"Yes, sir."

"See you mind then, damn it."

When they were alone, door closed behind the last of the departing ex-deputies, Dennison circled the desk, opened its central drawer, and swept the four badges out of sight with one hand. He then took a different badge from his coat pocket, this one stamped with the legend U.S. DEPUTY MARSHAL, and handed it to Slade.

The badge was small, but it felt heavy in Slade's hand.

"I've got an oath goes with that, when you're ready," Dennison informed him.

"No time like the present."

"Pin it on and raise your right hand then. We'll do without the Bible."

Slade pinned the badge to his vest, where his jacket would cover its shine if he felt so inclined, then raised his hand.

"Repeat after me," said the judge. "I, John Slade . . ."

Slade echoed him in fragments, swearing to defend the U.S. Constitution while observing and enforcing all laws passed by Congress in and for the Oklahoma Territory, without fear, favor, or any personal consideration. He decided that the last bit could be taken with a grain of salt, since his pursuit of those who'd killed his brother was intensely personal.

He had a hunting license now, but only if he used it wisely and within the law.

"You're sworn," said Dennison when Slade had finished with the oath. "Any more questions right away, before you catch a good night's sleep?"

"You said that I'd be working on Jim's murder," Slade reminded him.

"On that and Marshal Ford's, along with any other crimes that come along behind them."

"Do you doubt the murders are connected?"

"Doubt it? No. But I can't prove it, and it may turn out that both of us are wrong in that respect."

"About the Mathers gang . . ."

"They're definitely wanted on a list of charges that will hang them, if convicted. Even if they didn't kill your brother, I'd expect them all to swing."

"Which means they likely won't surrender," Slade observed.

"I would anticipate resistance," Dennison agreed. "But hear me now, and heed me well. *If* one or more of them resists you and you're forced to put the bastards down, I want it legal and aboveboard. Witnesses supporting your side of the story would be helpful. Failing that, I want it clear to any reasonable man that you had no choice whatsoever in the matter. Understood?"

"I hear you, Judge."

"It works to our advantage if you bring them in alive," said Dennison. "We hang our murderers in public, as an object lesson to society. Word gets around. Maybe it helps, or maybe not, but that's the law. Plus, there's a decent chance that one or more of them might sing to buy himself some extra time. May be the only way we'll find out whether they were paid to kill your brother, or just did it on their own account."

"I hear you," Slade repeated.

"Hear and *heed*."

"We understand each other."

"One last thing, before you go. If we can build a case against the men who killed your brother, there's a good chance you may need to testify at trial. Tell how you caught them, what they said in custody, describe the evidence against them."

"Fine."

"Just so we're clear," said Dennison. "Some judges may allow their officers to stretch the truth a mite or tell things as they *ought* to be, instead of how they are. But I'm not one of them. I'll slap a lawman with a charge of perjury as quick as hang a renegade. The penalty for lying in my court is five years, breaking rocks up in McAlester."

"You run a tight ship, Judge."

"It stays afloat," said Dennison, "and it's not swamped

with shit from men too lazy or dishonest to perform the duties they've accepted."

"I don't aim to let you down."

"Aiming's one thing, accomplishment's another. See you don't."

"Well, if we're done here . . ."

"Done we are. You'll find the office keys there, in your desk. Sleep well and get an early start tomorrow." Halfway to the door, Dennison stopped and asked him, "Am I right in thinking that you'll have another talk with Freeman sometime soon?"

"Tomorrow, if I can."

Nodding, the judge said, "I look forward to your first report. Be wary, Marshal Slade. Try not to die before you get your first paycheck."

Slade donned his gunbelt, found the office keys, locked up, and walked back to the Lawton Arms. Some of the folks he met along his way smiled warily, while others did their best to look through Slade, ignoring him. He didn't make a point of showing off his brand-new badge, trusting the gossip mill to spread that news without any particular display on his part.

Word would get around, starting with Curtis if Slade wasn't very much mistaken. Would it reach Doug Freeman's ears before he had a chance to see the badge on Slade's chest when they met again?

Was Slade in danger even now, before his first hour as a lawman passed?

Slade knew the answer to that question well enough. He'd been in danger from the moment he arrived in Lawton and began to nose around his brother's death. Slade had no doubt that Marshal Ford was killed for working on that case, despite the fact that he'd accomplished nothing by the time he died.

The killers would prefer it that way, questions without answers, tongues silenced by fear.

Slade still had no authority to force confessions from the guilty, but a badge might help him crack the wall of silence. And if Jim's killers tried to stop him, they would be forced to expose themselves.

And when they did . . .

Slade entered the hotel and went directly to the registration desk. The clerk was plainly shocked to see him, reckoning that Slade had changed his permanent address in favor of a jail cell. Shock turned into wonderment as Slade drew back the left side of his jacket to reveal his badge.

"Next time you feel like letting someone in my room, think twice," Slade warned.

"Yes, sir! But they were—"

"Wrong," Slade interrupted him. "Just hear me. Hear and heed."

Without another word, he turned away and headed for the stairs.

9

Slade woke near dawn, anxious to make a start but knowing that he couldn't rush the day. No matter how he felt, however keyed up he became, the pace of daily life in Lawton would remain unchanged.

Unless he started lighting fuses, seeing where they led.

Slade's first stop, with the shops on Main Street not yet open, was the office he'd inherited from Harmon Ford. He used his key, then locked the door behind him to avoid an early-morning interruption while he looked around the place.

It had the smell of every lawman's office Slade had ever visited—a mixture of aromas that included leather, gun oil, and a dash of fear-sweat from the prisoners who sometimes occupied its cells. Slade had been sweating some himself, when he was locked up in the back a few short hours earlier.

He checked the wanted posters briefly, disappointed to find nothing on the Mathers gang that might suggest a starting point for his projected search. From there, he scanned the office gun rack, where he found two lever-action rifles and one shotgun under lock and key. Boxes of ammunition occupied a drawer beneath the gun rack, also locked.

Slade had the keys. If he required a larger arsenal than this to deal with Mathers and his men, the cause was likely hopeless anyway.

Ford's chair—his now—creaked when he sat in it, and squeaked a little when he swiveled to the left. Oddly, it made no sound when he spun to the right, although it wobbled slightly near the completion of the circuit. Going through the desk drawers, he found pencils, one small pad of paper, a folding knife with the tip of its blade broken off, the emergency badges his captors had worn yesterday— and a small stack of files in stiff folders.

Slade spread the files out on his desktop, skimming the hand-lettered labels, searching for a dossier related to his brother's case. The disappointment hit him like a short punch to the solar plexus when he found Jim's name on none of them.

Had Ford kept other files, secreted in some other place? Could it be possible that he had *nothing* written down about Jim's murder?

"Damn it!"

Angrily, he put the files away and checked his watch. The nearby restaurant opened at six A.M., and Slade was there for breakfast when the boss lady unlocked her doors. Still early for the other stops he had in mind, Slade dawdled over ham, eggs, and potatoes for the best part of an hour while the waitress kept his coffee cup well filled and flirted with him just a little. If she'd heard about him being dragged to jail last night, she didn't let it show. In fact, Slade caught her sneaking glances at his badge and smiling in a way that made him think she leaned toward men in uniform.

Of course, Slade didn't *have* a uniform. Only the badge

suggested any change in status or authority, and that was easily concealed. As for the rest, he had two suits of clothes, and folks in town had seen them both by now. Slade reckoned he should get them cleaned and pressed when he had time, but at the moment he had other business on his mind.

Still killing time, he walked down to the barber's shop, found himself first in line for a haircut, and sat with a view of the street while the barber got busy. Slade's hair wasn't long, but he guessed that a lawman should think of his grooming more often than Slade did on long poker nights.

And besides, if the plan he was working should cost him his life, at least he'd be neat in his casket.

From the barber's, Slade walked two blocks farther to the Lawton post office. Inside, he spent a moment looking at the wanted posters on display, all duplicates of those found in his office. When the customer ahead of him was done, Slade braced the postmaster and let him see the federal badge.

"I need to find one of your leading citizens," Slade said, "and I don't have his address."

Bobbing his head birdlike, the postmaster responded, "Anything that I can do to help, Marshal."

"Name's Douglas Freeman," Slade explained. "I guess he has a spread somewhere nearby, but if he's got a place in town—"

"Yes, sir," the smaller man replied, not giving Slade a chance to finish. "He does, for a fact."

"Where might I find it?"

"Another block due east," the postmaster replied. "Free Range Society, he calls it, with his name right underneath. Can't miss it."

"And his spread? What was it called again?" asked Slade.

"The Rocking Y. After his brand, you know? Ride two miles north of town and you're on Freeman land, whichever way you turn. His house is three miles farther on."

"No fences?"

"Not yet, Marshal. With the free-range thing and all, I guess he doesn't like 'em."

No, Slade thought. *He wouldn't if the land's all his.*

The office wasn't large, but someone had spent time and money on the sign, some king of gold paint on the door's glass upper half, with fancy scrollwork. Freeman's name was half the size of the society's, a modest touch.

Slade tried the doorknob, felt it turn, and entered. At first glance, it seemed the tidy office was unoccupied, its two desks facing one another without anyone to keep them company. No bell was mounted on the door frame to announce him, and a moment passed before Slade heard soft humming, emanating from a room in back.

"Somebody here?" he called.

"Who's that?" Doug Freeman challenged, stepping into view. He flicked a glance at Slade's badge, then said, "Marshal Slade. Congratulations are in order."

"If you think it's good news," Slade replied.

"Good news for you. I don't see it affecting me much, one way or the other."

"No?"

"Why would it?" Freeman asked.

"No reason necessarily," Slade said. "I wanted you to know I've got a few new angles on my brother's killing. Turns out Marshal Ford kept files on his investigations squirreled away. It was dumb luck I found them, going through his things."

"I'm glad to hear it," Freeman answered stiffly. "We need law and order in the territory, if we're going to expand and thrive."

"I'm glad to hear you say so, Doug. I'll leave you to your business now, but maybe we'll talk later, when you have more time."

"About what, Marshal?"

"This and that. Who knows? I'll be in touch."

Slade smiled the whole way to the Gay Paree saloon, startling some passersby who craved more solemn faces at that hour of the morning. The saloon was open, ready to receive those customers who couldn't start the day without a shot or three. Hair of the dog that bit them and was gnawing at the inside of their skulls for more.

The place was quiet as he entered. No piano music in the daytime, and the working girls were all tucked in their beds, alone for once, after a hard night riding bareback. There were two old-timers drinking at the far end of the bar, served by the bartender who'd promised Slade to find out more about the Mathers gang.

The drinkers barely glanced at Slade as he approached the bar. Their fate and future swam within the amber contents of their glasses. They cared nothing for the new arrival or his badge, none of it having anything to do with them.

Slade took his stand well down the bar from them regardless, waiting as the bartender approached. The young man eyed Slade's badge and said, "I guess you're back about Dred Mathers then."

"You have some information for me?" Slade inquired.

"Guess there's no money in it for me, now you got that piece of tin."

"I said five dollars for a decent lead and nothing's changed. If you've decided not to deal—"

"Hold on there, Marshal. Don't be hasty." Glancing toward his other customers, the barkeep asked Slade, "Do you want a shot of something? Makes it look more natural."

"Bit early for the red eye," Siade replied. "Besides, I'm working."

"Hell, that never stopped your predecessor."

"He's not here."

"I guess that's right. Some coffee then? It's fresh, and they won't think you come to pick my brain."

"You think they care?"

"Most likely not, but who knows? Maybe somebody's watchin' you. They see you come in here, then ask around." The young man finished with a shrug and dour expression on his face.

"Coffee it is."

The barkeep poured it hot and black. Slade burned his tongue on the first sip and set it back to cool. "So, what's the word?" he pressed.

The young man kept his voice pitched low, using a rag to wipe the bar. "I asked around for Mathers and his boys, just like you wanted. Tryin' to be subtlelike, you know? He finds out I've been snoopin' and I'll wind up with a new hole in my head. It's risky if you get my drift."

"We settled on five dollars," Slade reminded him.

"I'm not tryin' to squeeze you on the price, Marshal. Just sayin' how it is—and why I couldn't get you much."

"Spill it," Slade prodded.

"Well, I got some names of boys who ride with Mathers now and then. No guarantee that any certain one of 'em is with him right this minute, but they're friends of his and done some jobs together off and on."

"I'll take the names."

"One of 'em's Wiley Grace, a mean drunk. Not too smart, but mean, they say."

"What does he look like?"

"Never seen him. This is what I *heard,* you know?"

"All right. Go on."

"Then, there's Frank Lugar. Him, I've seen. He's got a scar right here"—touching the left side of the chin—"where he got sliced somehow. Dark hair and crazy eyes."

"Who else?" asked Slade.

"The Chapman brothers, Quinn and Corey. Quinn's the eldest, but they both spell trouble. They've been banned from both saloons in town for bustin' up the furniture and customers. Don't turn your back on either one of 'em."

"Is that the lot?"

"Two more," the barkeep said. "Mack Riley I don't know, but talk says that he comes from Texas. If he's ridin' with the Mathers gang, you know he can't be good for much but stealin', maybe killin'."

"And the last?" Slade asked.

"Bran Huffman. He's been in here once or twice since I was hired. Good-lookin', in a man way. All the girls here seem to like 'im. Seems all right to talk to, but I wouldn't want to cross 'im."

That's my job, thought Slade. He asked, "Where can I find them?"

"That's the trouble, see. Nobody knows, or else they're scared of talking. I tried offerin' a dollar, but I got no takers."

Now you've got a bull's-eye on your back, Slade thought. "The names may help," he granted, "but without some kind of lead on where they go to hide—"

"Well, now, I might have something after all," the barkeep said.

"Don't play with me," Slade cautioned him.

"No, sir. Just saved the best for last. It turns out Mathers has himself a gal he visits when he's passin' by this way. Maybe she's on the game, but she don't work in the saloons. Name's Jenny Acton. S'posed to be a looker, but I've never seen her."

"If she doesn't work in town—"

"I'm there ahead of you, Marshal. She's got a place about a half mile out of Lawton, going south. Backs up against the woods down there, I understand. A cabin, nothing much. You oughta find it easy."

Slade delivered the five dollars, pinning it beneath his

index finger as he warned, "I'd better not find out you're stringing me along."

"Not me. No, sir," the barkeep answered earnestly. "I have to live here, Marshal. Maybe even when you're dead and gone."

It was a risky proposition, meeting Mathers in the middle of the open countryside, away from witnesses, but Freeman knew he had to take the chance. He'd hedged his bets a little, hiding two men armed with Winchesters inside a nearby copse of trees, but they would be more use avenging him than saving him, if Mathers had a mind to end it here and now.

Still, risk or no, meeting Mathers in town had been impossible, and Freeman didn't want him seen around the Rocking Y again, if he could help it. Mathers had the plague and it was spreading, with a new doctor committed to eradicating every stain.

Doug Freeman knew he wore the mark already, but there might be time to wash it off, if he moved swiftly and decisively enough.

It was a damned unpleasant twist, Judge Dennison releasing Slade and handing him a federal badge to boot. Killing the nosy twin was twice as hazardous for Freeman now. He would be suspect in the judge's eyes, of course. That part was unavoidable, but Dennison's own nature would prevent him from filing charges if he didn't have sufficient evidence to hang Freeman.

And without Dred Mathers, there would be no evidence.

The thought of killing Mathers made him smile, but Freeman knew he had to solve his problems one step at a time. Jack Slade was the most pressing threat, fired up with righteous anger at his brother's slaying, now empowered with a U.S. marshal's badge. He wouldn't really know the job yet, wouldn't be conversant with the law, but that only made him more dangerous in Freeman's view.

Judge Dennison would punish Slade if the new marshal overstepped his bounds. It was the old man's nature to observe each period and comma in the statute books, holding them sacrosanct and handing down the maximum permitted punishment to those who broke the code. But by the time he dealt with Slade, Doug Freeman could be dead.

And what good would it do him then?

He meant to cut the head off this snake in advance, *before* it bit him and he wound up suffering, or worse, from his timidity. One brother dead already, and another on the way to join him.

There was symmetry about it. Even poetry.

The afternoon was fading, but the sun was still damned hot as Freeman waited, sitting upright in his saddle like a soldier at attention. He had never served a day in uniform, but knew the value of a sharp appearance. First impressions were important to a businessman of his ambition. Last impressions too.

He thought again of killing Mathers on the spot, as soon as he arrived. Freeman had briefed his snipers. All he had to do was doff his hat and wipe his forehead with a sleeve. Before the swipe was finished, bullets would've hammered Mathers from his saddle, and the link that bound Doug Freeman to the marshal's murdered brother would be broken.

Maybe.

On the worried side, he couldn't know for sure if Mathers had discussed their bargain with his cronies, while they plotted to eliminate James Slade. If so, that still left half-a-dozen flapping mouths to threaten Freeman, and he couldn't truly rest until he'd silenced all of them.

That would require finesse, precision timing. Maybe he could get them all together for a celebration after Slade was dead, a party on some neutral ground where he could stack the odds against them. Set them up and knock them down, leave them to feed the buzzards or deposit them in one of Oklahoma's murky, cottonmouth-infested lakes.

Sounds like a plan, he thought. *But first things first.*

Freeman saw Mathers coming from a half mile out, his sharp eyes focused on the flyspeck that became a mounted rider, drawing closer by the moment. Mathers was alone, as far as he could tell, though others from the gang might well be circling wide around him, looking for a sniper's roost to cover him, the way Freeman was covering their boss.

"What's so all-fired important?" Mathers called to him when they were fifty yards apart.

Freeman sat waiting, so he wouldn't have to raise his voice. There were no innocents around to eavesdrop and report the conversation, but why take the chance?

When Mathers had reduced the gap to thirty feet, Freeman replied, "Judge Dennison surprised me yesterday. He's picked Slade's brother to replace the late, lamented Harmon Ford."

"Made him a marshal? Are you shittin' me?"

"I shit you not," said Freeman. "But we're in some if he stays around to do the job."

"This thing is getting complicated," Mathers said. "It was supposed to be a simple one-time job."

"That's life. Things change."

"You got that right," said Mathers. "And I'm thinking I could use a change myself. Look into someplace new and see what's what."

"You want to run out now?" asked Freeman, goading him. "Remember, that's a federal badge Slade's wearing. You won't be shed of him by riding five miles out of town—or all the way to California, for that matter."

"Hunting me and finding me are different things," Mathers replied. "There's always Mexico."

"And what then? Stay down there forever, eating beans?"

"I reckon they've got opportunities, the same as here."

Freeman reached for his hat, considered lifting it, then settled for a small adjustment, leveling his shade. "I guess you'll take the others with you then," he said.

"Why would I?" Mathers asked.

"Just thinking down the road," Freeman answered. "You leave them here, and Slade gets one of them to talk, you've got a hanging warrant waiting for you anytime you try to come back home. Six men, six coffin nails."

"I'm not afraid of them," said Mathers. "Anyway, it's five now."

"Somebody left already?"

"Didn't leave," Mathers replied. "But you could say he's gone."

"Who was it?"

"What's the difference?"

"None to me, but if the judge ties him to Ford—"

"You sweat too much, Douglas."

"Maybe. But Slade—"

"I'll think about him," Mathers said. "See what I want to do. If I decide to stick around awhile, maybe he'll have an accident. It wouldn't be the first time, eh?"

"You're right about that, Dred."

"But it'll cost you extra. Double sounds right, now that we've commenced to killing lawmen."

"Double."

Mathers shrugged. "It's all the same to me," he said. "You want to do the job yourself, go on and be my guest."

"Double it is," Freeman relented.

Thinking to himself, *And you can cash that check in hell.*

• • •

Slade followed the young bartender's directions, riding south from Lawton for the better part of half a mile, then veering well off course when he saw Jenny Acton's cabin standing in the distance, with a mass of deep, dark woods behind it.

He imagined it would make most women anxious, living in the open that way, on their own, removed from any kind of help. But then again, a woman who kept company with outlaws might not be the nervous type.

Slade circled to his left, eastward, until he reached the woods, then started heading west again, letting the tree line cover him. He took his time, no rush about it, watching out for traps or any signs of life besides the cabin proper and its rising plume of chimney smoke.

Woman alone. The Oklahoma Territory. Bad men everywhere. Slade took for granted that she would be armed and reasonably well versed in the handling of her chosen weapons. Stealth would get him close, and after that he'd have to trust his instincts.

What if she defied him? What if she was spooked by her first glimpse of Slade and opened fire? How would he handle it?

One way: Ride back and see the judge, swear out a warrant, deputize a posse, and return with witnesses—by which time Jenny Acton would most likely have a head start on her flight to parts unknown.

Or he could tough it out and see what happened, hoping that he wouldn't have to raise a hand, much less go for his gun.

When he was satisfied that no one lurked outside the cabin keeping watch, Slade left his horse tied to an ancient oak grazing, and took his rifle with him to advance on foot. When he was halfway there, the wind shifted and brought the smoke in his direction, carrying the scent of hearty stew.

Thanks for the supper invitation, Jenny. Don't mind if I do.

He reached the east side of the cabin, pausing at the sound of someone singing. Female intonation, unfamiliar lyrics. There was no window on his side of the structure, so Slade edged his way around in front and found the door propped open with a chunk of firewood.

Even standing on the doorstep, Slade still couldn't name the song. He finally decided she was improvising, something in the nature of a lullaby.

Jesus, he thought. *Don't let there be a baby in the house.*

Slade edged around the open door, prepared to rush or duck back out of sight, depending on what happened next. The woman's back—or rather rump—was toward him as she bent to stir the contents of a stew pot on the hearth. Slade sensed a slender, shapely body underneath the homemade dress. Dark hair fell nearly to her waist as she stood up, then turned—and froze at the sight of Slade filling the doorway.

He'd already seen her rifle, standing in the corner nearest to him, nearest to the door. One step into the room and he could block her access to the weapon, cut her off before she reached it. As for knives and such—

"So, who the hell are you?" she challenged.

Slade drew the left side of his coat back, hoping she could see his badge despite the sun behind him, casting him in silhouette. "Deputy U.S. Marshal," he informed her just in case. "Jack Slade."

"You're not the stew police?"

"No, ma' am."

"Then you won't mind if I remove my supper from the fire."

Slade left her to it, staying well back from the hearth, mindful that scalding broth could blind him, maybe leave

him scarred for life. Not that he'd live long if she reached
the rifle while he was disabled.

"Jenny Acton?" he inquired, watching her lift and move
the pot.

"You have a warrant to arrest me, Marshal?"

"No."

"To search my humble home?"

"No, ma'am."

"What brings you out from town then?" she inquired
while ladling stew into a metal bowl.

"I'm looking for Dred Mathers."

"Well, you missed him."

Slade could see that, but at least she hadn't lost her
voice. She sat, began to eat, Slade watching. "When do
you expect him?" Slade asked.

"He don't make appointments, hon. We should have
plenty time for business, but I want to eat my stew first."

Slade felt the color rising in his cheeks, angry that she
could pull his strings that way. "I'm here for him, not you,"
he said.

She shrugged. "Well, if you go that way, no skin off me.
I reckon you can use the bed for, say, a dollar."

"Maybe we should talk about this back in town," he
said.

The woman leaned back in her chair, arching her back
to emphasize her breasts beneath the wrinkled fabric of her
bodice. "You don't have a warrant, hon. Remember? Any-
how, you want to rough me up a little, here's as good a
place as any."

She startled Slade by swiveling her chair, legs scraping
on the dirt floor of the cabin, while she raised one leg and
braced her heel against the table's corner. The maneuver
left her skirt pooled in her lap, baring the upraised calf and
thigh.

"See anything you like?" she asked.

"I'd like to see your boyfriend at the short end of a

rope," Slade said. "I'm tracking him on murder charges, and the trash who's riding with him."

"And you're wanting me to help you fit him for the noose?"

"Just tell me where he's staying. You don't have to testify."

"That's mighty decent of you, dearie." Mocking him. "Just point you to him, shall I? Then sit back and wait for him to kill me when he's done with you?"

"Judge Dennison can offer you protection," Slade replied.

"That's just exactly what I need. Another man *protecting* me." She raised the skirt's hem to her chin. "Why don't you save some time and get it done, Marshal? Because I'm not about to tell you shit."

Slade turned away and left her on display. Her mocking laughter followed him as he retreated to the Appaloosa, and he fancied he could hear it halfway back to town.

10

Slade was angered and embarrassed by his failure to extract the slightest fragment of intelligence from Jenny Acton. It was not so much her mockery
that angered him—he'd been insulted by a few whores in
his time before that day—but rather the contempt with
which she'd treated his newfound authority.

Perhaps that disrespect was common with a certain
class of citizen. He'd known a few rough customers who
hated lawmen generally, without bothering to meet or
know an individual, and one or two had acted on that hatred to their ultimate regret. A gambler he had known in
Bisbee, Arizona shot a deputy who caught him dealing
from the bottom of the deck and wound up hanging, when
he could've simply moved along and found himself another town to plunder.

Stupid. But it hadn't been the lawman's fault.

With Jenny Acton, Slade supposed his cause was lost
before he ever reached her cabin, but perhaps he could've
done a better job. Persuaded her to—what? Trust him?

Not likely.

Thinking of the way she'd taunted him, putting her body on display, disturbed Slade. She was certainly attractive, in a scruffy, unwashed sort of way, and part of the embarrassment he felt came from the fact that she had managed to arouse him. Not that he was tempted, but the thoughts she stirred inside him shifted, features changing, so the face that smiled at him, the hands that beckoned him, belonged to someone else.

Faith Connover.

And that, in turn, stung Slade with unfamiliar pangs of guilt. Faith was his brother's fiancée, Jim's widow once removed. Pairing with her—assuming that she'd even have him—would've been an insult to Jim's memory, the life he'd built and left behind.

Slade had done many things he wasn't proud of, since the night he crept away from home and left Jim to his own devices, but he had to draw the line somewhere. In this case, he was drawing it around Faith Connover. It was a line he wouldn't cross.

Unless she asked him to perhaps? Unless she *begged*?

Slade nearly laughed aloud at that. The odds of any such thing happening were slim to none. He'd be more likely to produce straight flushes ten hands in a row, using a deck stacked by the house.

Still, there was something when she looked at him, when they were talking in the shade of dusk. As if she looked at him and saw . . .

She's seeing Jim, he thought. *That's all it is.*

And only gutter trash would take advantage of her momentary weakness. Slade was thankful to whatever gods there might be that he hadn't sunk so low.

Drawing his thoughts back to the moment with a mighty force of will, Slade tried to work out what, if anything, he'd learned from Jenny Acton. She'd revealed no information on the whereabouts of Mathers and his gang, but neither had she offered false denials of his presence in the area. That was encouraging, but still left Slade without a bird in hand that he could force to sing.

Could Jenny be of any further use to him?

Slade pictured two scenarios. In one, he found a vantage point from which to watch her cabin, spy on any visitors who came to call, and hope that Mathers was among them. If the outlaw came, alone or with his cronies, Slade could spring the trap and hope he wasn't so badly outnumbered that they put an end to him in seconds flat.

The other possibility was that she'd warn Mathers about his visit, leaving Mathers to decide on the next move. If he was spooked, Mathers might flee the territory, possibly forever, leaving Slade to gnash his teeth over lost opportunities. Conversely, Mathers might decide to kill him, as Slade reckoned he had done with Marshal Ford.

Bad bargains either way, but in the latter case, at least Slade had a chance of meeting Mathers, maybe even taking him alive and asking him some questions. Hearing Freeman's name from Mathers's lips and using it to get a warrant from Judge Dennison. Arresting Freeman on a murder charge and watching as he climbed the scaffold steps.

"Whoa, boy," Slade muttered to himself, and felt the Appaloosa shy. "Sorry," he told the horse. "Not you. Just talking to myself."

He still had a long way to go before he clapped the irons on Freeman's wrists, much less before he put a noose around the smirking bastard's neck.

And what if he was innocent?

Suppose, after all this, Slade got his hands on Mathers and the outlaw named some other person as the driving force behind Jim's murder. Someone Slade had never heard of, much less bothered to investigate while he was focused single-mindedly on Freeman?

No. It felt wrong.

Slade's hunches betrayed him now and then, sometimes with money riding on the line, but this was different. As if his twin had reached across the yawning gap of death to help Slade find his way, he knew one thing: Douglas Freeman was the man responsible.

And he would pay, no matter what Slade had to do to make things right.

"I'm sick of waitin'," Corey Chapman said.

"Go back and tell Dred that," his brother answered. "Find out what he says about it."

"I ain't quittin', dammmit! I just said I'm sick of waitin.'"

"We heard that the first three times," Mack Riley muttered, leaning from his hiding place to peer along the sidewalk, left and right.

"Don't gimme any lip!" Corey advised him, pushing off from where he'd slumped against a wall to stand upright. "You mightn't like what happens next."

"Shut up," Quinn told his younger brother. "We got work to do, and you're about to bring somebody down on us with all your gab."

"I just said—"

"Hush, for Christ's sake!" Riley ordered. "Someone's comin'!"

Quinn Chapman drew his pistol, listening to footsteps on the wooden sidewalk drawing nearer by the moment. Muffled conversation reached his ears, but he couldn't make out the words. Two people anyway, distracted by their talk.

There was no reason they should turn into the alley where he stood with Riley and his brother, three doors from the Lawton Arms. No reason in the world, unless they felt like it, or passing through the alley put them on some kind of shortcut going home.

In which case, they were in for a surprise.

The strangers, man and woman, passed without a glance in his direction. Chapman heard the woman giggle in a way that told him her companion had a lucky night ahead of him. Sugar for some, but Chapman had a job to do, and Mathers would be furious if anything went wrong.

"He's late," said Corey, bitching to himself again, as if Quinn hadn't warned him to be quiet. "Why don't we—"

"You say another goddamned word, we're gonna have a problem," Quinn informed him.

Corey made a little *humph*ing noise but shut his yap, at least for now. Riley was grinning in the moonlight, pleased to see the brothers squabbling, and it made Quinn want to punch him.

They'd been waiting for the better part of ninety minutes, since the sun went down and made the alley dark enough for them to hide in, unobserved by passersby. It was as close as they could get to the hotel and still be hidden from their target as he moved along the street. And Slade would have to pass this way, after he stopped in at the livery and put his horse to bed.

Mathers wanted the lawman dead, and that was good enough for Quinn Chapman. He could follow orders with the best of them, as long as he got paid. Go here, go there, kill this or that one. It was all the same to him.

Corey got on his nerves sometimes—*most* of the time, if he was being honest with himself—but they were family, and there was nothing he could do about it. Maybe kick his little brother's ass from time to time, but that was getting harder lately, Corey picking up new tricks, while Quinn felt weary, had less energy.

He reckoned whiskey had something to do with that, consumed in quantities that ranged from large to herculean, but he wasn't drunk tonight. Dred had explained the vital nature of this job, impressing Quinn with his desire that nothing should go wrong.

Or else.

Riley leaned out to check the street again, both ways, and stiffened in a semi-crouching pose. "I see him! Shit, he's on the wrong side of the street."

"The livery's on that side," Chapman reminded him. "He has to cross for the hotel."

"Listen, I know Dred said he was a twin, but . . ."

Riley didn't finish, forcing Quinn to ask, "But *what*?"

"How do we *know* he ain't some kinda ghost? It happens sometimes. Fellow dies the hard way and his soul don't take it right. He comes back to get even with the folks that done him wrong."

"Shut up that crazy talk," Chapman commanded.

"You ain't seen him," Riley whined. "He looks *exac'ly* like himself."

"Who else would he look like?"

Chapman and his brother crowded toward the alley's mouth, peering across the street to catch their first glimpse of the target. Quinn had barely known the lawman's brother, only seen him once, and that time over rifle sights and fifty yards. There was a similarity, of course, but—

"Shit!" his brother hissed. "That *is* him!"

"Don't you start now."

"But look at him!"

"Shut up, Corey!"

"I'm gettin' out of here," Riley announced.

"Like hell you are," Chapman replied, and pushed the quaking gunman out ahead of him, into the street.

Slade heard the scuffling argument across the street, and glanced in that direction as a man lurched from the alley, seemingly propelled from darkness. Even with the hat brim's shadow on his face, he looked familiar. There was something there, around the jawline. . . .

Two more men emerged behind the first, both glowering at Slade from thirty feet away. He didn't recognize them, though there was a vague resemblance between the two. Some kinship in their sour faces, as of siblings, maybe cousins.

All three were staring at him now and moving forward, with the middle man on awkward, shaky legs. Slade didn't need his badge to recognize an ambush, one man with his gun already drawn, the other two reaching for theirs.

Running wasn't an option. They could stand and shoot him in the back if he turned tail, no difficulty to it, even if it took them several tries to score a hit. The shops along Main Street were closed, no place for Slade to hide, unless he ducked into a recessed doorway that could turn into a death trap.

Slade drew his Peacemaker as one of the three gunmen fired a hasty shot. It missed Slade by a yard or more, smashing a window to his left and plowing on to strike a tailor's dummy standing in the dry goods store.

A second shot rang out, this one striking the roof above his head and somewhere to his right. Slade pivoted to face his would-be killers in profile, thumbed back his pistol's hammer, taking time to aim.

His first shot struck the gunman farthest to his right, their left. It was a solid hit and staggered him, but Slade guessed it was nothing mortal, since the shooter didn't fall at once. Instead, he fired a quick shot in return, cursing aloud to emphasize his point.

All three of them were blasting at him now, the night aswarm with bullets, breaking glass and drilling boards on either side of Slade. One whispered past his face, its heat reminding Slade of sunlight, as he fired again, then broke in search of cover.

Whether he had scored the second time, Slade didn't know. He scurried six or seven paces in a crouch, then ducked into the doorway of an assay office, locked up tight. His own office was two blocks farther east, its arsenal beyond his reach in time of need.

Four rounds left in the Peacemaker before he needed to reload, and still his enemies were slinging lead as if they couldn't count their shots or didn't care. They'd blasted out the windows of three different shops by now, and drilled their walls to boot. A couple of their bullets had come dangerously close to Slade, but he was still unbloodied, crouching in the shadow of his tenuous sanctuary.

Most of the Main Street shops had canopies or overhangs extending to the sidewalk's outer edge, supported there by upright beams. One of those beams was spoiling Slade's shot at his adversaries now, effectively concealing two of them, one trailing several paces in the others' shadows as they crossed the street.

Accordingly, he aimed at number three, steadied his gun hand with the other, and squeezed off a precious third shot to accompany the opposition's roaring fusillade. His target lurched, stumbled, and then surprised Slade by reversing his direction, running back across the street without a glance to see if his companions were behind him.

One of them noticed the runner breaking ranks and shouted after him, "Goddamn it, Mack! You yellow—" Gunfire punctuated the insult, kept Slade from hearing all of it, but the angry gunman's aim was still deficient. Running for his life, the sprinter disappeared into an alleyway where Slade supposed the trio had been hiding earlier.

Slade took it that the man was leaving, though he could've been mistaken. Maybe it was strategy, a cunning ploy to sneak around behind him somehow, but he didn't think so. Even in the dark, Slade knew fear when he saw it, and the shooter he had winged was running scared.

Which left two more, still mightily intent on killing him.

Slade wondered whether he should make a break for it. Three rounds left in his pistol. Maybe he could score a lucky hit or two if he emerged from cover. Clearly, neither of his adversaries was a marksman. Slade supposed they'd have no better luck with moving targets than when he was standing still. If he could make it to his office . . .

No.

They'd come halfway across the street by now, at least, and dumb luck said they ought to score a hit before much longer, if he didn't think of some way to outwit them. But if Slade dared not emerge to face them on the sidewalk . . . then what?

Groping blindly backward, Slade's left hand found a doorknob, confirmed that it was locked. There was a way around that, though. The top half of the door was frosted glass, already bullet punctured. If he cleared the lower window, Slade could reach inside and turn the latch, open the door, then put a wall between himself and his would-be assassins.

If they didn't drop him in the process.

Turning from the street, Slade swung his Peacemaker against the ruined, ornate glass. It fell in jagged shards, one snagging on his coat sleeve as he battered sharp-edged remnants from the frame.

Bill me, Slade thought as he rose from his crouch and turned his back reluctantly on those who sought to kill him, reaching through the window frame and feeling for the inner latch.

He found it, turned it, lunged inside, and locked the door behind him as another spray of gunfire raked the niche where he'd been huddled seconds earlier. Slade knew the door wouldn't delay the gunmen long, but he had an advantage now. Real cover, and a short time to reload his weapon.

Scuttling toward a nearby desk, he slid behind it and began removing cartridges from his gunbelt.

• • •

Quinn Chapman stumbled as he stepped up to the sidewalk, but his brother caught him, held him upright when he might've fallen otherwise.

"What's wrong with you?" asked Corey, hissing through his teeth.

Quinn pressed a hand against his side and held the crimson fingers up before his brother's face. "I'm hit," he said. "Don't worry, though. It ain't too bad."

"Jesus! You hit, and Riley run off like a goddamned—"

"Corey! Keep your damned voice down!" Quinn squeezed his brother's right arm with his bloody fingers, leaving dark stains on his sleeve. "We'll finish this, and after Dred sees how we done, we'll have a word with Riley. Don't you worry."

"Worry, hell," Corey replied, flashing a grin by moonlight. "I'll be glad to do the job myself."

"You keep loud-talking while he sits in there and listens to you," Quinn replied, "the only thing that's finished here tonight will be your worthless life."

Corey stood blinking, ready with a comeback, but he swallowed it and stepped in closer, whispering, "Okay, so what's the plan?"

Quinn clenched his teeth around a sudden jolt of pain, then answered, "Right. There's only one way into this place we know about. No time to run around looking for the back door." Already, he heard voices rising, up and down the street, townspeople gathering to find out what in hell was happening.

"Go in the front then," Corey said. "Good deal. You ready?"

"Check your loads first," Quinn advised him. "Going in there with an empty gun will only get you dead."

Quinn wiped the blood-slick fingers of his left hand on his pants, then thumbed open his six gun's loading gate and started prying out the empties, dropping them around his feet. Each empty chamber took a new live round, six chances to get even with the bastard who had stung him once already.

Quinn felt fear, as well as pain, but he refused to let it master him. He didn't want to think about the way the odds had shifted in the past few minutes, leaving him and Corey at a disadvantage with their target.

They had started out at three to one, with the advantage of surprise, but Riley's cowardice and clumsy shooting had prevented them from dropping Slade at once, before he could return fire. Now, Riley had left them in the lurch and Quinn was wounded, while their target had escaped into a darkened shop. He might have decent cover now, and he would surely see them coming through the doorway, back-lit by the moon, before they caught a glimpse of him.

"I'm going first," his brother said.

"Corey—"

"Don't argue with me now," the kid replied. "You're leakin', and that slows you down. Besides, I always was the better shot."

"Bullshit." Quinn forced a smile, not feeling it.

"Bullshit yourself," Corey replied, then turned away from him, crouching, prepared to rush the doorway. "Just keep up the best you can."

Goddamn it!

Quinn knew any further argument would only play into their target's hands, while vigilantes from the town collected weapons and closed ranks. It must be now or never, do the job or run like Riley and explain their cowardice to Mathers.

"Go then," he told Corey. "Get it done!"

Corey rushed forward, hit the door, his left hand groping for the knob, twisting it in vain. "Shit fire!" he blurted out. "It's locked!"

*   *   *

Slade crouched behind the desk, arms braced across it, holding the Peacemaker in a firm two-handed grip. He shot the gunman raging at the door, one slug from fifteen feet away that struck his target squarely in the chest and punched him over backward, out of sight.

Even with the gunshot's echo in his ears, Slade heard the body strike the wooden sidewalk. He was ready for the last man, sighted on the doorway, when a roaring from the street distracted him. It might've been a name, called out in anguish, or a simple snarl of rage. In any case, it issued from a throat strained to the limit by emotion and adrenaline.

The last man didn't rush the doorway, though. He learned from his companion's fatal error, turned around, and threw himself headlong against the tall front window of the assay office. It was bullet-cracked already and about to go. The shooter's plunging weight finished the job and put him in the middle of a glittering cascade, sharp edges snagging fabric, slicing flesh.

Slade winged a shot at the tumbling figure, unable to say if he'd tagged the intruder or not. He'd be injured by glass, if unscathed otherwise, but would that slow him down? From the sounds he was making, all growly like something that lives in a zoo, Slade supposed that he wasn't hurt badly enough to surrender. But was he determined enough to advance?

"That's my brother you killed," said the shooter, erasing all doubt. "Now it's your turn."

Slade waited, tracked the voice, his Peacemaker already cocked. Outside, he heard men's voices drawing closer, shouting questions back and forth across the street. He didn't want civilians in the line of fire, but there was nothing he could do about it at the moment, pinned down as he was.

Slade heard his adversary crawling, wondered if the man thought he was being quiet. Was he hurt, beyond whatever cuts he'd suffered coming through the window? Could he be the one Slade thought he'd hit on their advance across the street?

No answers. Only questions, as he waited in the dark.

A part of Slade supposed he should be paralyzed by fear. It was his first real battle, after all. Forget about the pig-sticking in Colorado and the barroom skirmishes he'd fought with drunken losers when the cards had gone against them. This time, he was fighting for his life and for the law, against assassins who'd been sent to kill him.

Sent by whom? Dred Mathers? Douglas Freeman?

Was there any difference between the two?

He'd find out soon enough, if he survived the next few minutes. Then, he'd have to find some way to make Judge Dennison believe he couldn't make the shooters drop their guns and march down to the jail, all peaceful and obedient.

Forget that now, he thought. *Just stay alive.*

As if the final gunman was a mind reader, he chose that moment to emerge from cover, bellowing and blasting with his pistol in the darkness of the assay office. His first shot was high and wide, but number two was closer, and the third one closer still. If he kept on that way—

Slade shot him from his crouch behind the desk, and knew it was a solid hit. The gunman staggered, cursing breathlessly, and fired another round that nearly grazed Slade's hat.

Dropping his pistol, Slade aimed his next shot well below the belt, firing into the shooter's hip, where pain and shattered bone were almost guaranteed to put him down. His target toppled, sprawled, and Slade could hear the pistol slithering beyond his reach.

Slade came around the desk, Peacemaker leveled at his fallen enemy, all cocked and ready for another shot if necessary. Voices from the street were closer now, edgy with worry and excitement mixed together. Someone said,

"That's *my* place!" and Slade guessed he'd meet the assay agent soon enough.

Slade's enemy was stretched out on the floor, bleeding from scalp to groin. The darkness wouldn't let Slade tell which wounds were caused by gunfire, which by falling glass, but raspy breathing told him that the man was badly injured.

Crouching at his side, Slade pulled the shooter's face around in his direction, asking him, "Who sent you? Whose idea was this?"

"You killed my brother," said the fallen gunman. "Good as dead, you are."

But it was *his* eyes rolling back, showing their whites, and *his* breath coming through the chest wall in a froth of scarlet bubbles now.

Slade pressed a hand over the sucking wound and leaned in close. "Don't die on me, you bastard!" he commanded, as if force of will alone could keep his man alive. "You hear me? Don't you die!"

Slade heard a scraping on the sidewalk, and a cautious voice inquired, "What's going on in there?"

"It's Marshal Slade," he answered. "Someone go and fetch Judge Dennison, right now!"

"I'm sorry, but I couldn't save him," said the doctor. He'd been introduced to Slade as Crenshaw. In his fifties, with a gray-streaked handlebar mustache below a drinker's nose, his hair unfashionably long in back. "Too much internal damage, bleeding, and what have you."

"All right then," Judge Dennison replied. "I'm sure you did your best in any case."

"Sorry," the doctor said again, before he shuffled out and left them in Slade's office, facing one another with his desk between them.

"Well," said Dennison, "this wasn't quite the first day that I had in mind for you."

"Nor me," said Slade. "I wanted one of them alive at least. No telling how the woman tipped them off so fast."

"Woman?"

There'd been no time to brief the judge on anything beyond the bare facts of the street fight, walking him around the scene, and fielding angry questions from the shop owners whose stock and windows had been shot to hell. The judge didn't appear to blame Slade for the shooting, but his disappointment showed in every move he made, each word he spoke.

"The whore who keeps Dred Mathers warm at night," Slade answered. "Jenny Acton. She lives out—"

"I know where Jenny Acton lives," said Dennison.

Slade caught his eyebrow on the rise and managed to control it, shifting in his seat. "All right. I found out she's been seeing Mathers, and I rode out there to ask about him."

"Any luck?"

Slade shook his head. "She's got a mouth on her, but all I heard was sass. She needs a good old-fashioned spanking."

"That'll cost you extra," Dennison observed, wearing the first wry smile that Slade had yet seen on his face. "I've got some good news for you, though, if we can call it that."

"Good news?"

"I know the two you killed tonight," said Dennison. "The Chapman brothers."

"Ah."

"You recognize the name?" asked Dennison.

"Bartender at the Gay Paree gave me some names of men who run with Mathers. There were Chapmans on the list."

"I'm not surprised," said Dennison. "A rotten family from the get-go. Father hanged for rustling some years back. The mother little better than a sporting woman. Corey was the younger, him they picked up off the sidewalk. Nineteen, maybe twenty. I could check his file. He's been in trouble all his life."

Nineteen, Slade's weary brain repeated. *Maybe twenty.*

"Too damned young," Slade said.

"I'd normally agree," the judge replied, "but strapping on a gun and plotting murder has a price. I would've rather sent him up for ten or fifteen years, but you were in the right. This time."

"The brother's name was Quinn, I think?"

"That's right. He's five or six years older. Did a two-year term, not long ago, for selling stolen calves. I'm not surprised the pair of them hooked up with Mathers. They were no great thinkers, if you get my meaning. Neither one of them could pour piss from a boot with the instructions printed on the heel."

"I get the picture." He had killed a pair of imbeciles apparently.

"The good news is that Mathers wants you dead."

"Hoo-ray."

"I would've thought you'd be more optimistic, now you've got your spurs into him. When a man gets scared or angry, then he starts making mistakes."

"I don't suppose that there's another Chapman brother?" Slade inquired.

"I'm proud to say there isn't. Why?" asked Dennison.

"There was a third man in the street tonight. He didn't stick around long. I suppose he must've been one of the others."

"You have names for those as well?"

"Bran Huffman," Slade replied. "Frank Lugar. Wiley Grace. Mack Riley."

"Wanted men, the lot of them," said Dennison. "Huffman and Riley have done time for rustling. Lugar paid a fine for battery, but I suspect he's done much worse. Grace is a no-account sneak thief. I wouldn't turn my back on him."

"I don't intend to."

"What about your other suspect?"

"Freeman? I dropped in to visit him this morning, showed the badge, and left him with the understanding that I meant to put his life under a magnifying glass. He took it pretty well, all things considered."

"Feisty, was he? Righteously indignant?" Dennison inquired.

"I got the feeling that he doesn't mind a challenge, now and then."

"He wouldn't, having carved an empire out of nothing on his own. What time'd you talk to him?" asked Dennison.

"This morning, after breakfast," Slade replied. "His office wasn't open long."

"So, then, he had all day."

Slade thought about it, nodding. Sure, why not? He'd jumped to the conclusion that Dred Mathers must've spoken to his woman, then dispatched his guns to Lawton, but the time frame didn't work. Unless the outlaws had a private telegraph, they would've had to pass him on the trail, racing ahead to lay their trap.

"Freeman," he said at last. "We need to have another talk."

"You can't accuse him without evidence," said Dennison. "Aside from being slanderous and downright rude, you stand a chance of jeopardizing any case you build against him later. If he goes to trial, Freeman could claim you had it in for him and fabricated evidence, pressured a witness into lying. Who knows what else he might say?"

"All bullshit," Slade replied.

"You know that, and *I* know it," Dennison agreed. "But twelve men on a jury might not see it that way. He could walk away scot-free."

"I need another angle," Slade acknowledged. "Maybe Mathers."

"If we take for granted that he's tried to kill you once and failed, he's only got two options left," said Dennison.

"Come back and do it right, or run like hell."

"My gut," said Dennison, "tells me he'll try again. Of course, I'm wrong from time to time."

"You know he murdered Marshal Ford as well," Slade said.

"I *feel* it, and I'll be hanging him for it," Dennison replied. "If Freeman had a hand in that, I'll hang him too. But first, you need to bring me proof."

"I'm working on it, Judge."

"Work harder, Deputy. Before the next men Mathers sends to kill you catch a lucky break."

"You had a visitor today," said Jenny Acton.

Mathers stopped dead on the cabin's threshold, studying her face. "What visitor?" he asked.

"A lawman. I don't recall his name."

"Would it be Slade?"

"That's it! Good-looking, young. I mightn't kick him out of bed, if he was smart enough to leave the badge at home. I liked his boots. You know the rule about big feet?"

Mathers ignored her prattle, wouldn't give her the reaction she was looking for. "You've seen the last of him," he said. "He's done, big feet and all."

"Something I oughta know about?" she asked him, standing there in front of him, hands on her hips.

"I don't see why you should."

"Maybe because he come out here and talked to me about your business," she replied. "Maybe because he told someone in town where he was going, and when you get done with him, the judge puts two and two together."

Mathers smiled. "You shouldn't talk to strangers, little girl. Didn't your mama ever teach you that?"

"My mama taught me how to keep my stepdaddy distracted when she didn't want him mountin' her. Now, what about this lawman?"

"Gone and soon forgotten," Mathers said. "Is that a stew I smell?"

"Could be," Jenny replied. "Unless you've got a taste for something sweeter."

"Starting with dessert? That's downright sinful."

"Makes it all the better," she informed him, reaching for his belt buckle. "You want a go, or not?"

"Darlin', I didn't ride out for your cooking."

"No, I don't suppose you did."

She led him to her simple bed and sat before him, nimble fingers busy. Mathers watched her, but he was distracted. "Tell me more about the lawman," he instructed.

"Gone and soon forgotten, you say," she replied.

"Tell me what *he* said."

"Let me think." She had his gunbelt off, and soon his pants were puddled on the floor around his boots. "I didn't note his words exactly, but he'd like to throw a necktie party for you. Maybe stretch the others while he's at it."

"Others?"

"Them you run with."

"Did he mention any other names?"

Her mouth was full, but Mathers tangled fingers in her hair and drew her face away from him. "Answer the question, damn it!"

"Ow! No other names," she said, and snapped her teeth at him, not altogether playfully.

He would've asked about Doug Freeman, but he didn't want her spinning thoughts in that direction, maybe talking out of turn next time a lawman showed up at her door. At least, if that happened, he knew it wouldn't be Jack Slade.

"Careful with those." He ran a fingertip along the sharp edge of her teeth. "You want to keep 'em, keep 'em to yourself."

Jenny went back to work. Mathers stood rigid with a combination of excitement and uneasiness. He knew Slade wouldn't bother him again, had seen to that himself, but complications troubled him.

Judge Dennison would find another deputy, of course,

and maybe he'd pursue Slade's line of thinking about Mathers. That, in turn, could lead him to Doug Freeman, and the rancher might decide to help himself by hanging Mathers out to dry.

"Damn it!"

"Too hard, baby?" she asked him.

"No, it's fine. Keep doing that."

Freeman paid well enough, but he was dangerous. Mathers had no illusions about Freeman's loyalty to anyone except himself. If he could hand the whole damned lot of them to Dennison and get a free pass out of it, he wouldn't hesitate.

"Bastard!"

"Mmph-umm?"

"Don't stop." He reached down with a hand to hold her head in place.

If Freeman thought that he could pull a double cross and get away with it, Mathers would happily instruct him on the error of his ways. Going that route might mean he'd have to leave the territory for a while, let things cool down, but he would risk it.

"Wait," he said. "Lie back there."

Jenny did as she was told, smiling. "I was thinkin' maybe you forgot me."

"What a notion."

Mathers climbed aboard, adjusted his position, searching for the rhythm. There it was.

"Oh, hon, that's good."

"Shut up a second."

"Anything you say, dearie."

"Damn it!"

"Just keep on doin' that. Right there."

"I said *shut up!*"

"I will, hon. Any minute now."

She vexed him, drove the thoughts of Slade and Freeman from his mind. It might be what she wanted, and if so he had to give her credit, but it galled him all the same. The more he tried to punish her, the more she babbled, telling him it never felt so good before, and could he do it just a little harder if he didn't mind?

Fact was, he didn't mind at all.

Mathers was lost somewhere, off hell and gone, when someone rode into the yard outside. He vaguely heard the horses snorting, stamping in the outer darkness. Heavy footsteps on the little nothing porch out there, and someone pounding on the door.

"Dred, are you in there?" Huffman.

"Just about!" gasped Mathers.

"Damn, I'm sorry, but we need to talk."

"Nuh-nuh-not now!"

After a hasty, whispered conversation, Huffman hollered back, "This really shouldn't wait."

"That's it, hon," Jenny urged him from below.

It tipped him over, squealing, going rigid as she clung to him. Mathers lost track of time, but heard insistent rapping on the door when he regained the full use of his ears.

"All right!" He threw the door wide open, standing naked with a pistol in his hand. Heard Jenny laugh behind him. "Now, goddamn it, what's so urgent?"

Huffman blinked at him and said, "The brothers didn't get it done. They're dead. And Slade, he's still alive."

Slade locked his office after Dennison departed, took a chance, and walked down to the bathhouse, situated next door to the barber's shop. Those individuals he passed along the way were careful not to meet his gaze for long, as if they feared the stain of violence might rub off on them and leave them tainted.

And for all Slade knew, they might be right.

So far, his poking into Jim's death had cost three more lives. How many left to go?

Slade ran the list in his head. Dred Mathers and his men, however many of them still remained. And Doug Freeman, the man behind it all.

The judge's words came back to haunt Slade: *Bring me proof.*

Now all he needed was a miracle.

Slade found the bathhouse open, tended by a man-and-wife team who were striking in their contrasts. He was tall and thin, almost insectile in his aspect and his movements, while she would've had to stand on tiptoe just to rest her head against his chest. The man was sour-faced, his mate a jolly soul who seemed to smile at everything.

Slade paid two bits for half an hour's soaking in hot water, with a bar of grainy soap for company. It cut the trail dust, but he couldn't seem to get the bloodstains off his hands. No matter how he scrubbed, despite the fact that lamplight showed his fingers to be spotless, Slade imagined them still crimson-smeared.

The more he thought about it, though, the less it bothered him.

The first time he had killed in self-defense, the rush of hot blood spattering his hand and knife had sickened him. Shooting was different, more remote, but Slade had still expected to feel more—feel *worse*—than he now felt.

Perhaps it was because the Chapman brothers might have murdered Jim, or played a role in it at least. Slade's hunger for revenge helped take the edge off any latent guilt he might've felt for gunning down two men who'd tried to kill him on the street. The bastards had it coming, likely had deserved far worse. Whatever guilt Slade felt or thought that he should feel would be misplaced.

He pictured Faith then, wondering how she would feel on hearing that he'd killed two men who might've murdered Jim. Would she be happy? Feel relieved? Or would she be disgusted with him for perpetuating violence in a place where she was working overtime to build a home?

Thinking of Faith took Slade in a direction that he didn't want to follow, most particularly in a public bath. A nagging question helped sidetrack that lurid train of thought: What would Doug Freeman do now that his bid on Faith's land once again had been rejected? Slade had witnessed her determination, so forged deeds would never do the trick. Before he could absorb the spread, Freeman would need to clear the field of obstacles.

He'd murdered Jim. Slade knew it, even if he couldn't prove it yet. Doing the same to Faith, with Slade and Dennison already watching him, would likely pose too great a risk for Freeman to consider it. There were intimidation tactics he could try—arson, rustling, a poisoned well—but once again he'd be the leading suspect, bringing more trouble down upon himself.

What then?

Slade deemed the riddle hopeless, with the information he possessed, and concentrated on a final scrubbing of his body with the homemade soap. It left him tingling in a sunburned kind of way as he rinsed off and dried himself on thin, rough towels before donning his clothes again.

The two mismatched proprietors wished Slade a pleasant evening, and he thought the woman might be serious about it. Stepping from the bathhouse, Slade tested the air, relieved to smell no trace of gunsmoke on the breeze. A sound of hammers told him angry shopkeepers were boarding up their windows, but the judge had told him to forget it. Money found on Quinn and Corey Chapman would be used to pay the undertaker and to compensate for broken glass and other damage to the Main Street stores.

All very civilized, thought Slade.

It was almost as if the shooting never happened, as if three men hadn't tried to kill him, two of them paying for the attempt in blood.

Three men.

Slade thought about the third man, wondering if there

was any way he could identify the runner. It might help if he was wounded, but he wouldn't go to Dr. Crenshaw for a patch-up. Slade had missed the chance to follow him, though some signs still might linger in the morning. He would check the alley, see if there was anything resembling a trail, and if so, where it led.

But Slade already knew that effort would be wasted. Number three had slipped beyond his grasp for now. The second question in his mind was whether the escapee would run back to Mathers with his news of failure or light out for parts unknown to save himself.

Slade reckoned it was fifty-fifty either way. He'd barely glimpsed the man this time, might never get another look at him, but it was Mathers who preoccupied him.

Mathers, and Doug Freeman.

Slade knew he would never rest until he'd seen both of them punished for his brother's murder. Still, the same problems confronted him: One of his targets was invisible, the other legally untouchable unless Slade found some evidence that linked him to the crime.

Ideally, a confession from Dred Mathers ought to do the trick. But realistically, the odds of that occurring were about the same, Slade thought, as striking gold on Main Street. Mathers was a hardcase, not the kind to spill his guts, even if Slade could find him, bring him in alive.

The plan still needed work, Slade realized as he passed through the entrance to the Lawton Arms. "Long day, Marshal," the clerk remarked in passing.

"You don't know the half of it," Slade answered, moving toward the stairs.

Another meeting on the sly, and Freeman had begun to wonder how much more he could endure. He watched Dred Mathers roll a cigarette, light it, taking his time.

"You want to tell me what went wrong, or am I here to watch you smoke?"

"What happened," Mathers said, "is that your marshal burned down Quinn and Corey—"

"I don't need their names," snapped Freeman, interrupting him. "I don't care who they were."

"All right." Mathers was working hard to seem unflappable. "The marshal killed two of my boys. There was a third, but I'm not sure what happened to him."

"What's that mean?" Freeman demanded.

"Just exactly what I said. The sawbones doesn't have his body, and he ain't locked up in jail. That tells me he's alive—or was when he lit out of town. As far as where he is right now, I couldn't say."

"Will he come back to you?"

A shrug from Mathers. "How'n hell should I know? If he's runnin' scared, I've prob'ly seen the last of him."

"Terrific. So, he's wandering around out there, half-crazed or drunk, for all we know, running his mouth."

"You worry too much, Doug," Mathers said. "I told you time and time again, the boys don't know who's payin' 'em."

"You *hope* they don't."

That made the gunman smile. "More like *you* hope they don't," Mathers replied. "But if they *do,* I'm tellin' you they didn't get the word from me."

"There's no one else besides the two of us," said Freeman.

"Then stop worrying."

"That's easy said."

"You want me to go lookin' for this boy who run away? I've only got two fellas left to help me, but I don't mind droppin' everything to beat the bushes for 'im, if you reckon it'll put your mind at ease. Course, that'll cost you extra."

"Everything you do costs extra," Freeman groused.

"Don't take it personally. I'm a businessman."

"Unfortunately," Freeman said, "you're not much good at taking care of business."

"Listen, just because—"

"No, *you* listen! I don't give a mosquito's fart about your two dead boys. I don't care if they *all* get killed before sunup tomorrow. What I care about is you doing the job I've paid you for. Doing it *right,* I mean, with no goddamned mistakes."

"You'll get your money's worth," Mathers assured him. "Next time, I'll be goin' for the marshal personally. He won't know what hit 'im."

"Forget about that now. There's something else I want to try," said Freeman.

"Just forget about my two men, lyin' dead up at the doctor's place?"

"You're getting sentimental now?" asked Freeman.

"Hell, no," Mathers sneered. "Your marshal's made it personal."

"By shooting men you sent to kill him? That's ridiculous."

"By makin' me look small!" Mathers retorted. "No sumbitch alive can get away with that."

"Listen, I don't care what you do to him, but do it *later.* I have something else in mind."

"Still thinkin' you can get his brother's land, I guess," said Mathers.

"What else was this all about?" asked Freeman. "Do you think I'm doing it for fun?"

"I'd be surprised if you knew what fun is."

"Maybe you're spending too much time, and too much of my money, having fun. Drinking, whoring around. I have to say, I'm losing confidence in you."

"Sorry to hear it, Doug," Mathers said. "But then again, who else you got?"

Freeman ignored the challenge, fought the urge to wrap his hands around the outlaw's throat and squeeze until the sneering face turned blue from lack of oxygen. Mathers would kill him if he tried it, if the gunman saw it coming.

Later. Freeman made the promise to himself.

He wouldn't need Mathers much longer if his new plan proved successful. Freeman wished he'd tried it first, but he'd been hopeful that Faith Connover would readily accept his offer for the ranch. Now that she'd turned him down repeatedly, he'd have to try another course of action.

"Well," said Mathers, prodding him, "you gonna tell me what you got in mind, or is it some big secret?"

"I'm going to distract the marshal," Freeman said, "while you ride out and see his brother's fiancée. You'll likely need more men. She still has hands out there who won't give up without a fight."

"You want her dead?" asked Mathers.

"No, Goddamn it! Get that straight. She isn't to be harmed in any way."

Now Mathers looked confused. "You're still not speakin' plain," he said.

"I need her breathing," Freeman answered. "And I need her in a frame of mind to give me what I want. Is any of this sinking in? She's no good to me dead, and if you tamper with her, she'll most likely fight me to the death just out of spite."

"So, I'm supposed to snatch her, but you don't want damaged goods," said Mathers.

"Now you're getting the idea."

"It may be tough, Doug. She's a looker, that one. Maybe just a little taste?"

"Do that, and there's no payday in it for you," Freeman promised him. "In fact, I'll put a bounty on you big enough to keep the shooters looking anywhere you go."

"Almost sounds like you want her for yourself," Mathers replied.

"You want to give the bride away?"

"Hell, Doug, I just want money."

"Then you'll do exactly as you're told, and don't make any more mistakes. We can't afford them."

"Thing about mistakes is that I always learn from them," Mathers replied.

"I hope so," Freeman said. "Because the next could be your last."

"I don't like threats, Doug. You should know that by now."

"Consider it a promise. Now, get out of here and find whatever men you need to do the job."

"When do you want it done?" Mathers inquired, resentment heavy in his tone.

Freeman removed his pocket watch, consulted it, and said, "It's almost midnight now. This time tomorrow, I'll expect to have a guest."

12

Slade had become a regular for breakfast at the restaurant across the street from his hotel. He knew routine was dangerous, with gunmen out to kill him, but part of Slade perversely wanted them to try again. He had survived the first attempt, put two of them in caskets, and now he needed contact with the gang again if he was ever going to complete his job.

Next time they came for him—and Slade had no doubt there would be a next time—he must try to capture one of them alive. That done, Slade reckoned he could find a way to make his captive talk.

And when the job was done—then what?

Slade hadn't thought beyond the task of tracking down his brother's murderers and bringing them to justice, one way or another. If he managed to survive it, he would have to think about what happened next. There was a world to see, card games to play, no end of jackpots waiting for a player who could make them his. Staying in Lawton barely crossed his mind.

Barely.

There would be Faith, of course, unless she changed her mind and sold the ranch, but seeing her was double torture, constantly reminding Slade of Jim, while taunting him with treasures he could never bring himself to claim. Better to ride away and never see her face again, he thought, than to remain and suffer daily while she went about her life, eventually found another man, and learned to love again.

No, Slade decided, he would definitely leave the Oklahoma Territory when his work was done.

Unless Dred Mathers or Doug Freeman killed him first.

Breakfast was steak and eggs, the usual pan-fried potatoes, Texas toast, and beans, washed down with coffee strong enough to keep him going all day long. When he was halfway through it, Freeman walked into the restaurant, stood checking out the tables for a moment, then made his determined way toward Slade's.

"Mind if I join you, Marshal?" Freeman asked.

"I'm almost finished here."

"Well, don't mind me. I'll just have coffee when the girl comes back around."

Instead of going with his first impulse, directing Freeman straight to hell, Slade shrugged and told him, "Suit yourself."

"Appreciate it, Marshal." Settling in a chair directly opposite from Slade, Freeman remarked, "That was a near miss you enjoyed last night."

"Point is, they missed," said Slade. "I didn't."

"No, indeed. And while I'm sure we're grateful you survived, there's still the question of a shoot-out on Main Street. I mean, is it a wise thing drawing violence into town?"

"You think I sent those three an invitation?"

"It's not a matter of . . . Did you say *three*? I thought—"

"Three shooters," Slade informed him. "Two went

down, one ran away. I think he's hit. If he turns up, I plan to have a talk with him. Find out who put him up to it."

"We wish you well, I'm sure. But still—"

"You have a tapeworm, Doug?"

Freeman blinked at him. "I beg your pardon?"

"You keep saying 'we,' but I don't see the others."

"Well, I'm speaking for the town, of course."

"I must've missed it," Slade replied.

"Missed what?"

"The big election where they made you mayor."

Freeman dredged up a smile. "You're in a testy mood this morning, Marshal. That's entirely understandable, of course. I simply wanted to communicate a citizen's concern about such incidents as last night's shooting fray."

"I was a bit concerned about it too," Slade said, "being the target."

"I understand. But still—"

"I don't think so."

"Excuse me?"

"I don't think you understand at all," Slade said. "When was the last time someone tried to murder you?"

"I only meant—"

"You don't want gunplay interfering with the town and cutting into business. It may come as a surprise to you, but I don't want that either. Maybe someone ought to tell the shooters that next time, before they ride in spoiling for a fight."

"That's your job, Marshal."

"I was thinking more of someone who's in touch with Mathers and his gang. Someone who tells them where to go and what to do."

Slade held the rancher's level gaze, determined that he wouldn't be the first to blink. A ruddy stain crept into Freeman's cheeks.

"If there was such a person, Marshal, he—or she—

would surely urge you to resign and leave your mission to professionals. This quest for vengeance—"

"I prefer to call it justice," Slade corrected him. "A murderer's supposed to hang. It shouldn't matter if he's two-bit border trash or dressed up in a fancy suit with money in the bank."

A blink from Freeman liberated Slade to take another bite of steak. The rancher said, "Speaking of money, marshal's wages must be quite a comedown from poker winnings."

"Beats hell out of losing, though."

"Until you lose it all," said Freeman, "on a wild-goose chase."

"It's good of you to be concerned," Slade said. "But I'm not hunting geese."

"A wise man knows when he's outmatched, Marshal. He finds a way to profit from the situation and move on, while there's still time."

"Guess I'm not very wise then," Slade replied.

"What would it take to get you off this thing?"

"Not much. The men who killed my brother and the man who put them up to it would have to see the judge, confess to what they've done, and take the legal consequences. Simple really."

"Not many men would put their heads into a noose," said Freeman.

"True. But there's a chance an early bird might save himself. Judge Dennison's suggested that the first one who steps up and makes a clean breast of it might get off with prison time. I'm hoping that might change some minds."

"Hope springs eternal. And I wish you luck."

Freeman rose from his chair. Slade aimed a steak knife at his chest and told him, "You forgot your coffee, Doug."

"Next time," Freeman answered. "I've got work to do."

Slade watched him go, a stately figure passing through the doorway, vanishing along the sidewalk.

So do I, Slade thought. *That's two of us.*

"We got a nice turnout this afternoon," Dred Mathers told the six new faces ranged before him. "Glad to see so many of you here today."

Huffman and Grace had brought the others, from saloons and dives where bad men gathered, spending their ill-gotten cash on women, booze, and games of chance. The six were nothing much to look at, not a decent shave among them, and collectively they smelled like two weeks on the trail without a bath. But Bran and Wiley told him they were cold, hard-bitten bastards not afraid to use their weapons in a cause that promised to put money in their pockets.

Mathers reckoned they would do.

"You don't know me," said Mathers, "and I don't know you. Fact is, that suits me fine. I'm hiring for a short-term job with risk involved, and I need men who'll lay it on the line for cold, hard cash, no questions asked. If anyone among you doesn't fit that bill, he needs to saddle up and leave right now."

None of them moved. A couple of them sniffed the air, catching the scent from Jenny Acton's kitchen, but they didn't ask if it was time to eat. The meal he'd promised them for simply coming out to hear his proposition wasn't ready yet. The pitch came first, and anyone who didn't buy it would be looking at a hungry ride back home.

If Mathers let him leave.

He told the newcomers, "This job we're gonna do—if you agree, that is—begins tonight and ought to finish up sometime tomorrow, next day at the latest. You won't get much sleep, but there's a hundred dollars in it for each one of you who comes along. Is everyone still with me?"

"What's the job?" a rangy redhead asked him.

"I'm gettin' to that. There's a ranch south of here, where we pick up some stock now and then. Time's come to try a little somethin' different," Mathers said. "Tonight, we're takin' the boss lady for a ride."

"You're payin' us to take her out?" a grizzled villain asked. "How ugly is she anyway?"

"I said we take her for a ride," Mathers replied. "Nobody's ridin' *her*. I want that understood by all concerned before we leave. Payment depends on her arrivin' at her destination fit and healthy. You want a poke, save it for later. I'll kill any man who tries to dip his wick."

The new men glanced around at one another, several of them frowning, but they didn't challenge Mathers. With a hundred dollars each, they could buy twenty whores apiece. Unless he missed his guess, one woman wouldn't drive them to the point of jeopardizing profits.

And if one of them couldn't manage to control himself, Mathers would leave the horny bastard where he fell.

"All right then, if we're clear on that, let's talk about the risk. Boss lady has herself some hands—I reckon six or seven anyway—who likely won't stand by and watch us take her from the place without a fight. That's why you're here," said Mathers. "Bran and Wiley tell me you've got grit. I take it none of you's got any scruples about killing."

"Not unless you want it done for free," the redhead quipped.

Mathers decided he'd enjoy paying this one in lead. Smiling, he said, "Don't worry. I'm not askin' anyone to work for free."

"So, where's this spread?" a long-faced blond inquired.

"About two hours south of here," Mathers replied. "Don't worry about findin' it. I'll lead the way. We're goin' in about midnight, so we've got time to kill, but I want everybody sober when we ride. The only way you're gettin' paid for dumb mistakes is with a bullet."

"When we get the hunnert dollars?" asked a stocky gun-man whose unruly hair appeared to sprout through moth holes in his beaver hat.

"One quarter now, and the rest when you're finished," said Mathers. "Unless you don't make it, of course."

"S'posin' I don't. Who gets my other eighty dollars?"

Mathers didn't make an issue of the gunman's poor arithmetic. "Nobody gets it," he replied. "This ain't a bank job or a ransom snatch. Each man is being paid for work done on the job. To get the full amount, you have to be alive. And you don't get any extra shooting members of the team by accident."

That earned a laugh from several of the new recruits, while others frowned in what he took for disappointment. Mathers didn't care. He needed men who'd work together, not be at each other's throats for ten or fifteen extra bucks.

The redhead raised his voice again. "Long as we're killin' time, have we got *anything* to drink around this place?"

"We're stocked with beer," Mathers replied. "Two bottles each. I want you sober when we ride out, like I said."

"Stew and a couple beers. That all?" the redhead pressed.

"What did you have in mind?" Mathers inquired.

Behind him, suddenly appearing from the cabin as if summoned by their conversation, Jenny Acton said, "Five minutes till we eat."

The redhead smiled. "Now that you ask," he said, "I wouldn't mind a piece of that."

Mathers saw Bran and Wiley tensing over on his left. His own gut knotted as he stood there, staring through the redhead for a long view of Boot Hill. His trigger finger twitched.

"You can't afford me," Jenny told the redhead, her sharp voice cutting through the tension like a razor through fresh cheese.

"How would you know that till you name a price?" the redhead asked.

"Ten dollars," Jenny answered, doubling her normal rate.

"Awright then," said the gunman. With a wink to Mathers, he told him, "Take it from the quarter of that hunnert you already owe me, will ya, sport?"

"You want your stew first?" Jenny asked him, totally ignoring Mathers now.

"I reckon it'll wait," the redhead answered. "I got a diff'ernt kinda hunger now."

Mathers stood fuming as the gunman sauntered past him, followed Jenny back inside the cabin, and the door swung shut behind them. Calling on his last reserve of self-control, he told the others, "Gentlemen, it seems that supper's been delayed."

Faith Connover was tired of sleeping by herself. She missed James fiercely, even two months gone, but now she was surprised to find her thoughts more often turning toward his twin.

It was completely natural, she told herself. Aside from being James's spitting image, Jack was helping her, when everybody else in town either ignored her plight or offered sympathy as if that was enough.

Except for Marshal Ford, she hadn't had a visitor from town since James was killed, and even Ford had only stopped by once, before the funeral. If it wasn't for Jack, her only contact with the outside world would be her rare trips into Lawton for supplies.

Now, Jack had nearly gotten killed himself. She'd heard the story from two of her hands, who'd been in Lawton for the evening when it happened. They'd cut short their visit, ridden back to stand watch on the property in case the shooting led to something worse, and they'd informed her of it in the morning.

Two men dead, from what she'd heard, but Jack had managed to come through it without injury. Faith thanked the Lord for that, but wished that he had ridden out to break the news himself.

You're being silly now, she told herself, plumping her pillow with impatient hands. *Why should he tell me every move he makes?*

Because she missed him, damn it. And it wouldn't do to tell him that. Not even if she wanted him to—

Stop that!

Going any further with the thoughts that roiled inside her head would feel like cheating on the almost-husband she would never see again. It struck her as preposterous, but that was what her life had suddenly become. She occupied a house and land belonging to a dead man who had loved her, while his twin risked death to punish those responsible. Small wonder that her feelings were confused.

Or were they?

Jack might be nearly identical to James on the outside—although Faith couldn't really judge that, with his clothes on—but the two of them were obviously very different men. James was a builder and a dreamer who had put down roots, with plans to forge a life, perhaps a dynasty. Jack was a drifter, going nowhere in a hurry when the news of tragedy had brought him to the Oklahoma Territory on a mission of revenge.

She couldn't count on Jack remaining when his work was done, regardless of the badge he carried for the moment. If it suited him, Faith knew he'd give Judge Dennison his notice and ride off to parts unknown without a moment's hesitation.

If it suited him.

But if he had some reason to remain . . . what then?

It would be scandalous, she thought, cheeks flaming, if

they started a relationship together. People in the town would talk, but did it matter? They'd been talking since she first moved in with James, starting the honeymoon as soon as he proposed, without the benefit of clergy. In some other countries, even parts of the United States, Faith knew that it was not uncommon for a man to wed his brother's widow. Some communities regarded it as normal, and if love grew from an act of charity, so much the better.

Love? Marriage?

Faith caught herself before the fantasy took on a whole life of its own. She had no evidence beyond her intuition that Jack felt any attraction to her, much less that he *loved* her. She had seen him glancing at her on the sly, of course, the way men look at women they desire, but otherwise he'd been a perfect gentleman.

Too perfect, if the truth be told.

Faith wished, just once, that he would cast propriety aside and take her in his arms. Allow his hands to—

The first gunshot brought her bolt upright in bed, gasping. Before a second echoed in the night, Faith was already on her feet and groping for her robe in darkness, pulling it around her with a haste that got her tangled in the sleeves. She struggled for a moment, cursing silently, then mastered the reluctant garment, belting it around her waist.

Outside, the gunfire sounded like a fireworks celebration, only louder. Other sounds now reached her ears as well. Men shouting, and the rush of horses galloping across the yard.

She reached for matches, then decided it might be a serious mistake to light the bedside lamp. Faith didn't know for certain who'd intruded on her land, but they could only mean her harm. She hoped her men could drive the shooters off, but if they failed for any reason, Faith intended to defend herself.

James kept his favorite rifle on the parlor wall, above the mantelpiece, but she'd removed it after he was killed and placed it in the bedroom they had shared. She crossed the room and took it from her cupboard now, a live cartridge already in the chamber.

Just in case.

James had instructed her in how to use the lever-action rifle, and she'd managed well enough when they were shooting cans and bottles out behind the barn. She'd balked at killing animals for sport, and never really thought she'd have to use the weapon on a human being, but since James was killed her attitude had shifted, undergoing a dramatic change.

If men had come to threaten her and her employees, possibly the very men who'd murdered James, Faith would be pleased to kill them.

All she needed was a fighting chance.

Dred Mathers was a self-taught strategist. He hadn't stayed alive this long while rustling and stealing for a living, dodging mobs and posses, without picking up a few tricks of the trade. Tonight, he'd split his eight-man team in two, three of the new recruits riding with Bran Huffman, the other three with Wiley Grace. Mathers himself led Huffman's team against the ranch house, while the others were dispatched to keep the widow lady's gunmen busy.

It had seemed a decent plan, as such things went, but even so, they got off to a rocky start. Two of her men were roving wide over the property—no trouble slipping past them, even with the moonlight—but he hadn't counted on a watchman at the house. That lookout saw them coming, fired on them without a warning from the shadows, and his first shot brought the others spilling from their bunkhouse in a rush.

Cursing the darkness lit with muzzle flashes, Mathers led his team around behind the house, hooves pounding on the hard-packed soil, dismounting when they reached the service porch. He left Wiley and his companions to eliminate the other guns, odds even for the moment, if the widow's outriders stayed clear.

Meanwhile, the prize he wanted was inside the house, and Mathers didn't know if she'd be covered by a bodyguard. He had to risk it, though, or go back empty-handed to Doug Freeman. And God only knows what *that* would mean.

"You hold the horses," Mathers told the redhead who'd gone first with Jenny for a ten-spot at the cabin. Any hatred for the man was lost now as Mathers concentrated on the moment, getting in and out alive with what he'd come for.

"Bran, the door!"

Huffman obeyed, putting his shoulder to it in a running charge that brought the door down, off its hinges, crashing to the floor. Bran fell on top of it, Mathers and his anonymous companions spreading out once they had crossed the threshold.

"Who is that?" a woman's voice demanded from the inner darkness of the house.

"Miz Connover," said Mathers, "we just need to have a word with you."

One of the others laughed at his ridiculous comment, but Mathers didn't have a chance to round on him in anger.

"Have *this* word," the woman answered, still invisible, before a muzzle-flash sent Mathers diving headlong to the floor. He heard the bullet sizzle past him, and a wet *smack* as it struck one of his men.

"Goddamn it!" wailed the shooter. "I been hit!"

"Shut up, you dumb—"

The second shot was aimed somewhere between their voices, missing flesh but shattering some kind of glass behind him. One of his companions fired a pistol, quickly followed by another, and he had to rage at them, inviting hostile fire to make them stop before they killed the bitch and ruined everything.

Her third shot almost nailed him, peeling back a six-inch strip of planking near his face, prompting Mathers to roll behind some kind of heavy chair.

"I'm bleedin' bad," the wounded shooter whined.

"Somebody shut him up!" snapped Mathers.

Faith accommodated him. Just as the injured gunman struggled to his feet, she fired again and dropped him in a twitching heap.

To hell with this, thought Mathers. Freeman might be angry if they injured her, but he'd be even more pissed off if they came back without the woman, shot to hell and spinning tales of failure.

Surging to his feet, Mathers fanned two quick shots in the direction of the rifle's muzzle-flash. He made them high on purpose, still intent on taking her alive, needing to close the gap. She fired regardless, falling back, but this shot was a clumsy effort, wasted on the ceiling.

Mathers saw her, a retreating shadow, grappling with her weapon, and he could've killed her then, but he had something else in mind. A headlong, snarling charge with outstretched arms, his Colt back in its holster, as he tackled Faith and brought her crashing to the wooden floor.

She fought him like a demon, cracking him across the forehead with her rifle's barrel hard enough to make his vision swim with glowing motes of light. He shook it off, cursing as if he couldn't draw a breath without some fresh obscenity to welcome it, wrenching the weapon from her hands and flinging it aside.

Her hands turned into claws then, raking at his face and neck. Mathers snapped at them with his teeth, but Faith avoided him, knocked off his hat and gouged his scalp, gripped handfuls of his oily hair and twisted painfully. One of her knees rose toward his groin, but Mathers used his own knees, wedging them between her frantic thighs, forcing her legs apart.

He didn't mean to take her, but the bucking of her body

underneath his, barely clad in nightclothes, still aroused him. Maybe she could feel it, from the way she started cursing him and sobbing all at once. He gripped her wrists, pinning both arms above her head, hearing the others close around them from behind.

"Somebody help me, dammit!" he commanded.

"Help do what?" Bran Huffman asked.

Panting from the exertion, Mathers answered, "Find something to tie her hands and feet. Hurry!"

Turning to speak, he dipped his head unconsciously, rewarded for the error by a savage bite along his jawline. She hung on until a gout of warm blood filled her mouth, then fell back retching in disgust. Mathers, enraged, drew back and butted her between the eyes with his forehead. Her writhing form went slack beneath him, leaving Mathers propped up on his knees and elbows, breathing heavily.

"I got some sash cord from the curtains," Huffman told him, thrusting out a limp snake from the shadows.

"Jesus," Mathers panted, rolling clear. "Just tie her up and let's get out of here."

"How 'bout the rest?" another of his gunmen asked.

"We'll flag 'em on the way out if we can," Mathers replied. "If not, they're on their own."

He sat on Faith while Huffman cut the sash cord with his bowie knife, then tightly bound her wrists and ankles. She was still unconscious when they hoisted her between them, bustling toward the door through which they'd entered.

On the way, they passed the crumpled body of their comrade. Mathers still had no idea what he'd been called, and didn't care. He would've liked to search the dead man's pockets for the fifteen dollars that was left after his go at Jenny Acton, but there wasn't time.

With gunfire echoing around them, they passed out into the darkness and were gone.

13

The rider tried Slade's office first, but even with the fall he'd suffered riding into town and all the time he'd wasted following his skittish horse on foot, he still arrived too early for the marshal. Dawn was barely breaking over Lawton when he rode in, slumped across his pommel, face half-buried in the pinto's mane.

He managed to dismount outside Slade's office, but forgot to tie his horse, and so it left him, ambling eastward along Main Street to the nearest water trough. That made no difference, since the rider's strength was failing and it would've been a hopeless challenge for him mounting up again.

He likely didn't even miss the horse after he tried the marshal's door and found it locked. The rider peered through Slade's front window, hands cupped to the glass beside his face, but there was nothing in the office to be seen. Nothing to help him anyway.

Frustrated, failing fast, he turned from Slade's doorstep and lurched along the sidewalk, westbound, in the general direction of the Dry Gulch and the Gay Paree saloons. Those two establishments were likewise closed.

In any case, he moved along the sidewalk, staggering, clutching his left side with a smudged and dripping hand, while bawling, "Marshal! Marshal Slade!" with all the strength that he possessed. He kept it up for two blocks, give or take, and then collapsed facedown, his right arm trailing in the dust of Main Street.

A pair of Good Samaritans retrieved him and conveyed him to the doctor's office. Only after Dr. Crenshaw had examined him and settled on a course of treatment was a runner sent to rouse Slade at the Lawton Arms.

The pounding on his door woke Slade with gun in hand, relaxing slightly as he realized that hired assassins likely wouldn't knock. He still used caution as he answered, standing well back from the door and to one side.

"Who is it?" he demanded.

"Billy McGiver, Marshal. Doc Crenshaw sent me to fetch you. He's got someone at his office shot up bad, asking for you by name."

"I'll be there soon," Slade answered through the door. "You go on back."

He dressed in haste, strapped on his gunbelt, let his hat conceal his pillow-tangled hair. Townsfolk were up and moving early, talking about the disturbance, many of them watching Slade as he proceeded to the doctor's office. There'd been no shots in the street this time, but he could almost hear them thinking, asking one another what kind of unruly hell he'd brought to town with him this time.

Dr. Crenshaw's office was behind a shoe store, with an alley entrance situated to provide his patients with a sense of privacy. Slade knocked once, standing in the shadows, and was summoned from within.

The door was barely shut behind him, when the doctor's

dry, familiar voice called out to him, "Back here." Slade crossed a small reception room, passed through a narrow corridor, and found Crenshaw at work in one of two examination rooms.

He had a cowboy on the table, shirt cut into tatters on the floor, blood smeared around his abdomen. Crenshaw and an assistant half his age were working to extract a bullet from the man's left side, the younger of the pair holding the cowboy down while Crenshaw probed his guts with shiny forceps. Slade hated to watch it, knew that he'd be skipping breakfast, but he waited all the same.

This man had asked for him. But why?

Something about the face tugged at his memory, though it was bathed in sweat, blotched here and there with trail dust, twisted in a snarl of agony. Slade tried to picture it relaxed, maybe smiling.

Where had he seen that face before? If not in town . . .

At Faith's place! This was one of the cowboys he'd seen outside her bunkhouse, watching him the first night they'd shared supper at the ranch. Now he was lying gut-shot on the doctor's operating table, and if he had come to town for help—

Slade moved closer, casting a shadow on the grisly scene, asking the doctor, "Has he spoken? Can you tell me what he said?"

"Nothing, except to call your name, then keep repeating, 'Trouble.'"

"Can I talk to him?"

"You may've noticed, Marshal, that I'm in the middle of an operation here. If you'd be kind enough to let me get this bullet out and stitch him up, then you can chat until the cows come home."

Crenshaw's reply seemed to distract the patient from his pain. The cowboy saw Slade standing over him and seemed to focus on his badge. "Ma-Marshal?"

"I'm right here," Slade told him, bending closer.

"Trouble. At the ranch. Miss Faith . . ."

"What happened?"

Dr. Crenshaw scowled at him. "Marshal, I must insist that you—"

"Shooters," the cowboy gasped, chest heaving. "Got past Shep and Woody. *Jesus!* Done our best. Took her regardless."

"Took her? *Who* took her?" Slade demanded. "Took her *where*?"

"Shooters," the wounded man repeated. "Rode off. I don't . . . I . . . God*damn* it!"

Crenshaw drew his forceps from the bleeding wound and dropped a bullet clattering into a metal pan. Slade stepped back from the table as the cowboy slumped, passing from consciousness to sweet oblivion, finding a refuge from his pain.

Of course he wouldn't know the men who'd kidnapped Faith, but Slade could guess at their identity. The ranch hand wouldn't know their destination either, and in that respect Slade shared his ignorance.

Ironically, he was encouraged that the gunmen had abducted Faith. It told Slade that they wanted her alive, for some reason, and might take steps to keep her relatively healthy. If they'd simply wanted to eliminate her, prudence would've made them kill her at the ranch.

So he had hope. But every moment Faith spent in the clutches of the Mathers gang left her at risk. Slade didn't want to think of what they might be doing to her, even now, but ugly images crowded his mind, unbidden, taunting him.

How could he find them? What should he do next?

The first step was so obvious that Slade couldn't ignore it. Leaving Dr. Crenshaw's office through the alley, he went off to wake the judge.

• • •

"Kidnapped, you say? And one man shot at least?"

"One man I'm sure of," Slade replied. He stood in front of Dennison, the judge seated and sipping coffee from a mug so large it nearly blotted out his face each time he drank. "I'm guessing there'll be others at the ranch. Doc Crenshaw's riding out there, once he gets his patient squared away."

"You should go with him," Dennison advised. "A crime scene needs to be examined while it's fresh, before the curious show up and trample on the evidence."

"I'm on my way," Slade said, "as soon as I make one stop here in town."

Dennison read his mind and cautioned Slade. "Be careful there. Suspicion—even if I share it, for the moment—isn't proof. You can ask questions, but harassment and coercion won't be tolerated. Understood?"

"I hear you. Asking's all I plan to do for now."

"Assuming he's involved with this, you think Freeman will tell you where the woman is?"

Slade shook his head. "I'm working on the same plan that I rode in with last week," he said. "If I push hard enough—"

"Within the law, that is," said Dennison.

"If I push hard enough, *within the law,* somebody might make a mistake."

"And if not?"

"Then I'll try something else," Slade replied.

"I'd feel better if we knew where Mathers might hide," the judge told him. "This woman of his . . ."

"Jenny Acton."

"Do you think he'd run back to her place by chance?"

"I've already been out there," Slade said. "It's the first thing he'd think of."

"I bow to your judgment in that case. But if you decide that she merits another visit, I can issue a warrant naming her as a material witness to the attempt on your life. The evidence supports that, I believe."

"I'll keep that in mind," Slade assured him. "Right now, I need to see a man about a kidnapping."

"Walk softly," Dennison suggested.

"I'll be on my best behavior, Judge."

Slade walked to Freeman's office under a foreboding sky, gray clouds blown into tatters by a fitful wind. The Main Street door was locked, but Slade cut through another alley, forced the back door open, and went on inside. Unseen, he entered Freeman's private sanctum, used a knife to spring the lock on his desk drawers, and rifled through them in a fruitless search for something, anything, that might direct him to Dred Mathers's hiding place.

It stood to reason there'd be nothing, and that was exactly what he found. Angry, Slade left a couple of the drawers ajar, their contents disarranged. If Freeman asked him to investigate the burglary, Slade would comply, and use the opportunity to grill the rancher about Faith's abduction.

In the meantime, he was needed at his brother's ranch—Faith's now, if she was still alive. There might be evidence, as Dennison had said. And if there was, if it could help him hang the men responsible, Slade meant to find it.

First, he walked back to his office, meaning to collect a shotgun and some extra ammunition. It was doubtful that he'd find a trail worth following, but just in case, Slade wanted to be ready for the chase and what would follow.

God help Mathers if he'd injured Faith in any way.

God help the bastards who had snatched her, when Slade had them in his sights.

Slade used his key, opened the office door, and heard the slip of paper scuff beneath his boot before he cleared the threshold. Stepping back, he lifted it, a piece of foolscap folded once, still thin enough to slip beneath his door.

Slade opened it and read the message printed there in crude block capitals.

WE GOT THE WOEMAN. IF YO WANT HERE COME ALONE AT MIDNITE TO THE OLD MILL SOTH OF TOWN. FIRST SIGN OF A POSSY AND SHE'S DED. REMEMBR WE MEAN BIZNESS.

Under other circumstances, Slade would probably have laughed aloud. It was a child's note, on the face of it, but deadly serious.

Interpretation was no problem. Slade read "yo" as "you" and "here" as "her." He guessed the mill was *south* of town, though he had never seen it and would have to ask directions. As for gathering a posse, Slade never considered it. He didn't know most of the townsfolk, wouldn't know which ones to trust, and he most definitely didn't want to see Faith "ded."

My job, he thought. And he would handle it himself.

Midnight was still a long way off. Slade had the better part of seventeen hours to kill, getting ready for his meeting with Faith's kidnappers.

It was a trap, of course. What else? He couldn't count on finding Faith at the old mill, but someone would be waiting for him there, likely intent on killing Slade from ambush, as they'd done with Jim. But when would they arrive and set the trap?

Slade doubted that the gang would be in place already. If he chose to disregard their warning, raise a hunting party, and surround the mill, they might be trapped, or else compelled to flee with trackers at their heels. It was more likely, he decided, that they'd scout the territory sometime after dusk, then settle down to wait in darkness, when a posse would be forced to blunder through the shadows and they could escape unseen.

Slade didn't have to wait for dusk, however.

He had business at the ranch, a search for evidence to carry out, but that would only take him up to noon, or thereabouts. With good directions to the mill, Slade reckoned he could be in place by two or three o'clock that afternoon, and waiting for his would-be killers to reveal themselves.

It was a plan at least. And at the moment, it was all he had.

Taking a shotgun from the rack, Slade hoped fervently, for Faith's sake, that it would be good enough.

During what seemed a long and hectic ride, bound to a horse facedown as if she was a corpse, Faith Connover swam in and out of consciousness, head throbbing from the blow that she had suffered, while the saddle underneath her bruised her breasts and stomach. She was ill upon first waking, retching bitterly, and then felt sorry for the horse that she had stained with bile. Another wave of nausea assaulted her, then quickly faded, leaving Faith to focus on her pain and fear.

She hadn't recognized her kidnappers during their battle in the darkness, and she couldn't see their faces now, bound as she was. It made no difference, if Jack was right about the Mathers gang, because she'd never met them anyway.

Faith had been snatched by strangers from her home, with blood shed in the process, and her anger at the memory was dwarfed by terror at the prospect of their plans for her.

If all they wanted was to kill her, Faith decided that they would've done it at the ranch. Kidnapping meant some hope of a material reward, or else a plan so fiendish that it couldn't be accomplished at her home, within the time allowed before help came from town.

Grim images flooded her mind, though she tried to suppress them. Faith had done her best against these men, had wounded one of them at least, but she was at their mercy now, helpless to free herself and fight or flee. Another chance might come, but for the moment she was trapped.

The rough ride seemed to last for hours, but it was still dark when the raiding party reached a combination cave and cabin, part of it protruding from a hillside, while the back rooms had been cut from soil and stone. Smoke streamed from a tall stovepipe on the roof. Three horses pawed the ground outside and watched the new arrivals warily. As the riders reined in, three men stepped from the curious dwelling to meet them.

"It's about time," one of them complained. Faith recognized the voice but couldn't name its owner sight unseen. "What took you so damned long?"

"Try doin' it yourself next time," one of the riders answered. "I lost two men, another wounded. If they'd followed us, we wouldn't be here yet."

"If you were followed," said the first speaker, "I wouldn't want you here. Bring her inside now. Hurry up!"

Strong hands untied the bonds that held Faith bent across the saddle. Others dragged her from the horse and set her on her feet, straying to pinch one of her breasts in the process. She jerked away and nearly fell, her hobbled ankles failing her. The hand came back to grope her once again, its owner snickering, before another man dressed all in black wrenched him away.

"Cut out that shit!" the black-clad gunman ordered. "You were warned, and once is all the caution I allow."

"I was just funnin'," said the other peevishly.

"Well, *fun* yourself, why don't you? We've got work to do."

The man in black produced a wicked-looking knife and held it inches from Faith's nose. "I'm taking off those hobbles now," he said. "But it you try to run, I'll cut your hamstrings. Understand."

She nodded jerkily, too frightened to respond in words. He stooped and passed the knife between her shins, cool metal slick against her skin. The hobbling rope parted and fell away.

Sheathing his blade, the seeming leader of her kidnappers clutched Faith's left arm and marched her toward the open doorway of the cave-house. "Mind your manners now," he cautioned her. "The man don't like to be upset."

Inside the main room of the dwelling, Douglas Freeman sat beside an old wood-burning stove, flanked by two standing gunmen whom Faith didn't recognize.

"I might have known," she said.

"You might've spared yourself this difficulty, Faith," he said. "That's what you might've done."

"Is this how you negotiate a sale?" she asked him, making no attempt to hide her sneer.

"We've gone beyond negotiations, I'm afraid," Freeman replied. "A long way past. It's more like war these days."

"You call it war," she said. "I call it kidnapping and murder."

"No one's murdered you as yet."

"I had in mind my fiancé and Marshal Ford, together with the men you slaughtered on my ranch tonight."

"They had a fightin' chance," her black clad escort said.

"Shut up," Freeman commanded. At her side, Faith felt the gunman stiffen, simmering with anger.

When her captor didn't answer, Freeman once again addressed himself to Faith. "Shall we discuss *your* ranch? I've made you several offers that were more than generous."

"And I've declined to sell. That ought to be the end of it."

"If it was only grass at stake," said Freeman, "that might be the case. What do you know about geology, Miz Connover?"

"It has to do with minerals," she answered grudgingly.

"Exactly. And are you familiar with the bounties of petroleum?"

"I haven't made a study of it," Faith replied.

"I have," said Freeman. "It appears that we inhabit oil-rich land here in the territory. Parts of it at least. My own reserve, on land that I hold title to, is sadly limited. Your spread, conversely, sits atop a veritable sea of what the Texans call 'black gold.' I'm counting on that sea to make me rich—well, *richer* anyway."

"And you're prepared to kill for it," she said, stating the obvious.

"Why not?" Freeman inquired. "We killed the red man for his open range. Your darling James was in the thick of it himself. How are his murders any different from my own?"

"I'm not surprised you have to ask," Faith said. But she was troubled by his question all the same.

"Alas, I didn't bring you here—at great expense, if I say so myself—for a debate that's better left to Congress. Thieves in Washington are paid to blather on for hours about nothing in particular. What I need from you, Miz Connover, is just a small thing. I require your autograph to verify a bill of sale."

"I'll die first," she replied.

"No, ma'am, you won't," Freeman corrected her. "You may die afterward, if that's your wish. May beg for it, in fact. But you most certainly will not die first."

"How come you let 'im talk to you like that?" Bran Huffman asked.

"Shut up, will you?"

In fact, Dred Mathers had been wondering that very thing himself. It galled him, having Freeman walk all over him, especially in front of men who were supposed to treat him with respect, acknowledge his authority. Each time the rancher shamed him, reading him the riot act or making stupid jokes at his expense, it wounded Mathers to the quick.

He'd swallowed it, so far, because Freeman paid top dollar for dirty work and had the law bamboozled into thinking he was honest. Now, Mathers could see all that changing with the new lawman, with his challenges to Freeman. Lately, Mathers wondered if the rancher had become a liability.

It might be time to fold his hand and find another game—but not before Jack Slade had paid his tab. The gambler-turned-marshal had killed two of Mathers's men and sent a third hightailing it for who knows where. That kind of insult couldn't be ignored, if Mathers wanted to maintain his reputation as a man who settled scores.

Slade had to die. And after him, perhaps Doug Freeman.

Unless, perhaps, the would-be oilman wanted to accept a silent partner in his great new enterprise. Mathers was willing to negotiate: one bloated, decadent life in exchange for enough wealth to keep Mathers smiling on Easy Street for the rest of his days.

Before they got around to that deal, though, he still had Slade to deal with. The supposed exchange was set for midnight, at the old mill south of Lawton. Mathers didn't know if Faith would be alive to see her hero riding to her rescue—that was Freeman's business—but he meant to have a warm reception waiting for Jack Slade.

Make that a *hot* reception, on behalf of Quinn and Corey Chapman, and in payment for the loss of status Mathers had sustained while running from a two-bit amateur.

Slade had been lucky so far, but his luck was running out. The marshal didn't know it yet, but any cards he drew from this point on would make a dead man's hand.

He heard a stifled cry from Faith, inside the cave-house, and ignored it. Wiley Grace turned toward the squat structure, scratching his jaw, and asked, "You think he's pokin' her?"

"What difference does it make?" Mathers replied. "There's none for you."

"Just wonderin', is all."

"Well, concentrate on what's important for a change," Mathers suggested. "Damaged goods or not, she's got the marshal comin' after her tonight. And I expect him to go down this time, if it's the last thing any of us do."

One of the three new men still on his feet and fit to ride chimed in, "I take it you'll be payin' extra for the killin', yes? I mean, our other deal was just to grab the woman, not dry-gulch no lawman."

"You'll be paid, all right," Mathers assured him.

"But the question is, how much?"

"The man's agreed to pay another hundred each for those still standing when it's over," Mathers said. In fact, Freeman had granted no such thing, but Mathers didn't plan on seeing any of the new men walk away.

He felt like cleaning house.

"A hunnert for a U.S. marshal might not be enough," the wiry redhead interjected.

"Well, then," Mathers answered, "why don't you go in and tell him that? I'm sure he won't mind bein' interrupted. Maybe he'll be so damned glad to see you that he'll double it."

The shooter paused, considered it, then shook his head. "I reckon not."

"So, are you with us then?" Mathers demanded.

"Hell, I come this far. Why not?"

"You others feel the same?" Mathers stood waiting while the redhead's two companions nodded, wearing sour expressions that he judged to be habitual. "Well, now we've got the hard part settled," he went on, "let's talk about how we're supposed to take this bastard down."

The mill he'd chosen for their fatal rendezvous with

Slade had been abandoned years before, some kind of plague blighting the grain that early farmers in the territory grew, before they pulled up stakes and journeyed farther west, leaving the open range to cattle and their masters. It was built mostly of stone, but leaked on rainy days through rotten timbers on the roof. Its windows had no glass, but they would serve as gun ports when the lawman came to call.

Mathers was confident that six men could dispose of Slade, as long as he obeyed instructions to show up alone. If, on the other hand, Slade brought a posse with him, it would be a relatively simple task to fall back in the darkness, slip away, and try for him another time. That way, the marshal would be left to speculate about what might've happened to his brother's woman because of his breaking of the rules.

And what *would* happen to the woman?

Mathers heard another squeal from the cave-house and turned a deaf ear to it. If she managed to survive the night, and Freeman deigned to send her on with Mathers to the mill, her fate was sealed in any case.

No witnesses.

It was a rule Dred Mathers lived by, and he didn't plan to break it now.

14

Slade reached his brother's former home a little after nine o'clock. He rode in slowly, giving every man still living on the spread a chance to recognize him and relax, put down the gun they kept constantly within arm's reach.

Arriving in the yard, Slade noted fresh scars on the house where bullets had impacted, chipping paint and gouging wood beneath. A couple of the windows had been shattered too, and Shade saw other battle scars on the bunkhouse. Much of the action had been centered there, he calculated, although Faith had doubtless been abducted from the house itself.

Four human corpses and a dead horse occupied the yard, while sullen men with rifles supervised them from the shaded porch. The horse was a roan gelding, gutted by a shotgun blast and finished with a close range pistol shot. Like the four dead men, it was now aswarm with flies.

Someone had taken time to separate the corpses. Two were laid out in a patch of shade, along the west side of the house, and covered from their waists up with a canvas tarpaulin. The other two lay twenty paces from the house, uncovered, drag marks in the dust revealing how they'd gotten there. Slade didn't have to ask which ones had been Faith's men, and which were from the raiding party that had stolen her away.

He paused beside the outlaws' bodies, leaning from his saddle to examine them. Slade didn't recognize their lifeless faces or their nondescript clothing, concluding that he'd either never seen these men before, or else dismissed them at a glance as individuals unworthy of his notice. Either way, he couldn't pin a name to either one of them.

He found Faith's foreman sitting in a rocker on the porch, his left arm in a sling and a Winchester lever-action rifle braced across his knees. Climbing the dusty steps, Slade heard the foreman say, "You missed 'em, Marshal. They already left."

"I heard that from your man in town," Slade said.

"Frank Beale. Doc Crenshaw says he'll be all right."

"Is the doctor still around?" asked Slade.

The foreman shook his head. "Already been and gone. I took the only hit of them still livin', and he couldn't help the rest."

"You taking care of them?"

"We plant our own," the foreman said. "Doc's sendin' out an undertaker for the trash."

"I don't suppose you know those two?" asked Slade, cocking his head toward the discarded corpses.

"Nope. They come in here last night with half a dozen more to steal Miss Faith. I'm mortified to say they did it too, but not without a cost. We hit at least one more I'm sure of, but the sumbitch got away."

"As to the others, did you get a look at any of their faces?" Slade inquired.

"I know the one who winged me right enough. Name's

Wiley Grace. I use ta see him now and then in Lawton, drinkin' at the Gay Paree."

"One of the Mathers gang," Slade said.

"That's what I hear these days. He won't be part of no one's gang next time I see him. Fair or foul, that bastard's going down, I promise you."

"That's not the sort of thing you want to tell a badge," said Slade.

The foreman gave a stiff, one-sided shrug. "They wanna stretch me for it, guess they'll have to catch me first. I shoulda been more help to Miss Faith when they come for her. I let her down, but if I see that Wiley Grace again—"

"With any luck," Slade interrupted him, "you won't."

"Well, if you get him first, it's all the same to me. Just so he's dead and roasting down in hell."

It was too much to ask, but Slade would feel remiss unless he tried. "You wouldn't know where they were taking her, by any chance? One of the riders calling to the rest, something like that?"

"If I knew *that*," the foreman said, "you'd have to eat my trail dust, broken wing or no."

"And none of them left anything behind, I guess? By accident?"

"Just one fair horse and two dead bags of shit."

"All right then. If I manage to lay hands on Wiley Grace, I take it that you'd testify against him for Judge Dennison?"

"To see him swing, I'll say 'bout anything you want me to, Marshal."

"The truth is all I want," Slade answered, "if it comes to that."

"Then, truth it is."

"I'll need to have a look around inside the house."

"Go on then. Anything to help." As Slade moved toward the front door, Faith's employee said, "They went in through the back and got 'er, while we fought the rest of 'em out here."

Slade turned and walked around the west side of the house, skirting the bodies with their legs protruding from beneath the tarp. This brought the score to seven dead since he'd arrived in Lawton with no thought to joining in a local war. For all he knew, Faith Connover was number eight, though something still told Slade the kidnappers must have a use for her alive.

Slade found the back door off its hinges, lying in the middle of the floor and scarred by boot heels. There was blood and plenty of it farther in, with drag marks showing Slade where one of the dead raiders had been hauled outside. Beyond the killing floor, he found five cartridge cases from a rifle, marking the position where some member of the household stood and fought.

One of the hands outside? Or Faith?

Aside from bearing witness to a fight, the rooms told Slade nothing. He found no objects left behind by those he hunted, no convenient carving on the wall to say, MATHERS WAS HERE. Slade *knew* it, but he still had nothing against any of the gang but Wiley Grace. And where was he, now that the damage had been done?

With Mathers and the rest, no doubt, wherever *they* were. With Doug Freeman possibly.

Another question mark.

Slade thought of stopping at the Rocking Y to ask if Freeman was at home, but he imagined it would be a wasted effort. If he found the rancher there, Freeman would strike a pose of innocence and call his hands to testify that he had never left the ranch all night. If he was gone . . . well, then, what of it? Any man was free to come and go at will, unless he left some clue behind that linked him to specific crimes.

No Rocking Y today, Slade thought. He had another er-

rand to perform, which weighed more heavily upon his
mind.

Before leaving the spread, Slade stopped back at the
front porch and inquired about directions to the old mill.

It was a good four-hour ride, skirting the town, but Slade
had time to kill. He didn't want to stop in Lawton on his
way, for fear of getting sidetracked with some other chore,
perhaps waylaid by Dennison for a report on his visit to the
ranch.

More to the point, there was at least an outside chance
he might be followed, and Slade didn't want a tail as he
prepared to lay his trap.

The note left at his office had instructed Slade to come
alone, and he was glad to keep that bargain. What he
wouldn't do was let Faith's kidnappers dictate the hour of
arrival. Slade would be in place, with any luck at all, before the gang showed up to take their own positions in the
mill. It would be his game then—or at the very least, he
would've shaved the odds.

Stopping in Lawton would've granted any spies in town
a chance to shadow him, reporting when he left and which
road he had taken out of town. This way, if there were
watchers waiting for him, they could only say that he had
ridden out to Faith's ranch in the morning and had not been
seen again.

That message could make Mathers nervous in and of itself, but Slade trusted the outlaw's arrogance to make him
feel superior. Mathers would think he had Slade covered,
beaten, bowing to his will before ever they met. Faith was
his hole card, and the kidnappers would count on Slade's
reluctance to place her in further jeopardy.

They'd be right to a point, but just so far. Slade hoped
that Faith was still alive, but he couldn't be sure of it until
he'd seen her in the flesh. Meanwhile, he could only take

for granted that she might be dead, or else subjected to continuing, life-threatening abuse by her abductors. And with that in mind, whatever risks Slade took to set her free were justified, from his perspective.

Whether Judge Dennison would share that view or not was anybody'd guess, but Slade was more concerned with Faith's well-being than his badge or any repercussions he might face for acting on impulse.

It was approaching two o'clock when Slade sighted the old, abandoned mill. Half-hidden among trees, it stood above a rushing stream that would've turned its grinding wheels in other days, before harsh Nature called a different game and put its owners out of business, through no fault of their own.

Slade studied its stone walls and vacant windows from a distance, seeking any sign of movement and detecting none. Still being cautious, he rode slowly closer, taking care to leave the mill well screened by trees, so that a watcher in the ruins couldn't follow his approach. If anyone had glimpsed him yet, Slade took for granted that they'd open fire soon and eliminate him if they could. When nothing happened by the time he'd closed the gap to something like one hundred yards, he reckoned he was safe.

For now.

Slade found a place to tie his Appaloosa, where it would be hidden from the mill and from the two main access routes. Both roads were long-disused and overgrown with weeds, but Slade still noted them without much difficulty and arranged himself accordingly.

His horse had grass and water handy where he left it, trusting that it wouldn't raise a fuss if he was gone awhile. Next, he crept closer to the mill, finding an elm that suited him and climbing halfway up the ladder of its branches to a perch where he could watch the mill and yet be unobserved.

From that point, he could watch and wait for Mathers or
whoever did his dirty work to come and lay their trap. They
might bring Faith along, or they might not. Slade wasn't
counting on it, though he still hoped for the best.

Once they arrived and settled in, it would be his job to
approach them stealthily and render them defenseless, by
whatever means he could devise. Faith's presence would
increase his risk, even as it spurred him on to greater effort,
more subversive guile. And whether she was there or not,
Slade's final goal remained the same.

He needed one live prisoner at least. Alive and talking,
that would be. If Faith was missing, then Slade needed to
find out where she was. If he recovered her, alive or dead,
he needed testimony for Judge Dennison to name the other
men responsible for her kidnapping, for Jim's murder, and
for the other slayings that had happened afterward.

One man, alive and talking for the judge.

The rest of them, Slade thought, could all go straight to
hell. And he'd be pleased to send them there himself.

Faith wasn't tied across the saddle when she left Doug
Freeman's cave-house hideaway. She was relieved of that
indignity at least, although her wrists were tightly bound to
the pommel of her saddle, leaving one of her abductors
with the reins that led her unfamiliar mount. Each time
they broke into a gallop or went plunging down a hillside,
Faith half-feared, half-hoped that she would tumble from
the horse and break her neck, but she was not to be permitted that escape.

Her mind and heart were caught up in a maelstrom of
emotion as she rode, surrounded by her captors, through a
zebra landscape of moonlight and shadow. Part of what she
felt was rage, competing with a not-so-healthy dose of
shame and deep, abiding fear.

The anger was directed at her kidnappers, at Freeman

for employing them, and also at herself. She hated all those men who had disrupted and despoiled her life, from killing James to this night's filthy work. Given a chance, Faith thought she might've killed them all and never lost a wink of sleep. Might've been proud, in fact, of what she'd done.

The anger at herself was sparked by what she viewed as weakness. She had signed the papers Freeman brandished at her, after hours of abuse and torment, knowing that a signature obtained through fraud or through coercion was invalid on its face. Freeman could never truly claim her land while Faith was still alive to challenge him, but he had broken her, and she could not forgive herself for bending to his will, regardless of the force employed.

Shame sprang from that encounter too. The memory of Freeman's groping, probing hands humiliated Faith. He hadn't done his worst, though God alone knows what had stopped him, but things Freeman *had* done were bad enough to haunt her dreams for months or years ahead. And when she'd steeled herself against the intimate assaults, his face had reddened, big hands turning hard instead of hungry. Slapping. Punching. Twisting.

Somewhere in the midst of it, she'd reached a limit never tested in her life before, unrecognized until she met it, like colliding with a stout brick wall. One moment, she was glowering at Freeman through a blur of tears, with blood smeared on her nose and lips; the next, Faith realized that if he struck her one more time, she would start screaming and might never stop.

So she had signed his bill of sale, ceding the land, buildings, and stock to Freeman for a moderate amount of cash she'd never see. Her signature quite literally wasn't worth the paper bearing it if Faith chose to contest the "sale."

But to dispute it, she would have to be alive.

And Freeman had already thought of that.

Her kidnappers would soon become her executioners, and Faith imagined she'd be lucky if they only shot her, without taking time for any brutal games beforehand. But that still wasn't the worst of it.

The worst was that they planned on using her as bait, to kill Jack Slade.

Freeman had kept that information from her, but the man in black—Dred Mathers, she now realized—couldn't resist the urge to brief her on the details of their vile conspiracy. They'd gotten word to Jack, somehow, that Faith could be retrieved by meeting them at midnight, at a landmark south of Lawton. He'd been told to come alone, and Mathers seemed to think that he'd obey.

Faith prayed that her kidnapper was mistaken, but she wondered whether bringing extra men along would make a difference. Mathers had picked the meeting place himself, and therefore must feel confident of its ability to serve him, even if Jack happened to ignore the rules. With five men to support him, he could lay a deadly ambush in the darkness, killing twice as many men perhaps before they could defend themselves.

Again, Faith wished that she could simply plummet from her horse and end it now, but even if her hands were free, she understood that Mathers would go on without her. He might even be relieved, one less potential complication while he lay in wait to spring his trap. No risk of screams to warn his victims as they rode in to their deaths.

At last, after what seemed like hours on the trail, Faith saw the mill ahead. In daylight, she supposed it would be just another old, abandoned building, but by night, it made her skin crawl. She imagined snakes, spiders, and scorpions nesting inside, emerging from their holes at sundown in an endless quest for prey. She didn't want to join them, but the good news was that any venomous inhabitants might target Mathers and his gunmen while they hunkered in the shadows, waiting for Jack.

Not likely, Faith decided. *Vermin knows its own.*

Their group approached the ruins from a rough southeasterly direction. Mathers led them to the mill's back door, dismounted there, and walked his horse inside, passing beneath the archway of a door that had accommodated wagons when the mill was functional. The door was gone now, but its gaping maw still beckoned them, resembling the black maw of a cave or mine shaft.

Faith couldn't dismount with hands tied to her saddle horn. She watched the others step down from their animals, wishing that she could turn and bolt while they were at a disadvantage, but her grinning escort kept a tight grip on her horse's reins.

Helpless, she waited until the man drew a knife and slit her bonds, then put his blade away and offered Faith a helping hand, which she ignored. He tried to slip the hand beneath her skirt, while Faith had one foot in a stirrup, and she turned to strike at him, then lost her balance, tumbling painfully to the ground. A couple of the other gunmen laughed at her predicament; then Mathers was among them, shoving, hissing curses.

"I told you to keep your goddamn mouths shut, didn't I? Next one who makes a noise, I'll bleed him out."

That said, Mathers reached down and pulled Faith to her feet. He steered her toward the doorway, with a shove to prove there was no sympathy behind his intervention with the others, then turned back to face her escort.

"Bring her horse, if you can manage it," said Mathers, then showed the young gunman his back.

Faith stepped into the mill and felt its dampness settle over her. She wondered if the crumbling hulk would be her tomb.

Slade hadn't quite believed his ears at first. The whicker of a horse might prove to be a bird's call or the trilling of an insect, misidentified. Only when he had heard the sound repeated, closer than the first time, did he tolerate a sense of hope. And when a second horse answered the first, he was convinced.

Sound helped him track the new arrivals, but it wouldn't do the job alone. Moonlight was sparse beneath the tree-tops, but it still existed, offering brief, fragmentary glimpses of the riders as they closed in on the mill. Even at that, however, it was only when they cleared the trees entirely and approached the mill's back door that Slade saw Faith and counted her escorts.

Six men, with one whom he assumed to be Dred Mathers in the lead. He couldn't verify it, but Slade's common sense told him that Mathers wouldn't miss the action when his plan was carried out, nor would he trust another to ride point when they were this close to the finish line.

When seven riders and their mounts had disappeared inside the mill, Slade fought the urge to climb down from his tree and seek another vantage point. Instead, he waited for the shooters to arrange themselves inside the mill, saw match light flare and vanish just as quickly, while they checked for stumbling blocks and wildlife hiding in the corners.

That done, darkness settled in once more. Slade could imagine faces peering from the several windows, though he couldn't see them. Any one of them could drop him if Slade dropped his guard while crossing open ground, and Slade believed that he was Faith's last hope of living through the night. That meant he had to stay alive for her, no easy task with odds at six to one.

Waiting paid off as Slade saw one of the gunmen emerge from the direction of the mill's back door. The shooter looked around, nervous in moonlight, then jogged briskly toward a large tree situated twenty paces from the mill's southeastern corner. On arrival there, he hunkered down among tall ferns that ringed the tree, thus vanished from sight.

He was the rear guard, situated to prevent rescuers from

sneaking up behind the Mathers party, while his friends waited to ambush Slade. A gunshot or a shouted warning would alert the others, maybe bring them to his aid if they were so inclined. But the alarm might also trigger action against Faith, and Slade sought to avoid that at all costs.

He didn't know what she had suffered since her kidnapping, had tried his best not to consider it, but he supposed that there'd be no time for distractions now that Mathers and his men had reached the ambush site. That made her safe, after a fashion, but she'd have no more protection once the battle had been joined.

Slow steps then.

He had time to spare. The riders hadn't spotted him on their approach, and Slade still had the best part of three hours left before he was supposed to meet them. He had surveyed the ground by daylight, had its pitfalls memorized, and barring some freak accident, Slade knew that he could reach the gang's rear guard unseen.

What happened after that depended on his stealth, strength, and determination. If he managed to dispatch the lookout silently, he had a chance to infiltrate the mill and take the others by surprise. Darkness might work against him, but his enemies had the same handicap.

Slade descended with care, keeping the main bulk of the tree between himself and the mill's staring windows. Upon reaching the ground, he spent another moment waiting for his muscles to relax, his pulse to normalize. Excitement was his enemy tonight. He'd need the same icy calm he felt at the card table, when he held a winning hand and knew the pot was his.

This time, of course, the odds were all against him. He was facing six armed men, and Slade assumed that all of them had more experience in combat than he did. A life outside the law would do that, teaching down and dirty tricks to win a killing confrontation, while Slade's own experience ran more toward talk and dealing cards.

Still, he had done all right in his first meeting with the Mathers gang. He'd handled three of them, put two in caskets, while the third had run away. He couldn't count on any of these hombres running, but at least his victory the first time out encouraged some degree of confidence.

Watch that, Slade warned himself.

A cocky attitude was every bit as dangerous as freezing when an adversary made his move. If undue hesitancy was a killer, so was overconfidence. It made men reckless, prodded them to actions that increased their risk for no good reason.

And he still had Faith to think of, more important to him than his own safety.

Faith, and the quest for a surviving witness who could help him put a noose around Doug Freeman's neck.

Which one would that be? Slade supposed he'd have to try for Mathers, though the bandit leader would be the toughest of the lot to crack. And Slade supposed that he would only reach his man by going through the others, killing or disabling each one of them in turn.

Judge Dennison wouldn't approve, but he was safe at home, reading his newspaper, maybe relaxing by the fire. Slade had a bloody job of work to do.

And he was running out of time.

15

Slade hadn't done much big-game stalking—one brief hunt for mule deer, if that even counted, when he'd last seen Jim four years ago—but he was skilled enough to know his various advantages and disadvantages as he crept closer to the gunmen in the old, abandoned mill.

The good news first. Unlike most animals, they wouldn't smell him coming. Likewise, in the dark their eyes would be less useful than an animal's. They still might hear him, if he rushed or let himself get careless, but he'd spent time covering the ground in daylight for that very reason, to avoid deadly mistakes. If he could only watch his step, make progress with a minimum of noise, Slade had a chance to reach his target without being spotted.

Now, the bad news. While most animals would bite or sting if they were cornered, and a few were powerful enough to rip Slade limb from limb, they didn't carry guns and couldn't riddle him with bullets at a hundred yards.

The men whom he was stalking did, and could, if he provided them a target.

Easy does it then, Slade thought, creeping along at a galling snail's pace. He wanted to charge, hell-for-leather, shouting and blasting the men who had killed Jim, kidnapped his fiancée, but that course of action would only mean death for himself, and for Faith.

It took Slade ten minutes to cover a distance of seventy yards. At that, he sometimes felt as if he was rushing too quickly, inviting a mishap with noise to betray him, but nothing went wrong. The first leg of his journey completed, he crouched in deep shadow behind an oak tree, fifteen feet from the gang's outer guard.

For some reason, the man seemed focused solely on the trail by which his party had arrived. Slade tried to work it out, couldn't decide if Mathers was expecting reinforcements, or somehow believed that Slade would try to come in from behind him. Maybe neither one was true and the appointed sentry simply didn't know enough to look in various directions while he was on watch. In either case, his failure was Slade's gain.

The problem now was how to take him down. Slade couldn't shoot him without warning Mathers and the other outlaws in the mill. That also meant he couldn't give the guard a chance to cry out when Slade made his move. Slade had to silence him at first contact . . . but how?

One answer was the knife sheathed in his boot. Its six-inch blade could stifle any argument or warning cry the lookout might attempt to make—but stabbing him might look bad to Judge Dennison. Slade spent another moment wondering how much he cared, then finally decided he would use the dagger only as a last resort.

That left a bludgeon of some kind. His rifle seemed ideal, especially since it had once been Jim's. If he was careful not to damage it, applied the proper force on the target without hesitation, it should work all right.

And if it didn't, all he needed was a moment's interval in which to draw his knife and make the killing thrust.

Slade clutched his Winchester, eased forward from the oak's sheltering cover, moving toward his adversary in a crouch. Each step was torture as he feared that a twig or pebble might betray him, or that some sixth sense would warn his quarry of the danger creeping up behind him.

Almost there . . .

A thorny bush reached out to snag Slade's trousers as he took one final step and placed himself in striking range. It rustled softly, brought the lookout's head around as Slade put all his weight behind a sharp swing with the rifle's stock.

It struck the guard flush on the left side of his jaw and whipped his head another forty-five degrees off center. The stunning impact pitched the gunman over backward, sprawling in the dust with arms outflung, no seeming thought for either of the six-guns holstered on his hips.

He might've been unconscious, but Slade couldn't take the chance. Stooping, he raised the Winchester again and slammed its butt into the lookout's face, feeling his nose and something else crumple on impact. Half afraid to check the guard's pulse, Slade took his two guns instead, and tucked them down inside his belt around in back.

It was the best that he could d.o.

Still less than satisfied, Slade turned and started for the dark mouth of the mill's back door.

There's something wrong, Dred Mathers thought. He couldn't put his finger on it, would've looked a fool trying to spell it out for Bran or Wiley, but he *knew* it, just as sure as he was standing in the dark, waiting to kill a man he'd never seen.

Something. But *what*?

It might've been a sound, so faint it barely registered,

but Mathers couldn't trace it to a source, or even start to say what he had heard—if anything.

Was it a smell?

He sniffed the air and shook his head. Nothing he hadn't smelled within the past two hours, whether it was grass or dirt, snake shit, the woods outside, or Faith Connover's womanly aroma drifting to his nostrils from the point where he'd commanded her to sit when they arrived, ten feet off to his left.

They could've found a better way to pass the time than staring out a vacant window into dappled moonlight, but a slip in that direction could destroy his hope of bagging Slade.

Hell, it might even get Mathers killed.

He'd staked one of the new men out to watch their backs, cover the various blind side approaches to the mill. Its architects had work in mind when they were building the stone edifice, so windows weren't positioned as a sniper might've liked. Still, he and his men would make do with what they had, and Slade would never know what hit him if they played their cards right.

If.

Mathers came back to what had troubled him, and couldn't pin it down. If they could risk lights in the mill, perhaps he'd see something that struck him wrong, but in the darkness he could only guess—

A sudden scuffling noise surprised his straining ears. It sounded like boot heels on sand or gritty stone, accompanied by heavy breathing and a grunt of effort, maybe even pain. A brief, erratic *thump-thump-thump* of solid blows.

Mathers sat clutching his rifle in white-knuckled hands, paralyzed. In that instant, he couldn't decide what to do.

If he ordered a roll call, the sound of his voice would betray him—either to intruders in the mill, or to watchers outside, assuming that the scuffling noises were a false alarm, one of the new boys dozing at his post and waking with a start. In either case, a spoken word could ruin every-thing, might even bring a bullet homing toward his face.

But what else could he do? Ignore it? That was crazy. If the marshal was *inside* the mill, it meant their plan had gone to hell. All bets were off, and the sooner his men started shooting, the better. Mathers preferred to take his chances with a ricochet, rather than enemies inside the mill.

And yet . . .

The matter was decided for him in another heartbeat, as a pistol shot rang out. The muzzle flash came from his right, the same direction as the scuffling noises, though he would've placed it closer if he'd had to guess on sound alone. The bullet wasn't aimed at Mathers, but was angled skyward, where it loosed a dribbling stream of sawdust and termites from the mill's rotten roof beams.

"Jesus!" someone shouted from his left.

Another pistol barked, immediately followed by the sharp *crack* of a rifle. Mathers held his fire, ducking un-consciously to make himself a smaller target. Mouthing silent curses, he pushed off from cover, lunging toward the spot where Faith sat waiting for him, huddled in a clench of fear.

Slade hadn't really counted on surprising anybody else. He knew five men remained inside the mill, all armed, and that Faith Connover was also hidden somewhere in the pitch-black shadows there. Stray beams of moonlight through a couple of the westward-facing windows helped him navi-gate a little, once he'd crossed the threshold, but his mem-ories of touring the mill by daylight were distorted now. It all seemed different in the dark.

Slade found his second man by accident, nearly tripped over him while inching step-by-step along one wall. The windows were his targets, since he calculated that the men who hunted him would be in close proximity to firing ports, but Slade wasn't adventurous enough to strike off through the darkness in the middle of the vaulted chamber. He would take the slow way, hope to bag another man or two before the frantic shooting started, and feel lucky if he got that far.

If he found Faith—

The soft collision with a human body, and a muttered, "What the—?" brought his rifle slashing toward the faceless target at around gut level. Slade connected with an arm instead, rewarded with a grunt of pain, and felt his man twisting away, palming a weapon.

Slade charged, ramming his Winchester broadside into the stranger's chest, as if it were a fighting staff. Foul breath washed over him, a hissing curse without sufficient wind behind it, as Slade smashed a knee into his adversary's groin. That brought a whimper, but the man kept reaching for his gun. Slade heard him cock the hammer, felt the weapon jabbing upward, toward his face.

He took a half step backward, ducked, and swung the rifle underhanded, striking at his enemy's gun arm. He connected with an elbow, made the other squeal, but it was lost in the explosion of a pistol shot aimed toward the ceiling. Deafened, Slade swung his rifle butt in the direction of a face briefly illuminated by the muzzle-flash.

He struck the shooter's face, swung *through* it, driving head and Stetson hard against the nearby stony wall. Slade heard a cracking sound that could've been old mortar or a human skull. There was no time to wonder about it as his enemy collapsed and other weapons started spitting death inside the mill.

Slade hit the floor, worming his way around the limp form of his fallen adversary, following the wall. A slug struck stone somewhere above him, close enough to sting his face with razor shards, and Slade hunched lower still, keeping his cheek pressed to the earthen floor.

Muzzle-flashes surrounded him, at least three weapons peppering the inner walls. Slade couldn't watch them all at once, crawling along the west wall with his face down in the dirt, but still he did his best. At one point, when a shadow-shape loomed over him, two pistols glinting in the moonlight from a nearby window, Slade rolled over on his side and shot the man at point-blank range, his rifle's muzzle almost pressed against the target's buckskin shirt.

That muffled shot produced another ragged burst of firing, handguns with a rifle for support, while Slade tried marking their positions from the muzzle-blasts. At least one man was unaccounted for, not firing yet, but Slade couldn't predict who that might be. The head count went to hell regardless, if his enemies were moving or if one of them was packing two guns, like the guard outside.

And where was Faith, with all that shooting going on?

A grim thought struck him, wondering if Mathers had dispatched her silently once she had stepped inside the mill. That way, he wouldn't have to think about her when the shooting started. Half his bloody work would already be done.

Slade clenched his teeth around that thought, willing it to be wrong. If he called out Faith's name, he'd make himself a target, draw the fire of every shooter still alive and functional inside the mill. He couldn't risk it, couldn't sacrifice himself until he knew for sure that Faith was past all hope.

And then?

Get on with it, Slade urged himself, and crept on toward a goal he couldn't see.

Faith had stifled a scream at the first sound of gunfire, then gasped as someone clutched her right arm in the darkness, dragging her bodily from the stony corner she had occupied since Mathers brought her to the mill. Her legs were stiff and that nearly made her stumble, but Faith kept her balance with the aid of her unseen escort, who gave her arm a painful wrench.

"Stay on your feet, damn it!" the disembodied voice hissed at her. Mathers? She believed it was, but couldn't be certain. "This way!"

She let the gunman steer her while, around them, muzzle-flashes lit the darkness with a strobe effect, bullets whining in ricochet from stone walls that surrounded them. Faith sobbed in fear, but clapped a hand across her own mouth to contain the sound, afraid some gunman would be drawn to fire at her if it was audible.

Tears stung her eyes, but vision was irrelevant inside the mill. Faint shafts of moonlight fell through windows here and there, but otherwise the mill's interior was pitch-black, like the bottom of a well at midnight. Faith had no idea where her captor was taking her, but he appeared to have a destination that would leave the worst gunfire behind.

Lie down, she thought, and almost spoke the words aloud. *We should be lying on the floor.*

But aimless ricochets could find her even there, Faith realized. The mill's interior was like a dreadful echo chamber, amplifying each gunshot and crack of lead on stone until they deafened her and threatened to disrupt her sanity. A rock slid out from underneath her left foot, made Faith slump against her captor, but he jerked her roughly upright with another warning.

"Watch your step, will you?"

"How *can* I?" she responded in an angry whisper of her own.

"Shut up!"

As if the terse exchange had put them on some sniper's map, a muzzle flash exploded to Faith's left. She heard and felt the bullet pass before her face, its heat like the caress of fevered fingertips against her cheek. Beside her, Mathers, or whoever, cursed and staggered, then swung her around ninety degrees and fired a shot back toward the source of that report.

Faith couldn't tell if he had scored a hit or not, but suddenly her captor started running, pulling her along behind him in a rush. She kept up for a few strides, then fell heavily, skinning her knees. The deadweight in his grasp made her kidnapper hesitate; then he began to drag her after him, panting and wheezing from the effort.

I wish I was fat, Faith thought, and nearly cackled in hysterics at the image of Dred Mathers dragging her obese form through the darkness.

When it felt as if her shoulder might be separated from its socket, Faith somehow contrived to get one foot beneath her, then the other, and began to run again. Almost immediately, her abductor veered off to the right, and Faith could feel the earthen floor sloping away beneath her. She hadn't seen this portion of the mill's interior before the gang had doused their lights, and she had no idea where they were going. Only—

Something struck her in the face, a solid blow, or maybe she collided with a solid, stationary object. Either way, Faith staggered from the stunning impact, felt her knees begin to buckle, and could only use one arm to catch herself as she collapsed. The wet warmth on her forehead felt like syrup, freshly heated on the stove. Faith scraped her palm and barely felt it as she hit the ground with force enough to punch the last air from her lungs.

Drowning, she thought distractedly. *I'm drowning now. How can that be?*

Survival instincts made her cough and gasp for breath, but it was an unconscious reflex. Faith felt nothing as Dred Mathers, cursing bitterly, used all of his remaining strength to drag her through the shadows.

• • •

Jesus Christ! thought Mathers. *This bitch weighs a ton!*

Objectively, he knew that wasn't true—she was quite slim, in fact—but objectivity had long ago deserted him, and rationality itself was hanging by a thread. Pained by the bullet that had grazed his arm, he struggled on for five or six more paces, hauling Faith's inert form after him, then found by touch a low retaining wall to shelter them from aimless shots and ricochets.

Huddled behind that bulwark, Mathers clutched his Colt with one round gone and wished he had a bat's eyes, anything to help him see through midnight darkness, separating friends from enemies.

Jack Slade was somewhere in the mill. Mathers took that much as given, but he couldn't tell if Slade had come alone or with more guns to help him. How he'd gotten past their lookout was a question for another time, if Mathers lived that long.

Unconscious, Faith was little use to him, but nothing happened when he lightly slapped her cheeks or pinched her breast. She was out cold, as far as he could tell, after colliding with a stone wall several paces from the point where Mathers crouched now, hidden—so he hoped—from any enemies. He wouldn't travel far with Faith in that condition, but he *didn't* need to travel.

All he needed was a clear shot at the marshal. Just one chance to put him down.

Mathers leaned out to scan the eerie battleground, with no real hope of seeing anyone or anything. Bright muzzle-flashes still winked in the darkness, giant fireflies with a deadly sting, but Mathers couldn't tell whose guns they came from, or what targets drew the fire.

It struck him that his men might all be trading shots with one another, burning up their ammunition while Jack Slade sat back in Lawton, safe and warm in his hotel room, but that painful image didn't take account of the first sounds he'd heard, the noise of two men grappling in the dark before the first shot echoed through the mill. Unless his boys had started fighting hand to hand, then switched to guns, that meant they had at least one adversary with them in the dark.

Unless he's dead already, Mathers thought, pulse quickening. Maybe a lucky shot had gutted Slade—perhaps his own, a moment earlier—and Slade was bleeding out right now, unseen in the confusion. Mathers didn't know the definition of *ironic,* but his brain could grasp the sense of it, and he supposed that something must be done to take stock of the carnage here and now.

He couldn't strike a match and give himself away. That would be tantamount to suicide, even if his men were the sole survivors in the mill. His own shooters would likely fire at the first flare of light, and never know the difference until it was too late.

That thought made Mathers wonder if he'd shot an ally moments earlier, but the idea didn't disturb him. He was still alive and well, despite the shallow graze, and Mathers meant to stay that way, no matter who he had to kill.

What could he do?

In front of him, no more than fifteen feet away, he heard a scuffling sound of footsteps as two men approached each other in the darkness. One hissed out, "Who's that?" before they both cut loose with six-guns, blazing at each other from a range of three or four short paces.

By the light of muzzle-flashes, Mathers recognized Bran Huffman and another of his riders, one whose name he'd never taken time to learn. He couldn't tell if they'd glimpsed one another, but it hardly mattered. Both of them scored close-range hits, and Mathers watched them topple over into darkness, while their last shots echoed through the mill.

"Enough!" he shouted. "That's enough, goddamn it! Hold your fire!"

And as a testament to trust, he struck a match.

• • •

Slade didn't recognize the voice, but since it was a man's and wasn't his, he knew it was an enemy's. Crouching behind the rusted hulk of some great grinding tool, he sighted in the general direction of that voice, then blinked as someone struck a match, holding its feeble light aloft.

"Who's left out there?" Mathers demanded.

Glancing left and right at scattered bodies, Slade replied, "It looks like you're alone."

Mathers was quick, dropping the match and bringing up his gun, but not quite fast enough. Slade had him sighted, and he dropped the hammer with a gentle squeeze, knowing as darkness fell again that he had done his best.

A cry of pain confirmed it, and the sound of Mathers thrashing on the ground. That could all be an act, but Slade was disinclined to think so. He'd been aiming for a solid hit and reckoned that he'd made one. His concern now was that Mathers might've flinched as he recoiled, and made the hit a fatal wound.

It wasn't meant to be.

Slade still needed a witness against Freeman, someone who could link the rancher to Jim's murder and the death of Marshal Ford. Who better than the leader of the gang Freeman had hired to do his dirty work? But if Slade killed him, that potential evidence went up in smoke. And even Faith, if she was still alive, couldn't supply the proof he needed for a murder charge.

"Mathers?" he called out to the shadows.

"I'm still here," the outlaw answered, sounding winded. "You're a piss-poor shot."

"So, you're not leaking then?"

"Not so's you'd notice, lawman."

"Then I don't guess you'd be interested in a deal."

"The only deal I want," Mathers replied, "is you dropping before I ride the hell away from here."

"That's not going to happen," Slade assured him. "You're already bleeding out."

"Like hell!" Almost a gasp.

"Yeah, I can tell you're healthy by the way you sound."

"Maybe I'm acting, lawman."

"Spare me. I already know how this show ends."

"Did I forget to mention that I've got your brother's girlfriend here? Or maybe I should call her yours these days?"

"You're looking at a rope already, Mathers, for my brother and the marshal. Why add any more?"

"The way I understand it, they can only hang me once."

"And I was thinking, maybe, that you shouldn't hang at all."

Mathers delayed responding for a moment, then asked Slade, "What's that supposed to mean?"

"It means I'm offering a deal. You testify against whoever paid to have Ford and my brother killed, and I'll persuade Judge Dennison to give you prison time, instead of stretching rope."

"Sounds like he ain't persuaded yet," Mathers replied.

"He wants the man behind the killings more than he wants shooters. We can deal, or you can die."

"How 'bout I do this little honey while I think about it, just for old times' sake?"

Was Faith alive, or was the outlaw bluffing?

"If you do," Slade said, "I guarantee you'll never leave this hole alive."

"I might not anyway," Mathers allowed. "Your aim ain't quite as poor as I let on."

"Then end it now," said Slade. "It's up to you."

"Sounds like a plan," Mathers responded, then came rushing at him through the darkness in a hobbling run, firing in the direction of Slade's voice.

Slade dropped his aim a yard below the outlaw's muzzle flashes, squeezed off two quick shots, and found his

mark with one of them. Dred Mathers cried out one last
time as he pitched forward, falling headlong in the dark.

Slade risked striking his own match then, holding the
flame at arm's length from his body while he aimed his
Colt at Mathers, lying facedown on the ground. Slade
kicked the gunman's six-shooter away and rolled him over
with a boot toe, picking out the shoulder wound he'd first
inflicted, and another in the bandit's left leg, just above the
knee.

Before the match died, Slade reached down and pulled
a dark bandanna from around his quarry's neck. He lit one
end of it and draped it carefully across the crumbled corner of a nearby wall. Using the wick for light, he took a
piece of rawhide from his pocket, crouched beside Mathers, and bound the outlaw's hands behind his back.

"That's wasted effort for a dead man," Mathers said
with a grimace.

"You're not dying," Slade informed him. "Not until the
judge decides it anyway. Where's Faith?"

"Find her yourself," Mathers replied.

Slade did, a moment later, feeling something close to
heartbreak when he saw her lying crumpled on the ground,
inert. And it was something close to heaven moments later,
when her eyes opened and she pronounced his name.

16

Slade argued past Judge Dennison's suggestion that he should delay the raid on Freeman's Rocking Y until more deputies arrived. Waiting for Aaron Price and Luke Walker meant sitting on his hands for two days, more or less, while nothing but sheer arrogance prevented Freeman from abandoning his spread and vanishing beyond Slade's reach.

No, that was wrong.

Wherever Freeman tried to hide, Slade meant to root him out, with or without a badge to make it legal. If he had to chase Freeman beyond the limits of the territory, anything could happen. Mathers might escape from custody or change his mind about accusing Freeman at his murder trial. Some means might even be devised to silence him in jail. Faith Connover, for her part, would remain at risk so long as Freeman was alive and capable of hiring men to carry out his will.

That power would be broken once Judge Dennison had dealt with Freeman from the bench, but in the meantime,

Freeman was as lethal as a rattlesnake. He might attack head-on, or slip away and strike from ambush later, when he felt the time was right.

With Mathers and his battered lookout under lock and key, and Faith confined to Slade's room at the Lawton Arms with guards outside her door, Slade followed Dennison's directions to the Rocking Y. Before he left, the judge admonished him once more to use only the necessary force required for an arrest.

"You did a good job at the mill," said Dennison, "although I wish you'd asked for my advice to start with. Running off that way without a by-your-leave, and no one knowing where you'd gone, it could've been the end for you *and* Miss Connover."

"But it wasn't," Slade reminded him.

"By pure, dumb luck. It's also your good fortune that those idjits started shooting one another in the dark. The way I see it, you killed one of four dead men and brought two out alive. Under the circumstances—"

"Hold that thought," said Slade. "I'm still not sure how many shooters Freeman carries on his payroll."

"Right around a dozen, I'd imagine," Dennison replied. "So, if you've changed your mind and want to wait—"

"We've covered that," Slade interrupted. "Every hour I wait gives Freeman more time to get away. I'm taking him tonight, if he's not gone already."

"Well, you've got your warrant, Deputy," said Dennison. "Just keep it clean. Remember that you serve the law."

"I'm not forgetting anything," Slade said in parting as he set out on the forty-minute ride.

He watched for traps along the way, made detours when a certain stretch of countryside seemed too inviting for an ambush party. Slade couldn't have proved that Freeman's men were laying for him—not until they opened fire at least—but he was counting on a warm reception at the ranch.

And he was hoping Freeman might have thinned his troops by sending some of them to watch the trail between the Rocking Y and Lawton. They could wait all night, while Slade used Dennison's shortcut and added some refinements of his own along the way.

Slade wasn't sure how many gunmen would oppose him at the ranch. Judge Dennison had guessed a dozen, minimum, but Slade thought some of them would be dispatched to guard the spread's perimeter. Others might balk at finding out Slade was a lawman, frightened of a hanging rope where killing rustlers or trespassers would've rested lightly on their conscience.

Maybe.

But if Freeman threw a dozen or two dozen shooters at him, Slade still had to bring him in. He owed that much to Jim, to Faith—even to Harmon Ford, although he'd barely known the man.

Slade wasn't sure exactly when he crossed the unmarked boundary onto Freeman's land. The first outriders that he saw were some two hundred yards away, small figures etched in moonlight shadows, riding in the opposite direction. Slade sat still and waited for the pair to pass from sight, then rode on toward the ranch house.

From a quarter mile away, it looked serene. Lights showed from several of the windows, but the barn and outbuildings were dark, no shooters visible around the place. Slade didn't know if that meant Freeman had departed, or if he was just a cool head when it came to baiting traps.

One way, Slade's ride would be a waste of time. The other, it could get him killed within the next few moments.

Either way, it was something he had to do.

Slowly approaching from the east, Slade started looking for a place to leave his Appaloosa, hidden at least from casual observers, while he made the final trek on foot.

•   •   •

Doug Freeman paced the polished floorboards of his study, drawing furiously on a fat cigar. Tobacco calmed him generally, but tonight it wasn't working. Supper sat like lead weights in his stomach, and he jumped at every little sound the house made, settling after yet another day.

No word from Mathers yet, and that could only be bad news. Freeman had broken two appointments scheduled for that afternoon, afraid to visit Lawton until Mathers let him know the job was done, that Slade was dead and Faith Connover was gone without a trace. Until then, all his plans could still go sour, and the bill of sale bearing Faith's shaky signature was only good for fireplace tinder.

If she was alive and talking to the law . . .

His first impulse, as daylight came and went without a word, had been to cut and run. If it had been some minor score, a common range feud winding down, he might've taken a vacation. Head to Texas for a while, or even down to Mexico, until the dust settled and everything was right again. But this was different: a deal worth millions, kidnapping, a U.S. marshal and at least one other innocent already dead by Freeman's order. If he fumbled now, if Mathers let him down, the dust would never settle.

Not until grave diggers shoveled it on top of him.

Freeman gave up on the cigar, pitched it into the fireplace, and retreated to his liquor cabinet. With a double shot of bourbon underneath his belt, he felt a bit more confident.

Who was Jack Slade? One man, with or without a badge, who sought revenge for his brother's death. A local jury might believe that he'd become obsessed with punishing the guilty parties. So obsessed, in fact, that he had been susceptible to spiteful lies told by his brother's almost-widow. Freeman could claim Faith hated him for spurning her affections and had taken up with James Slade afterward, poisoned his mind against a blameless neighbor, and provoked a pointless feud between them. She might even be responsible herself for killing James, to get his land and livestock. After that . . .

What then?

Of course! She'd hired the Mathers gang to murder Marshal Ford when he began collecting evidence that would've sent her to the gallows. Jack Slade, blind with grief over his brother's death and lust for Faith, had been a simpleminded pawn in her malicious game. She'd come to Freeman, offered him the ranch, then staged her own kidnapping, using Mathers as her stooge. If Mathers lived to testify, his record could be used against him, painting him as a no-good who'd tell a jury anything to save himself.

That much at least was true.

Faith's motive for conspiring against Freeman was simplicity itself. She'd learned about the oil that lay beneath both properties, and wanted it all for herself. With Freeman dead or locked away for life, she could acquire the Rocking Y at bargain rates. Who'd even bid against her, after all that she had suffered?

Yes, he thought, pouring a second glass of amber fire, *it just might work.*

And if it seemed that Mathers might give Freeman too much trouble on the witness stand, then he could be eliminated. What jail was really safe? Mathers might have an accident, or try to flee and stop a bullet in the process. Anything could happen in the months while well-paid lawyers stalled a trial.

But in the meantime—

"Freeman!"

Someone calling to him from the yard outside, a voice he didn't recognize at first, without the *Mister* he'd expect from one of his hired hands. Freeman stopped dead, the whiskey glass poised at his lips, a sudden tremor in his right hand sending ripples through its contents.

"Freeman, this is Marshal Slade! I have a warrant here for—"

Gunshots echoed in the outer darkness. Freeman dropped his glass, barely aware when it smashed at his feet, dousing his boots and trouser cuffs with bourbon. Darting toward the nearest window, he peered out between drawn curtains, just in time to glimpse a figure running for the barn. Two of his men were in pursuit, firing six-shooters as they ran.

"Trespassing," Freeman muttered to himself. "He came out here at night, didn't announce himself. What could my people do?"

It sounded reasonable. Any member of his staff who valued steady work would play along, forget whatever he had heard that contradicted Freeman's story. Slade's death would be a tragic accident at worst, perhaps the fitting disposition of a madman seeking vengeance from an innocent.

And if his men had trouble finishing the job? What then?

Freeman was out the study door and running by the time the thought took shape. "I wasn't even here," he told himself, as if repeating it would make the fable true. "I wasn't here at all."

Slade had surprised a group of Freeman's hands while they were playing poker in the bunkhouse. Four of them were seated at a smallish folding table, one of those with folding legs that could be put out of the way at need. They gaped at him when he intruded on their party, covering the quartet with his Winchester while he explained his business at the Rocking Y.

The four had doubted him at first, despite the badge pinned on Slade's vest, and that was only natural. Doug Freeman was the font of everything they had in life, had been for years, while Slade was an armed stranger who arrived in darkness, telling tales. The warrant changed their minds, after the single reader in the group pored over it and told the others what it said.

Murder. Kidnapping. Fraud. Grand theft.

The cowboys took Slade at his word that they could leave, unarmed, and come back for their hardware later. While they got dressed for the ride, their spokesman told Slade there were nine more hands employed by Freeman on the Rocking Y. Six of them had been packed off to patrol the spread at dusk, which still left three at large somewhere in the compound.

Slade wasn't sure if he could trust the four, but he had risked it, walked them to the barn, and watched them saddle up, then ride away. If they came back with reinforcements, he was finished, but there'd been no place to lock them up, no quiet way of silencing four men without alerting others on the grounds.

He'd wasted no time searching for the others, knowing they'd find him once he had made his move. Instead, he'd called to Freeman from the yard outside the rancher's house, identified himself in no uncertain terms, mentioned the warrant loud and clear.

The last bit had been interrupted by gunfire, and a fast retreat to Freeman's barn. Two shooters followed, firing as they came, clearly intent on killing Slade before he reached their boss.

So much for doing things the easy way.

Slade ducked inside the barn, then turned and raised his Winchester. His two pursuers couldn't see him, standing in the shadows, as they veered in opposite directions, fanning out to flank the barn. Slade tracked the taller of them, led him just a little with the rifle, and squeezed off a shot that dropped him in mid-stride.

Wounded or dead, Slade couldn't tell, but either way, the man was down and lying motionless. His partner didn't hesitate, fanning three shots in rapid fire before he disappeared around a corner of the barn.

Coming around behind me, Slade thought. *Or he might want me to think that. Double back and catch me with my back turned.*

Slade moved quickly to a nearby empty stall, concealed himself, and waited for his enemy to reappear. Their gunfire would've drawn the other shooter from his rounds, and Freeman might be arming servants in the house, for all Slade knew. He didn't fancy squaring off against a cook or chambermaid, but he'd face anything Doug Freeman threw at him and give it back in spades.

A rush of footsteps on his right warned Slade of company coming, even as a door creaked somewhere to his left. Two shooters then, and if his first informant had been truthful, dropping them would clear the way to Freeman's doorstep. If he did it fast enough, before the outriders returned.

Something made Slade give them a final chance.

"Before you do another thing," he called out in the darkness, "know that I'm a U.S. marshal with a warrant to arrest your boss for murder, kidnapping, and robbery. Maybe you didn't hear before, but now you know."

"We know, all right," the shooter on his left replied. "We just don't give a damn."

"Your funeral," Slade said.

"We'll see about that, lawdog."

Slade figured one of them had probably reloaded on his walk around the paddock, while the other hadn't fired his pistol yet. Twelve rounds, at least, against fourteen in his Winchester and six more in his Colt, but numbers didn't tell the story. One shot was enough to end him, if his adversaries found an opening.

He shifted in the stall, moved toward the slats along the left side, crouching low as shots erupted from both sides. Slugs tore the wooden slats and set Doug Freeman's horses clamoring inside their nearby stalls.

Slade aimed between the nearest slats, tracking a

shadow-shape and muzzle-flashes, triggering a round from ten feet that tore through his target's chest and spun the man like something caught up in a whirlwind. Turning instantly, before the first shooter collapsed, Slade caught the other coming for him, snarling curses as he barged into the stall.

Slade fired into the open mouth at something close to point-blank range, his muzzle-blast lighting the startled face. A momentary drumming of the dead man's boot heels faded into silence, leaving Slade still breathing in the barn.

Uncertain what awaited him outside, Slade decided to leave that place of death and move back toward the house.

Before fleeing the house, Freeman paused long enough to grab a gunbelt, strap it on, and check the load of his hand-engraved, pearl-handled Schofield revolver. All six chambers of the double-action pistol were loaded, and Freeman handled it carefully as he snugged it into his holster, securing the hammer thong to hold it in place.

From a wall rack, he also chose a Henry rifle, giving him some range, and filled the pockets of his coat with extra cartridges. Now Freeman rattled when he walked, but he felt better, more secure.

Leaving his house by the back door, he followed the sounds of gunfire, realizing for the first time that his men had chased Slade into the barn. It was no problem for him if they killed the marshal there, but if they only pinned him down, that meant Freeman would have to pass within a few feet of Slade's gun to reach his favorite horse.

Cursing, he turned away and left them to their killing. Freeman had a whole corral of saddle-broken horses waiting for him, with spare saddles and the other gear he needed in a nearby tackle shed. He'd have to leave Wildfire, his jet-black stallion, behind. Freeman reckoned that

was only temporary, until Slade was dealt with and removed.

He could come home then, and begin the legal battle
that, with any luck at all, would see him vindicated and en-
riched beyond his wildest dreams.

But first, he had to put some ground between himself
and Slade, leave the new marshal to his own devices with
the gunmen of the Rocking Y. If Freeman met any reinforcements in his flight, he would send them back to help
the others at the house. If not . . . well, he supposed the
men already stalking Slade could handle him.

And there were always more where those came from.

Bypassing the corral at first, Freeman went straight to
the equipment shed, hauled out a saddle, bit, and reins,
then carried all the gear back to the paddock gate. He set it
on the ground, reached for the latch, then froze.

No shooting from the barn.

He turned slowly and stared across the yard, considering the various scenarios that came to mind. In one, his
men killed Slade and dragged his body off somewhere to
feed the buzzards and coyotes. In another, Slade and Freeman's men killed off each other, and his other hands were
forced to handle the disposal. The scenario he dreaded was
the third one, Slade emerging from the barn alive and coming after Freeman in a rush of hate-fueled bloodlust.

Check it out, a small voice in his head demanded.

"No," the rancher whispered to himself.

But he couldn't afford to run. Not now. The battle in the
barn was over, one way or another. If his men had finished
Slade, there was no reason for him to evacuate the Rocking Y. If they had failed, Slade would most likely overtake
Freeman while he was picking out a horse, trying to saddle
it.

Nowhere to run. No time to get away.

His hope, if Slade still lived, was to move in and
take the marshal down himself. It didn't have to be close

work, a classic showdown. He could find some cover, hunker down in darkness, waiting for the target to reveal himself.

Waiting.

But what if Slade was wounded, lying in the barn disabled? It was Freeman's job to finish it, administer the coup de grâce and put this part of the nightmare behind him.

Do it! the small voice ordered. Freeman took his Henry from the pile of saddle gear and started toward the barn slowly, circling around toward the back door with all the stealth that he could manage.

"Don't go anywhere," he whispered to a man who might be dead. "I'm on my way."

Slade checked the two slain gunmen, making sure he hadn't left a live one by mistake to follow him, then turned toward the barn's front door. He tried to calculate where Freeman might have fled by now, but couldn't work it out with his scant knowledge of the Rocking Y.

If he was running on four legs, the rancher wouldn't have his pick of horses in the barn, but there were plenty more outside. Slade didn't know about saddles, but he would check the paddock first, and keep a sharp eye on the barn meanwhile, in case Freeman was still inside the house and waiting for his chance to make a break.

If Slade let him get away on horseback, Freeman had a chance to leave him in the dust, since Slade's Appaloosa was tied a hundred yards out from the house and barn. By the time Slade retrieved it and went in pursuit, a good rider would have a half-mile lead, and Slade wouldn't be sure in which direction Freeman had escaped.

The only way to stop that nightmare coming true was to find Freeman here and now, keep him from getting to a horse. Stop him before he had a chance to run. And if he had more gunmen waiting in the shadows, maybe riding back from other stations, Slade would deal with them as well.

He'd nearly reached the barn's front door when someone fired a shot behind him, missing Slade by inches, blasting splinters from the doorjamb. With a startled curse, Slade ducked and lunged off to his left, rolling behind a pyramid of hay bales.

Damn it! He'd been sure the two gunmen were dead. Now, he'd be forced to go back and—

"You comfy back there, Slade?" Doug Freeman asked him from the far end of the barn. Advancing, by the sound of it, but slowly. Cautiously.

"Never been better," Slade replied.

"Really? I thought you might've had some injuries by now. I've come to ease your pain."

"Don't do me any favors, Freeman."

"No," the rancher answered, definitely closer now. "This is a favor to myself. I'm going to put you out of my misery."

"Think it'll help? You think Judge Dennison will just forget he sent me out here with a murder warrant?"

"I'll leave that to my attorneys, Slade. Right now, I'm cleaning house."

"You'll find yourself shorthanded."

"That's no problem. Shooters are a dime a dozen. Marshals too."

"Meaning there'll be another if you kill me, and another after him. You're finished, Freeman. Time to smell the lilies."

That provoked a shot, but the hay bales absorbed it. Slade rolled clear of cover, squeezing off a quick round from his Winchester while Freeman pumped his rifle's lever action. Even though Slade missed, the shot drove Freeman to take cover, breaking for the shadows of a nearby empty stall.

"Looks like we've got a standoff," Slade advised him. "You're not getting past me, and Judge Dennison knows where I am. If I'm not back in Lawton come the morning, he'll be sending out a posse and we'll break the stalemate then."

"They won't find you," said Freeman, still defiant. "I've still got riders out, and they'll be checking back before daybreak. You want to walk away from this, your best chance is to leave right now."

"But then, I'd miss your necktie party," Slade replied.

"You think a judge and jury in this godforsaken place will hang *me*, Slade? I own more land and stock in western Oklahoma Territory than my closest five competitors combined, and now there's *oil* under our feet. I'm filthy rich, Slade!"

"Well, at least you got the first half right."

Freeman responded to the insult with a barking laugh. "I'll *buy* that jury, you dumb bastard. No one's hanging me for anything. You may as well accept that now, and try to live with it while you've still got a chance."

"Or maybe," Slade responded, "I'll just deal with you myself. Right here, right now."

"Try it!" the rancher taunted him. "Come on!"

Slade took a hay fork from its place beside the stack of bales, reared back, and pitched it overhand into the stall adjoining Freeman's. Freeman yelped in panic, started rapid-firing through the wooden slats between the stalls, and suddenly appeared in front of Slade, still pumping bullets into empty space.

Slade shot him in the left thigh, saw a spray of blood as Freeman went down with a squeal. The rancher lost his Henry, falling, but he still had grit enough to scrabble for the Schofield. Slade got there ahead of him, aiming the Winchester between his eyes from seven feet away.

"Your call," he told Freeman. "But if you really trust that jury, you may want to reconsider dying here tonight."

"You're right," Freeman replied after a tense delay. He lay back in the dust, wincing, and raised two empty hands. "I'll call that bet and raise you everything I own."

"I'm in," Slade told him, stooping down to lift the six-gun from the wounded rancher's belt.

17

Jury selection for the trial of Douglas Freeman took the best part of a Tuesday morning, wrapping up in time to break for lunch. His pair of lawyers—one from Oklahoma City and the other brought in special from St. Louis—seemed disgruntled by the speed with which Judge Dennison impaneled jurors, but their various objections were dismissed with smart raps of the gavel.

As established after due consideration, Freeman's panel would include six farmers, four of Lawton's merchants, a schoolmaster (school was not in session at the moment), and a handyman who doubled as an elder of the local Baptist church.

Freeman's defenders had come looking for a change of venue, but their motion was denied on grounds that they would find no other court within the western half of Oklahoma Territory, and Judge Dennison assured them of a fair, impartial trial. Next, they attacked the jury composition, noting that eleven of the twelve had once known Harmon Ford, and half of them considered him a friend. Judge Dennison had gaveled down that argument as well, responding that it was a miracle they'd found one man in town who *hadn't* known the marshal, while their friendship toward the victim played no part in judging any certain suspect's guilt or innocence.

"It might affect the fixing of his punishment, in the event of a conviction," said the lawyer from St. Louis, Armon Trout.

"Then let me put your mind at ease," Judge Dennison replied. "The jury in this case will not be fixing punishment. I take that burden on myself."

Slade, watching from a bench behind the prosecution's table, thought he saw a little color drain from Freeman's jowly face at that. The rancher had gained weight in jail, waiting for Dennison to finish up the paperwork and fix a trial date, pick the jury pool, and serve those on the list with proper notice to appear in court for questioning by the attorneys on both sides.

Fatback and beans must've agreed with him to some extent, thought Slade, although Freeman had lost most of his outdoors color in the lockup, waiting for his day in court.

The first few days in custody, he'd worked the angles, variously taunting Slade or offering to make him wealthy in return for help. Suggestions varied as to what that help might be—a cell door left unlocked, a change in Slade's remembrance of Faith Connover's abduction, sudden and complete amnesia—but he had given up on all of it after his lawyers brought their circus into town.

The rest was all newspaper interviews, predictions that the great man would be vindicated and his false accusers brought to book, and that the "real killers" of Marshal Ford and James Slade would be brought to justice somewhere down the line. Of course, they questioned Marshal Slade's involvement in his brother's case, citing poor judgment, shaky ethics, and whatever else was stored in their vocabulary, but it all boiled down to hinting at a frame-up, with their client as the victim.

Now, with twelve good men and true impaneled on the jury, they would have a chance to prove their case.

There were no women on the jury, since Judge Dennison selected jurors from the voters' roll and Oklahoma women weren't allowed to vote. The twelve faces were white for the exact same reason, and because the local Powers That Be were set against blacks "meddling" in what they labeled "white folks' business." Slade supposed both bars would fall in time, when people deemed that change was overdue or someone forced their hand, but social protest was beyond his personal experience.

Right now, his focus was on seeing justice done to those who'd murdered Jim and Marshal Ford, who'd kidnapped Faith and tried to take her land by force, who'd nearly murdered *him* on two occasions. All those charges were enumerated, bundled into an indictment that included murder in the first degree (two counts), conspiracy to murder, kidnapping, conspiracy to kidnap, fraud, grand theft, assault, and two counts of attempted murder. If convicted on all charges, Freeman theoretically could hang three times at least.

But Slade thought once should be enough.

The prosecution's witnesses, besides himself, included Faith, Dred Mathers, and a drifter named Elijah Poole, who'd been the lookout Slade coldcocked outside the mill the night he'd rescued Faith. Mathers was crucial as a witness to the murder and conspiracy indictments, linking Freeman to the various events that Slade and Faith described from firsthand knowledge. Poole, meanwhile, was kept on ice to help hang Mathers if the outlaw leader changed his mind and couldn't find his voice when he was called to testify.

So far, Mathers had lived up to his bargain. In return for testifying truthfully, Judge Dennison had promised not to hang him for the murders Mathers had confessed to. His sentence would be life imprisonment, accompanied by Dennison's suggestion that he be considered for parole after a term of twenty years. Conversely, if he swung the other way in court and tried to change his story, Mathers would be tried with no restrictions on whatever charges Dennison and Slade might file, and his confessions would be used as evidence against him, guaranteeing him a noose.

Slade wore his poker face throughout the trial's preliminary motions and procedures, seeming as if nothing touched him, nothing mattered. And in fact, he wasn't greatly worried by the trial's outcome. If Freeman was acquitted somehow, in defiance of the evidence, that simply meant that Slade would have another shot at him, out in the world.

And next time, there'd be no attempt to bring the rancher in alive.

The trial was Slade's first time in court, aside from being fined in Wichita two years ago for his disorderly behavior in a barroom fight. Despite his inside view of the proceedings this time, there was still a sense of apprehension as he entered Dennison's courtroom—and sneaking little shivers of relief that *he* was not on trial.

The cases heard before this court were serious, matters of life or death. Slade wanted no part of it, beyond sitting in the witness chair.

He listened closely to the opening remarks, both sides vowing to prove their diametrically opposed positions with "a clear preponderance of evidence." Slade reckoned that was bluff coming from Freeman's team, since they were fronting for a guilty man. Still, strange things happened at the bar of justice every now and then. Slade watched and waited, shifting midway through the arguments to find a place where he could also watch the spectators.

Slade didn't think Freeman was fool enough to try escaping from the courtroom, but he couldn't absolutely rule it out. If trouble started, and it seemed about to go that way, Slade made a promise to himself that Freeman wouldn't taste the air outside.

Faith Connover was first in line to testify, describing her abduction and her meeting with Doug Freeman, where he'd brutalized and badgered her into signing a false bill of sale for her land. From there, she sketched events leading up to her rescue at the mill, drawing a link between Freeman and the attempt to murder Slade. Freeman's defense attorneys planted a suggestion that the man who'd battered Faith inside the cave-house might've been some crafty lookalike, but they stopped short of calling her a liar, probably because attacking a young woman on the verge of tears would poison any possible goodwill from members of the jury or the courtroom audience.

Slade was the second witness called. Guided by questions from the prosecutor, he described the various events that had occurred since he arrived in Lawton, asking questions privately about his brother's death, accepting Harmon Ford's commission when the marshal was assassinated, killing two known members of the Mathers gang in town, then facing half a dozen more to save Faith Connover from certain death.

"Or maybe worse," the prosecutor added, leaving every man in court to stretch his own imagination, muttering among themselves until Judge Dennison stepped in and gaveled them to silence.

"Order in the court!" His voice was stern and sharp-edged from the bench. "One more demonstration and I'll clear this room."

Freeman's attorneys didn't wear kid gloves with Slade. The Oklahoma City lawyer, Crane Jessup, was first on the

attack, asking if Slade had loved his brother well enough
to lie or break the law while tracking those who'd murdered him. Slade answered that he might've, but it wasn't
necessary when the men responsible took pains to make
their guilt so obvious.

Jessup suggested that he harbored animosity against
Doug Freeman. No more, Slade replied, than he might feel
for any man who killed his brother, tried to murder *him,*
and then kidnapped his dead brother's fiancée. If that
stacked up to a grudge, then he'd plead guilty and be
damned.

Was it a wise move, Jessup asked him, for an untrained,
lifelong gambler to become a lawman solely to pursue the
men who'd killed a sibling? Slade replied that no one else
had seemed to want the job, once Harmon Ford was killed.
If Jessup wanted to contest Judge Dennison's selection of
his deputies, go right ahead.

That put the Oklahoma City lawyer in his chair, but
Armon Trout was on his feet before Crane Jessup's
trousers lost their crease. Wasn't it true, he asked, that
Slade harbored improper feelings toward Faith Connover,
his late, lamented brother's fiancée? Wasn't it fair to say
that Slade would lie, cheat, even kill to keep Faith happy?
And while they were on the subject, had she shown any
"peculiar gratitude" to Slade, after he'd saved her life or
any other time?

Fuming despite his best intentions to stay calm, Slade
kept his seat with effort and denied each allegation in its
turn. That done, he offered Trout a lesson in respect for decent women, if the lawyer chose to meet him elsewhere
during the next recess.

This time, the gavel stifled laughter and the warning
was reserved for Slade alone. Leaning across his stately
podium, Dennison advised Slade to remember his position
and refrain from any loose talk in the court or elsewhere.

Slade agreed, with proper counterfeit repentance, and was soon dismissed when Trout ran out of innuendoes.

There was only one more witness left to call, and it was Slade's job to retrieve him from the lockup. Dennison allowed a recess while Slade went to fetch Dred Mathers from his cell. It was a short walk, but he made the most of it, breathing deeply, rolling his shoulders to release the pent-up tension from his session on the witness stand.

The guard on watch was Marshal Aaron Price, called in from Enid for the trial, so that security for Mathers wasn't left to amateurs. Slade found him smoking on the sidewalk, taking in the sun.

"Time for your guest to earn his keep?" asked Price as Slade approached.

"They're waiting for the star attraction," Slade replied.

"He's been asleep since lunch," Price said. "I guess the deal he made saves him from any worries."

"For another twenty years at least," Slade said, and passed inside.

Mathers was lying on his cot, back turned to Slade, inert and silent. "Rise and shine," Slade ordered, jangling keys. "Your audience is waiting."

Mathers didn't move. Calling his name again, with no result, Slade used his key and stepped inside the cell. Cautious of any tricks, he kept his right hand on his Peacemaker, using the left to shake Mathers, then roll the inmate over on his back.

Slade didn't need a medical degree to recognize a dead man. Mathers had gone blue around the lips, and he was cooling to the touch. There was no pulse when Slade pressed fingers to his throat or wrist.

"Goddamn it!"

"What's the matter?" Aaron asked him from the doorway.

"See for yourself," said Slade. "And call the doctor over

when you've had a look. I have to tell Judge Dennison his key witness is dead."

"Your prisoner was poisoned," Dr. Crenshaw said. "That's really all I know, except he wasn't stung or bitten. I've been over him from scalp to soles, and all I found was some postmortem bleeding from the . . . er . . . his fundament."

"What's that?" asked Slade.

"His ass," Judge Dennison replied. Then, to the doctor, "Nothing else?"

"It wasn't violent. He didn't thrash around or soil himself, which rules out strychnine. The blue lips reveal a lack of oxygen. Essentially, he suffocated."

"And the means of poisoning?" asked Dennison.

"Presumably ingestion. That is, something that he ate. You said he had lunch shortly prior to the collapse?"

"I was in court," Slade answered, "but the other marshal mentioned it. We feed our prisoners from Crowley's down the street."

"I won't believe that Amos Crowley had a hand in this," said Dennison. "One of his staff perhaps. You'll have to question everyone."

"I've already been down there," Slade replied. "No one saw anything that they'll admit to, but I saw two people come into the kitchen through the back door in the twenty minutes I was there. It looks to me like anyone could dose a plate, if they knew which one would be coming to the jail."

"A thing like this, the risk involved," said Dennison, "it had to cost a pretty penny."

"Freeman's got the bankroll for it," Slade remarked.

"I can't debate a suspect's guilt or innocence. That's for the jury to decide." Scowling, the judge stood up, then hammered Slade's desk with his fist. "Goddamn it all to hell!"

"What will you do?" asked Slade.

"The only thing I *can* do, in the circumstances," Dennison replied. "Ask if the prosecution has more testimony to present, which they do not, then hear from the defense. They'll likely move for a dismissal on the murder charges anyway."

"Can you avoid that?" Slade inquired. "Just let the jury vote?"

"I'm bound by law and precedent. Beyond a certain point, my hands are tied, and any fancy tricks would get the whole case thrown out on appeal.."

"So, we just keep out fingers crossed?" asked Slade.

"Unless you know a special prayer," said Dennison.

When court convened at half-past three o'clock, Judge Dennison explained the loss of Mathers to a courtroom hushed by shock. Slade watched Doug Freeman, looking for the smirk that would betray him, but the rancher seemed surprised. Slade took it for an act, but his suspicion wouldn't build a murder case.

As planned, Dennison asked the prosecutor whether he had any further evidence or testimony to present. Upon receiving the expected negative reply, he turned and said, "Counsel for the defense may now present its case."

The two attorneys huddled for a moment, whispering; then Armon Trout stood up. "Your Honor," he declared, "because the state has manifestly failed to prove its case . . . we rest."

Dennison hammered down the swell of muttered comments with his gavel, frowning at the lawyer from St. Louis, then replying with a muted, "Very well."

"And," Trout continued, "we would move to have the murder charges stricken, since the prosecution has revealed no evidence linking our client to those crimes. Nothing. Not one—"

"I heard you, Counselor." Judge Dennison looked like a man who'd bitten into a ripe apple, only to discover it was filled with worms. "Under the circumstances, I have no choice but to grant the motion. Charges of murder in the first degree, concerning victims Harmon Ford and James Slade, are hereby dismissed without prejudice. Should further evidence be found, the prosecution may refile the charges at some future time. There is no statute of limitations on murder."

Facing the jury, Dennison continued. "Gentlemen, in just a moment you'll retire to consider your verdict, but first I'm obliged to explain certain fine points of law. Although two charges were dismissed, the defendant still stands accused of multiple crimes. You, in your wisdom and upon consideration of the evidence, have sole discretion to convict or acquit him on any particular charge. All defendants are presumed innocent before the court, and need not testify or summon witnesses on their behalf. It is the prosecution's burden to present sufficient evidence of guilt to prove the case."

Pausing to scan the faces in the jury box, he took a breath, then forged ahead. "It may be that you feel the prosecution has presented evidence enough on one charge, but has been deficient on another. You may acquit on one charge and convict on others, if you feel the evidence is strong enough. You are not asked, nor have you been empowered, to decide on penalties for any charge where you find evidence sufficient for conviction. That's my job. Now, are there any questions?"

There were none.

Escorted by a bailiff, the twelve jury men retreated through a side door, off to argue in the soundproof jury room. Slade watched them go, disgusted by the turn events had taken. There was nothing he could do about it now, except to wait and hear the verdict they returned.

And after that?

He couldn't think beyond the grim-faced members of the panel, trying to imagine their debate, wondering if Freeman had managed to taint the panel with his money, the same way he'd reached out to silence Mathers.

Judge Dennison recessed the court, and Slade wandered outside to get some air. He found Faith on the sidewalk and they stood together, neither speaking, as the shadows along Main Street slanted eastward, heralding the day's decline.

Slade checked his watch at one point, found the jury had been out for only fifteen minutes, and was putting it away when the bailiff emerged to announce their return.

Moments later, Judge Dennison gaveled the courtroom to order, while his bailiff called for silence. The jurors returned, single file, and eased into their chairs. The foreman stood alone as Dennison asked whether they had reached a verdict on the charges.

"Yes, we have, Your Honor."

"And how do you find the defendant, in respect to the kidnapping charge?"

"Guilty."

"As to the robbery?"

"Guilty."

"And the assault?"

"Guilty, Your Honor."

Freeman and his attorneys rose upon command, facing the bench. Judge Dennison surveyed them for a moment, then intoned, "Douglas Freeman, you have been duly convicted by a jury of your peers. I hereby sentence you fifty years confinement at hard labor, to begin immediately. Marshal Slade, take charge of the defendant and prepare him for transport."

"Yes, sir," Slade replied.

"And watch what you feed him, meanwhile," the judge added. "We don't want to lose him."

•   •   •

"So, what will you do now?" Faith asked.

They stood outside Slade's office, in the cool of early dusk. Inside, Doug Freeman huddled with his lawyers, talking strategy for his appeal with bars between them, Aaron Price on hand to make sure nothing more than words was passed between them.

"Well, first thing will be transporting Freeman to McAlester," Slade replied. "That's the—"

"Territorial prison," she finished for him. "Yes, I know. And after that?"

"I hadn't thought about it much," he lied. "Come back and get my things, I guess. Talk to Judge Dennison. I never planned on sticking with the marshal's job once this was done, but I can't leave him in the lurch."

"It would be rude," she granted.

"He'd most likely find me in contempt."

"Well, he can't *force* you to remain as marshal. I mean, that would be the same as slavery."

"No," Slade granted. "I suppose he wouldn't do that."

"And he wouldn't want you if your heart's not in it anyway."

"I guess that's right."

"So, you're inclined to leave?"

"Well, I . . ."

"You wouldn't have to be the marshal just to stay in Lawton. I imagine that a gambler could make his way quite nicely here. Or you could try your hand at something else."

"Cardplaying's all I've ever really done," Slade said, "except a few odd jobs along the way. I have to say, it used to be more fun."

"You're tired of gambling then?" Faith asked.

"Not tired, so much as . . . well, let's say it doesn't hold the same surprises as it used to anymore."

"You like surprises, Jack?"

"Sometimes. Depends on what they are, of course," he

said. "I've had a few the past two weeks I could've lived without."

She laughed and said, "Amen to that!"

"And what about yourself?" Slade asked, uncomfortable with the sudden scrutiny. "I guess you're free to sell the ranch now, if you want to."

"Sell it?"

"Well, with no one forcing you. It's your choice now. If you'd prefer to let it go and get on with your life, forget about—"

"Your brother?"

"That's not what I meant," Slade answered. "My failing has always been with words."

"I disagree," she said. "You manage to express yourself quite clearly when you choose to."

"Well . . ."

"In any case, I'm in no hurry to sell out," she said. "The land still holds too many memories. My dreams are rooted there. They haven't vanished, only changed."

"I see."

"Do you?"

Slade felt a flush of color rising in his cheeks, and he was thankful for the fading light that helped conceal it. Changing subjects once again, he said, "I guess Judge Dennison will want to have a word about the job when I get back."

"I wouldn't be surprised."

"Gives me something to think about."

"It's good to know your options, think them through," Faith said.

"No point in rushing things, I guess."

Her hand found his, squeezed lightly, then withdrew. "No point at all," she said, and left him standing on the sidewalk, staring after her.

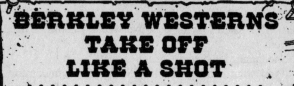

BERKLEY WESTERNS TAKE OFF LIKE A SHOT

- LYLE BRANDT
- PETER BRANDVOLD
- JACK BALLAS
- J. LEE BUTTS
- JORY SHERMAN
- ED GORMAN
- MIKE JAMESON

Don't miss the best Westerns from Berkley.